JESSICA JAMES

Foiled

First edition

ISBN: 979-8-218-77669-5

This book was professionally typeset on Reedsy.
Find out more at reedsy.com

For all the villain magnets.

High adventure and stupefying risks
are my métier.

—ERIC OVERMYER,
On The Verge

Contents

1

Foiled Again

Viridian

"I can't do this," I found myself in the small kitchenette in the back of the funeral home. Falling to the ground in sobs.

Collin scooped me up in his arms before I realized they were his. This amount of grief. This emptiness. He didn't say anything. There wasn't anything he could say. It had been a hard year. Right when I didn't think it could be any worse.

Connor was dead.

Collin was stone. Weirdly unaffected by everything going on around him. Connor is his twin brother. Why isn't he freaking out like me?

This is the second funeral I've been to this year, I thought as I sat comatose in the last row of the chapel. The tears were dried to my face, Collin held my hand in both of his, as if he were protecting it somehow. He needed me to be okay, but I wasn't.

How many loved ones am I possibly going to lose? Is Collin next?

I shut down that thought quickly.

How am I supposed to go on? Everyone is going up to the altar to say wonderful things about Connor. I can't even move. I should be up there. But I can't speak. I can't do this. Through my borderline catatonic-state I see his ex-girlfriend, Winona, go up there like she knows a damn thing, and I just snap up from my seat, startling Collin next to me.

"What?" he just says in surprise.

"I'm gonna go have a smoke," I whisper.

"Right now?" He questioned me disapprovingly.

I'm so annoyed by his response I don't even reply. I collect my bag and head out the main doors out to the parking lot. My cigarette is lit by the time the doors close behind me. I know I caused a disturbance and everyone saw me storm out of there. I don't care.

"That'll kill you, ya know," A low voice from behind me.

I turned around, and leaning against the building was one of our old schoolyard pals. He looked the same except now he has more tattoos. His hair was dark and trailed past his chin, a scruffy face, not quite a beard, and he towered over me like a giant. He had a cigarette of his own in between his lips.

I smile slightly, "Juniper," I say with joy. He brings his cigarette out of his mouth and brings me into an embrace. "I'm happy to see you."

"Sorry for the circumstances," He said softly into my hair. I pull out of the hug and puff on my cigarette.

"How long has it been?"

"Six years. I moved my sophomore year of high school."

"I can't believe you made the trip. Who told you?"

"I found out through social media actually. It's crazy how when someone dies, all these people that never really knew them come out of the woodwork to say 'RIP' and all that."

I frowned. "I'm sorry that's how you found out."

"It's better than how Collin found out."

I was taken aback. Noticeably so. Juniper was never especially sensitive. I could always count on him to say the wrong thing, to be honest.

"It's all over the internet, Vee. The whole story," He said quietly.

"I couldn't expect anything less," I sighed. "I broke my phone a few days ago. I may have like. Carelessly threw it to the ground on purpose. Needless to say, I haven't been on the internet in a few days. Of course, everyone is talking about Connor. Everyone loved him."

"Not like you did, though," Added Juniper.

I inhaled some of my cigarette. "Maybe," was all I said.

Collin came out the main doors and saw me with Juniper. His eyes lit up. And brought his hand out to greet him.

"Hey, man," they shook hands. "Thanks for coming, so glad to see you."

"My condolences, brother. Connor will be missed by so many."

I ditched my cigarette.

"I know this is exactly how Connor would see it going down. The only person that's missing from our old gang is Charlie."

"Yeah, where is that little weirdo?" Juniper jokes.

I snorted. "Last January she bought a healing crystal and some sage, now she's somewhere in I believe Nepal? She told me she left to open her third eye and she isn't coming back until... it was open?"

"None of us have heard from her since mid-May," finished Collin.

"So she'll be popping back up in no time," Juniper stated, joking but also serious.

Collin and I suppressed a low chuckle. "Basically," I answered.

"No one's been able to reach her. To let her know about Connor," I say softly. It's quiet for a moment.

"I have to go back inside. Don't make me face these people by myself," Collin pleaded to us.

Lingering in front of this place was getting old. Juniper and I followed Collin inside and faced his family and our friends. I can't believe this is happening.

This ache in my heart that tells me that this isn't real. Ever since I was a little girl, I knew it was supposed to be me and Connor. It was supposed to be us. And now it never will.

There was a large reception at Connor and Collin's parent's house. A lavish mansion to say the least. Perfect for intimate gatherings of 100 people or less. Memories rushed back to me. This is the home that I truly grew up in. I lived next door to the Parrish's.

Winona, Connor's first girlfriend, decided to show up. They were together for three months but acted like they were soulmates. It's horribly annoying. I held my tongue. I'll get back at her my own way. Winona and I had our own history. We were really close when we were little, but our friendship ended well before middle school.

I found a moment alone and went to the coat closet. I snuck by very sneakily and ninja-like to not get caught. Let's see what she thinks is important to bring to a funeral. I found her leather trench coat with the authentic rabbit trim. I dug into the pockets and found nothing.

"Viridian?"

Shit.

"What are you doing?" It was Juniper.

I plaster a huge fake smile as I turn around and attempt to *not* look like I was just searching Winona's jacket. "Um, just checking to see if I left something in here. I didn't," I say as I try to exit the coat closet.

"Well, Klepto, seems like you're back at what you do best, huh?"

I scowl. "I'm having a rough day. A rough fucking year. Leave me alone." Juniper was among the people that knew I had a stint in my teenage years where I had this insatiable urge to steal things from peoples homes. There was just something in my brain, just knowing I could get away with it. It was never anything big. They were always knick knacks, small trinkets, trophies for me. They were mementos.

"I'll never understand you rich girls. Stealing stuff even though you have all the money in the world."

"Don't even try to understand me, June. Also, how dare you put me in the Rich Girl box? Like that's all I am?" I said infuriated, getting closer to his face.

"That's big talk coming from someone who's searching through people's coat pockets, *Gwenore.*"

"DO NOT," I was fuming. "Call me that."

"It's literally your first name."

"I will not be called that name," I said tensely.

"Hey, guys," suddenly Collin appeared through the doorway. "Oh. Um. What's going on here?"

"Nothing," I said, me being a terrible liar.

"We were making out," said Juniper matter-of-factly. Me, instantly punching him in the arm.

"Collin, we were NOT making out."

Collin smiled a genuine smile, "Okay - I don't care what you were doing. I was just going to see if you wanted to go somewhere? I need to get out of this house. I cannot handle another 'He's in a better place now.'"

Juniper piped in immediately, "We should go to Presley's!"

I smiled softly, I haven't been there in years. The five of us used to go there as kids all the time. We'd all get chocolate peanut butter banana shakes. It's a diner like place, Elvis-themed of course. It was located just a few blocks from here.

Collin agreed, "That's a great idea. Vee? You in?"

The three of us got settled into a booth. Juniper sat on one side and Collin and I sat on the other.

"This seemed like such a great idea, but I seriously can't eat anything," I said softly. I looked around at the restaurant. Not very busy. Two families with kids and a couple sitting near the door sharing a milkshake. Looks like there was only one waitress going around tonight.

"I know what you mean. Let's just get one of our usual shakes and like some fries to share," said Collin.

"And nacho cheese for the fries. Connor never went without."

Collin and I both smiled. I started tearing up again. I tried not to draw attention to myself but, "Today was so hard.," I said. I try to smile through the tears, to make the best of the situation.

"Whoa," said Juniper, suddenly getting up from his position.

"What's wrong?" Collin asked with concern.

From behind us there was a shout, "Hello, my star children!" The sugary voice echoed through the little nostalgic diner. We both turned around and there was our Charlie Locke. I forgot how short she was. Her little figure ran towards us, no taller than four foot eleven. Her once shortly cropped blonde hair was now down past her shoulders, and her hazel eyes beamed at us.

"Hey! Weirdo!" Juniper greeted her.

She laughed as she took a seat next to him, "How did I know that I'd find my pals here?" Her face softened when she saw the fresh tears still on my face. "What's going on, Vee?"

Collin came to my rescue and chimed in "I'll tell her, Vee. Why don't you and Juniper go outside for a smoke. You just... look like you could use a break."

He was completely right.

"Yeah, not a bad idea. Juniper, do you want to go outside?" I said.

"Yeah, let's go."

Collin let me out of the booth. Juniper and I trailed outside and took a seat at the little bench near the main entrance where we lit both of our cigarettes and savored the taste.

It was quiet for a moment. I was taking in the scenery. Nothing like a usually busy street completely quiet. It's a strange feeling. The other shops on this block were turning off their neon open signs. Presley's was known to be open later. A shiver ran down my spine. The cold October air always got to me. I just didn't feel it before. Juniper didn't say anything, but he removed his jean jacket and put it over me. It smelled like cloves.

"You didn't have to do that."

"It's no problem."

"How much longer are you going to be in town?"

He sighed. "I leave first thing in the morning."

"What's home for you right now?" I asked.

"This town will always be home," He emphasized. "But lately I've been living in LA," he expressed like he was under duress.

"You sound so abused," I teased, "What are you doing there?"

"I have this little start-up company. We develop software to find missing people and other things. Sometimes we use it to find criminals specifically. It's nothing major yet."

"That honestly sounds like amazing work. I haven't really worked since my dad died, to be honest," I admitted to him.

"Your dad died?"

"Last January," I skipped over the on-my-birthday part.

"Viridian. I'm so sorry. This year has really been a tough one for you. I really can't imagine."

I took another drag of my cigarette. "Let's go back in. I'm sure Collin has explained everything by now," I tossed my cigarette into the street and gathered myself. I stood up and turned to head in.

"Wait," Juniper grabbed my hand. I turned and looked him straight in the eyes. I went to speak but he spoke first.

"Don't go back in. Just. Come to LA with me," His voice was concise and serious. Almost tense.

I laughed. Trying to break the tension. Trying to understand him. "You must be kidding. You're joking, right?"

"Look there's nothing keeping you here. You aren't working, and the love of your life just died. Why not? Start over with me."

I closed my eyes slowly trying to process this. I haven't heard from Juniper in years. And now he just? What? I can't even comprehend this.

"Look, June. I'm just going to pretend you didn't say this. I'm going back inside. Please don't make me do this alone." The last sentence came out as a plea. He understood that I needed to pretend that he didn't say that. That I couldn't take in another thing. I can't believe he referred to Connor as the love of my life. I mean, was he wrong? Not really. But Connor never gave me the time of day. He didn't want me that way. He was my best friend.

I sat down next to Charlie this time when I got in there. Juniper was seated next to Collin. I rested my head on her shoulder. "Don't ever leave me ever again," I said weakly.

She wrapped her arm around me in a nurturing way. "I promise, my little sun baby."

"How was Nepal?" I asked.

"I was in Peru, ya dumb."

"What? What happened to Nepal? I swear to god you said you were going to Nepal."

"Oh, well, I listened to the voice deep inside myself and traded my plane ticket in for one in Peru. And my god, the ruins were amazing. I brought back some special tequila. You're going to looooove it."

I sighed and shook my head. "You are so crazy. So I assume your third eye is now open?"

"Bruh, my seventh eye is open. It was the tequila, Vee. You have to try some."

"Do you guys want to head back to my place for a few drinks?" interjected Collin.

I made a face of rejection, but Collin continued, "Look, if you guys don't come over, I'll just end up drinking by myself."

"I could go for a Gin and Tonic, myself," concluded Juniper.

I sighed reluctantly, "I'm in. We'll have to start with that tequila."

"Can we walk there?" Asked Charlie, "The bite of the air is quite infectious tonight. I love it."

No one had the energy to argue with Charlie. I paid our bill and headed down the street. I walked up the sidewalk with Charlie. Our arms interlocked to keep each other warm. I was a little concerned for Juniper, I was still wearing his jacket. He's too much of a guy to complain about the cold.

We walked a few blocks without really saying anything. Silence was better than talking about Connor. It hurt too much. But I must be here for Collin. He basically let me throw a tantrum all day. When he was the one that lost a brother. I lost a best friend, but that was his twin. They shared a womb. Why isn't he freaking out? Why isn't he falling apart? I just don't understand.

"Stop. Guys," Charlie has us stopped on the pavement.

"What?" said Collin.

"The old Zoo," She pointed. "Let's see if we can get in!"

"Charlie...I really don't want to. It's closed down for a reason," I tried to argue. But she was already basically dragging me to the end of the alley where it was located. You could see the old carousel from the end of the road.

"Come on! We can totally make it over that fence! We've done it before. It'll be like nothing," She said excitedly. The boys were catching up behind us. I groaned as she dragged me towards the fence. Just a normal chain link fence. She was right, it would be like nothing at all. We had done this when we were kids many times. The zoo was shut down for mistreatment of the animals, so it was basically a ghost town. It had been shut down for at least 5 years at this point. In high school a bunch of our friends had snuck in through this very spot for skip day. One of the tech students figured out how to turn on the carousel. It was a fun day. Connor and I graffitied the old monkey house.

The memory crashed over me like a tidal wave. We were just a bunch of kids. There were maybe a dozen of us. Some kids I knew well, others I had maybe a class or two with. We all got in through this very spot. Collin jumped over the fence and Connor had helped guide me over it, and I grabbed Collin's hand to secure my landing over to the Zoo. All of us ran in different directions, discreetly to not get caught, muffling our joyful laughter to the best our teenage bodies could handle. I was about to follow Charlie and Collin over to the Lion's Den when Connor had stopped me with a devilish grin. He opened his backpack to reveal four cans of spray paint. All of them were red. I remember what I had said to him.

"Red?"

"I like red."

"What if we get caught red handed?"

His smile beamed, "What if we do?"

I smile thinking back, because that's all he had to say to convince me. Just the two of us, tagging the inside of the monkey house. Connor had a very specific art style where he would find murals of animals and he would illustrate lit cigarettes dangling out of their mouths. I've never been as creative, I painted flowers and hearts. I'll never forget what he wrote over one monkey that seemed bigger than the other monkeys. He drew in his eyes red, and added devil horns on the top of his head. Then a speech bubble to the side of him that spoke, "FOILED AGAIN."

I laughed aloud, "How do you think of this stuff?" I said through giggles.

"He just looked like a villain," He shrugged, and smiled smugly.

"You wrote them a new destiny," I said referring to the other monkeys, all smoking cigarettes of course. Looking back, the "good" monkeys were the ones smoking cigarettes and I couldn't help but recognize a tad bit of irony.

"I couldn't let him win."

Charlie climbed over with little effort and Juniper followed after her. I was brought back to the present day and Collin helped me over and trailed behind me.

"Let's go to the butterfly house!" Hollered Charlie ahead of us.

"The make out spot?" Laughed Collin. He wasn't wrong. A lot of the younger couples would go there to kiss their lovers. It was a notorious spot.

"There's something I want to show you! Did you know that Peru is home to like twenty percent of the butterfly population of the world? I want to see if they have one of my favorites," she insisted.

There was no arguing with her. "Fine, but we're hitting up the carousel next," I said giving in to her. I'm sick of complaining.

Through the old beaten up path, that was once freshly concreted, is now filled with cracks and debris strung all over it, we followed her to the Butterfly Exhibit.

We stepped through the netted door, inside was once a butterfly paradise, one straight yellow-bricked aisle. Along the corridor was once 50 different varieties of plants and thousands of butterflies living their little butterfly lives. The walls are painted with them, and scientifically labeled. Now the floor was more of a gray. Seldom broken terracotta pots lined the aisles, dead plants and dried up soil. And not a single fluttering butterfly in sight.

We spoke little until Charlie piped up. "There," and pointed. The blue Morphos butterfly. "Named after Aphrodite. And so recalled as Morphos because of its ability to transform, so-to-speak. It's not really blue. It's how the light is reflected from it that makes it look blue." She began digging from her bag, and pulled out a little bottle with the Morphos butterfly on it. "The tequila I was talking about. Let's all take a swig. Right here! Right now."

She held it to the air. Knowing I was about to protest, she bellowed, "To Connor!" and took a sip from her little bottle. Juniper shook his head and grabbed the bottle from her.

"To Connor, the most magnetic person I have ever known," and sipped from the bottle.

He handed the bottle to Collin who looked at it skeptically. "Connor would never say no to tequila. To Connor," and sipped. He grimaced slightly. We all laughed. Collin never drank as much as the rest of us. He handed it to me.

"To Connor, the love of my life," No one looked surprised. Common knowledge apparently, that had never been said aloud before. I didn't think anyone knew about my devotion to Connor, a boy that I had loved my entire life. A boy I had never kissed, never shared a romantic moment with, yet every moment spent with him felt intimate somehow.

I drank the rest of it down. They cheered me on.

I remember the moment that I knew I loved him. We were in fourth grade. On the school bus we were headed to the capitol building on a field trip in the dead of winter. We didn't get to choose where we sat on the bus. I was sitting in the back because I was one of the first kids in line. Connor was one of the last to get on the bus and he was closer to the front. I was okay, I had a book to read for the bus ride but I couldn't help but peek at him every now and then. Then I saw the girl he was sitting next to peck him on the cheek so fast. My eyes widened and my jaw nearly dropped.

I didn't even know this girl. I remember thinking how did he even know her? Did he know her? I was cold to him the entire field trip. He tried to get near me and I would keep my distance. After the field trip was over and we had returned to school he finally confronted me. He begged me to explain what was going on and I asked him about that girl. He swore up and down that he was just as surprised as I was and he didn't even like that girl. I went home feeling so confused, I didn't know why seeing him be kissed made me so upset.

But he came knocking on my door, asking my dad if I could come out and play. I was hesitant but I put on my snow pants and my boots and bundled up and headed outside. That's when he took me to the ice patch in his backyard, and he taught me how to ice skate. He had some old skates that didn't fit him anymore and somehow fit perfectly over my feet. He held my hand the entire time, and he didn't let me fall once. I was mid-glide when I realized my feelings for him. Deep down, I knew how safe he made me feel. And now it's like I will never feel safe again. He let go of my metaphorical hand, and in no time at all I'm sure to crash into the ice cold pavement.

I looked around at my dear friends, bringing me out of my warm memory of Connor. Each of them always supporting me. Even when I push them away. The last thing I remember was coming into an embrace with them. The night faded out.

There I was waking up in the arms of my lover. We were up all night mostly talking and drinking red wine. I woke in a haze, through a thin veil of a hangover. Walter was now in his 50s while I was in my early 20s. He took really good care of himself. I admired him for it.

Walter was all I knew.

Every Wednesday during college, he came to town for business. I always made sure that I only had morning classes on Wednesdays, so we could spend the rest of our time together at the local Marriott.

I was pursuing my master's degree in Computer Science. But of course, I was minoring in business for my father. But that's only because he knew I'd be getting his half of Viridian Corp when he retired, he wanted me to know what I was doing. But I've always excelled when it comes to things on the black mirror, the dark web. I had entangled myself into it ever since I was young.

I think it started when I was six and I took my father's blackberry apart. He was so angry. But I got away with most things like that when I was younger. I always had a way of getting what I wanted.

I think Walter is a result of that. Walter Valentine was my father's business partner. I can't recall who pursued who. I was pretty young when our affair began. It was after my last debutante ball. I ditched Skye Young, the guy responsible for courting me, and snuck out to the back parking lot. Walter was there, and he gave me my first cigarette. He treated me like an adult. I think that's what I needed. Someone who took me seriously.

The sun peeked through the thick hotel curtains. I got up and did the cute-girl routine before he woke up. You know the one. You slowly get out of bed, brush your teeth, spray on his favorite perfume, straighten your hair a little and put on some mascara; then sneak back into bed so when he wakes up he sees you way more gorgeous than you'd be normally. One difference that morning is I also started the coffee pot. He knew my cute girl routine, he wasn't completely obtuse. I'd still do it anyway. I wanted him to know I always tried to be as beautiful as when he met me.

I slipped back under the covers and cuddled up next to him, my butt rubbing up to his groin. With my eyes closed my mouth turned into a mischievous little grin, I did this to him every Thursday morning. He stirred next to me and moaned.

"Not this morning, Honeybunny. Daddy has a lot on his plate today."

And I knew what happened every time we made love. It was a recipe for him to pass out as quickly as possible. "Finishing him" was my favorite double entendre.

I turned to him, my forehead pressed against his and I grimaced. "You know I hate it when you call yourself Daddy. " I joked with him. He turned and kissed my cheek.

"Let me have my fun." He whispered through his coarse, sleepy voice. I shook my head.

"Apparently there's no time for fun." I teased. "But never mind, I made coffee. Wake up, sleepyhead."

I got out of bed and out of his embrace.

"You have a big day yourself, don't you?"

"What do you mean?"

"Well, you're graduating tomorrow. I'm sure that you have tons of preparation you need to do. Aren't you packing up your dorm and coming home?"

I started preparing my coffee with creamer and sugar. "Speaking of that, the ceremony is at five. I'll be one of the last people to go up, but I'm sure Dad has room in his row for you to come," I took a sip of the shitty hotel coffee. I grimaced but I'm not picky when it comes to coffee, I've definitely had worse. I began searching in my bag for my cigarettes, Walter was silent until I lit mine up.

"Sweetheart. I wanted to talk to you about something," He said softly, rising from bed. "I don't think It'd be appropriate for me to show up at your graduation."

My heart had dropped. how did I not see this coming? "Why? I don't understand? Don't you want to be there?" How did I not see this coming?

"Of course I do. It just doesn't make sense for me, your father's partner, to show up in Davenport, Maine for my partner's daughter's graduation."

I sat up from my slumped position. Trying to remain composed. "I just thought that because you came to my high school graduation and you were there for all of my birthdays..."

"It wasn't just your graduation. I was there for Winona. And all of your father's business associates showed up at those parties. Everyone in town would show up."

Winona Valentine. Connor's first girlfriend. And the daughter of my secret lover. My childhood best friend. Beautiful and stupid, it's no wonder that she never figured it out. Winona Valentine — who got everything I wanted.

"I just thought... that maybe. Just maybe, you could make an exception. That you could be there for me," I stabbed out my cigarette and began gathering my stuff.

"I don't want to upset you, Honeybunny. You mean so much to me and when you get back home I'll make it up to you."

"You always say that, Walter," I said putting my jeans on and a thin tee-shirt. I ran to the bathroom and threw all the free toiletries in my bag, and the towels, whatever, let them charge his credit card. I don't care.

"But I always make it up to you! Remember that vacation in Aspen? That was a lot of fun!"

I ignored his pleas. "Is this even worth it to you anymore?" I say coming out of the bathroom. "Or do you just expect me to be your dirty little secret forever?"

He was silent. "Gwenore, this isn't fair. You know that I can't—" I stopped him right there.

"I'm done, Walter," I slung my bag over my shoulder.

"Done? What do you mean?"

"Don't call me anymore. Don't contact me. You treat me like nothing – so I'm leaving this just like that. Nothing," my heart was pounding out of my chest. I couldn't believe I was doing this.

"You don't mean that, baby. Look, in a few days you'll be home and we'll do something special and romantic and I'll make it up to you," he pleaded to me as he got up from his spot in bed. He made his way over to me. I stood there ready to leave by the door.

"Don't come near me, Walter. I mean it."

"You've said all of this before and you always come back. You know you can't make it without me," he reached out and tried to grab my hand, as if touching me would change everything. I snapped away from him.

"I need you to take this seriously," I told my 50-year-old, ex-lover.

His eyes softened. "You can't be serious. All because I can't come to your graduation?"

"I'm as serious," I said sternly, "As statutory rape. So you best stay away from me, Walter."

His soft tone took a quick turn for the worst. Instantly enraged by my threat. "You better be careful saying stuff like that, little girl," he grabbed my wrist and I instantly fought it out of his grasp.

I stood rigidly, one hand on the door knob. I turned my back to him as I opened the door. "I'm not a little girl anymore. You made sure of that," I stepped through the door.

"Gwenore! God damn it. Viridian!" He hollered behind the closed hotel room door. Steadily and calmly I tried to remain composed as I headed toward the elevator with my luggage in hand.

I made it to the elevator, beginning to breathe faster, harder. My throat felt tight, like someone was strangling me. Inches from the elevator to be closed, it began to glitch and falter allowing Walter access. He quickly slid into the platform and the doors closed around us.

"This is not over," he insisted. "Viridian, Honeybunny. I love what we are. You give me everything I need."

I try to respond, choking back tears. "Walter - This can't be all you want. Because I want more. I know I do. I want to get married. I want to show you off. I want a family. But you won't let that happen. I've always known it."

Walter was red in the face, panting from chasing me to the elevator. He stood there preventing the elevator from closing. "This isn't worth giving up on! What we are doing now works! Don't you see that?"

I cracked right up and laughed in his face. "This is functional to you? What are we? A 30-year age gap and a secret relationship?"

"Baby, this is the most functional relationship I've ever been a part of."

My laughter had finally just turned into tears. I muffled sobs. "Just let me go home! I don't even want to look at you," I tried to push him out of the entryway but he wouldn't budge.

"Look, I was going to wait for your birthday...but I've had this on me for weeks already...in case the right moment came up," He stepped into the elevator, in nothing but his pajamas, and got down on one knee. The elevator began descending to the main floor.

I gasped and my stomach dropped drastically. "No way," I

whimpered.

"Yes," He returned softly. He took a small box out of his pants pocket. I gasped again in absolute horror.

The elevator doors opened and coincidentally as the box came into view I swat it right out of his hands and the box sat in the corridor in front of us.

"Viridian! I'm trying to propose to you!"

"I know!" I exclaimed. "And no. No, Walter. Not trying to be engaged to someone that doesn't even exist. I'm done," I cried.

I ran out of the elevator that was then surrounded by a small group of hotel employees. One of them returned the ring box to Walter while I bolted out the main doors.

I did the right thing, I did the right thing, I did the right thing.

I kept repeating it in my head even though none of it even felt real. I felt lightheaded like I was going to pass out any moment.

He would propose to me while I'm breaking up with him. That absolute dickhead. But aw, he was going to propose to me on my birthday this year. That's so sweet. Ugh, I'm so angry.

I stepped into my little silver car and allowed myself to mourn my relationship. Or lack thereof, if I'm being honest with myself. Tomorrow, I will graduate college. Next week, I'll begin at V Corp. Then I'll annoy Walter out of his partnership with daddy.

I didn't want to cry because my youth was wasted. I wanted to cry because I wanted to believe what we were doing was okay. That our love was strong enough. I didn't know what we were, but I knew that we did love each other. Love isn't love unless it hurts you as much as it fills you up with warmth. Because it did both perfectly.

No one will see it that way if it gets out. I'll be called a whore. I'll be accused of having "daddy issues." They won't necessarily be wrong. But it's no one's business.

I'll never go public. I'll never hurt Walter like that. He's never betrayed me in that way.

I sat in my car for what felt like an hour, fighting the urge to pass out while I let the tears stream freely down my face.

The light from the sun through Collin's bedroom windows woke me up. Why are all my dreams just flashbacks of things that hurt me? How did I even get here? Where was I last? The butterfly room. Tequila. Oh my God, that tequila.

Blinking my eyes open next to me in bed is Charlie and to the other side is Juniper. We're all fully clothed, so that rules out the possibility that we all had some weird, alcohol-induced threesome. So that's definitely a plus. I was still in Juniper's jacket. Charlie literally drooled into my hair. She's lucky I love her and I've missed her so much.

I grimaced as I slowly rose from between them, trying to avoid waking them. I wanted to find Collin. It was rather peculiar that we woke up in his own room without him in it. Sitting up I noticed him through his sliding doors. Sitting on his terrace overlooking Rock Island. Charlie made a small snore and Juniper slept soundly. I climbed the rest of the way out from between them and snuck out the front of the bed. I straightened my clothes from the night before and pushed my fingers through my messy dark hair. The underneath was tangled into a nest of dreads. I quickly gave up on the idea of untangling my hair before I made my way out to see him.

Collin wasn't like Connor. Connor had this way with words. He was poetic to a fault. Collin was the music, and Connor was the lyrics. He was gifted in a way that could only be compared to that of a prodigy. He just... somehow picked up any instrument, and played it like it was him and that instrument connecting him to the earth. He was a man of few words. He let his abilities do the talking. He was always the smartest in school, and super athletic, but somehow always stayed out of the limelight. He just left that up to Connor.

The two were identical to most, but of course I'd know how Collin holds himself, and how Connor would smoke his cigarette. Of course, Collin never picked up that vice. Collin had a very small beauty mark above the left corner of his lip. Something no one would notice unless you were looking for it. They both had textured, sandy blonde hair, and earthy brown eyes. They would both tower over me but they weren't as tall as Juniper.

I made my way through his sliding door, and he noticed me immediately, I nearly startled him. I closed the door softly behind me.

"Morning, Coll," I greeted drowsily.

He smiled softly, "I thought you guys were never going to wake up."

"What time is it?"

"Where's your phone?"

I shook my head, "I threw it out my window, don't you remember?"

"You really need to get a new one, this is ridiculous," he scolded. "And it's around ten."

I sighed and made my way to the railing where he rested against it. "I need coffee. Should we wake them up?"

Collin inched closer to me. "Not yet. I need to talk to you about something."

Immediately I'm concerned, "Is everything okay?"

"I mean...obviously not."

I responded by cringing. That was a dumb question.

"No, sorry I didn't mean it like that. I just..."

My eyebrows furrowed, "What is it?"

"I know Juniper asked you to go back to LA with him."

I sighed, knowing exactly what he's going to say next. "Collin, you have nothing to worry about. I'd never leave you at a time like this. He was probably high when he said that to me," I said, writing him off.

"No," he persisted. "I don't think it'd be a bad idea for you to get out..."

My mouth fell open, speechlessly.

"You should get out of Rock Island for a while. You've had such a rough year, and I just want what's best for you. I'll be fine. I can distract myself with work. And Charlie is finally back from wherever. You aren't even working, and V Corp is being run by Walt just fine. It's not going anywhere. You've had to deal with so much."

I shook my head at him. "That's no excuse, Collin. You're my family. I can't leave you right now!"

"I'm not asking. I'm telling you."

I huffed at him and tried to decide how I would even respond. "If *you think for one sec-*"

"Go," he interrupted me. "Just spend a little time in LA, I know you've missed being behind a computer. Juniper has a start up that you could really make come alive. You know it."

There was silence. I sighed loudly. "I need coffee. I can't deal with this right now."

How could he be like this? How could he possibly think that this is the answer? Why does he want me to go away?

I quickly turned around back to the doors that lead to his room. I opened the door swiftly, making enough noise to wake up Charlie and Juniper.

I stepped in and Collin came in behind me, closing the door. Charlie shot right up from her slumber, eyes wide like a feral cat. While Juniper made a groan from his direction.

Charlie turned to see Juniper and gasped, putting both hands over her mouth. "I didn't?!"

I laughed softly, "No. You didn't have sex with Juniper."

She untensed her body and let out a huge breath, "Thank God."

"Yeah. Thank God," grumbled Juniper through his hungover voice.

Charlie instantly reacted and smacked him on the shoulder loudly.

He stirred from his laying position and surrendered. "Alright. Alright. I'm up," and sat up slowly putting his eyes into his hands and rubbing softly.

Once his eyes were on me I simply announced, "Coffee?"

Juniper and I got our coffees first. We both just got grande black coffees while Charlie and Collin got weird, girly, complicated drinks. We found a shaded area near the coffee shop and took a seat on a bench. We figured we'd at least smoke a cigarette while we waited for those two disasters.

It was oddly warm compared to last night. We were lucky. Juniper said very few things to me on the way to the coffee shop. We sat quietly on the bench smoking our cigarettes slowly.

"I missed my flight this morning," he said indifferently.

"Oh. Oh no," I swallowed a sip of my Kenyan dark roast.

"I'm booked for the red eye back tonight. I have to go back to work tomorrow. There's just a lot of people counting on me."

"No, of course," I said. "It was wonderful seeing you, Juniper. Really. I just wish the circumstances were different."

A moment of silence had passed us. "I bought you a ticket. I want you to come back with me."

"Juniper," I turned to him.

"No, hear me out," he started, leaning in closer to me. He tossed his cigarette into the street and grabbed my hand. "There is something special about you. Don't you know that?"

I shook my head. "What?" I was confused.

"Viridian, you are capable of something that I can't even properly explain. I know you don't see it. But I'm so inexplicably drawn to you."

I was so taken aback. That last sentence...Walter used to say something like that to me. He said that I pulled him in like a magnet?

"Just give me and LA one chance. That's all I want. You won't regret it."

I gave in.

2

Rough Landing

Viridian

I woke up on the airplane, next to me was Juniper. He slept soundlessly next to me. This allowed me to do something I hadn't thought of before. To really see him. To study him. He let his dark hair grow out long. And his eyes were framed with dark, luxurious eyelashes. He had dominant, Chuck Bass eyebrows. And his cheekbones were sharp enough to cut diamonds. He was really quite thin and slender. His white skin draped over his bones.

What was I doing?

I guess I was good at making rash decisions in the face of uncertainty. I shouldn't be going to LA. I should be going back to work. A place I had been neglecting for months. Doing the absolute bare minimum, attending a couple board meetings here and there, sure. But even with Walter being my former paramour, I let him solely run my father's business. It was half his business after all. It wasn't like he was going to let it go under. It was his business too.

"Vee?" his eyes fluttered open and he collected himself in his seat. "How much longer do you think we have?"

"I think we have a good 20 minutes before we prepare for landing."

He sighed and stretched. "I'll just be awake then. We have a big day ahead of us."

"What's on our agenda?"

"Oh, we're absolutely not going to do any work, by the way. We're on bereavement leave."

"June, the whole reason I left Rock Island was to do some work for you and keep my mind off things."

"Tomorrow, I promise, will be all about work. Today, I want you to get settled in, dive into the local culture, maybe get a few drinks-"

I cut him off, "I understand getting settled in but really I just want to see your set up and see how I can help. I promise we'll do all the fun stuff later but this is really important to me."

He was quiet for a moment, but he seemed to understand. "I hear you. I really do. We'll stop at my place, I'll show you your room, get settled and then we'll get straight to business."

Suddenly the plane began to shake with some uncomfortable turbulence and I nearly jumped out of my skin. My hand immediately grabbed Juniper's and I waited for the rough air to pass. It stopped and I carefully removed my hand from his. I realized I stopped breathing altogether and I exhaled involuntarily and began to catch my breath.

"That didn't feel normal," I said collecting myself.

"My apologies, passengers," said the pilot from the overhead speaker, "There is more rough air ahead so expect some more turbulence, we should be preparing for landing within the next 30 minutes."

Juniper's face turned white. He unbuckled his seat belt quickly.

"What are you doing? He just said–"

"I'll be right back," He got up from his seat and bounded towards the head of the plane.

I felt so confused. What in the world does Juniper think he's doing? I watched as he disappeared into the cockpit of the plane. Is he insane? Is he trying to get arrested?

Without fail the rough air came back in full swing and began to shake the plane, the lights flashing on and off and the passengers began to panic. I was beginning to panic myself. The shaking subsided and I impulsively unlatched my seat belt and went after Juniper.

Shakily I scurried across the narrow pathway to gather Juniper and hopefully save him from some sort of legal action. I have to figure out what he could possibly be thinking. I grabbed the latch on the cockpit door and swung the door open to see Juniper and the Pilot in a screaming match.

"Juniper!" I was exasperated. "What is going on?"

Him and the pilot look at each other and then they look at me.

"Vee, go back to your seat. We're about to land. Come on, I'm coming with you."

When I turned around the lights were still blinking on and off and I felt panicked to a certain level of paralysis. Juniper came from behind me and guided me forward.

"Let's go, Vee!" and he shoved me and my feet into working again and we both hurried into our seats. I sat next to the window and he sat in the seat next to me. My hands were shaking and I struggled with my seat belt. Juniper locked his seat belt in place and then got mine for me.

Without fail the oxygen masks fell from the ceiling and Juniper came to my rescue in this account as well. He put his around his face and then helped me with mine as my mind just seemed to fail. I felt myself slipping out of consciousness, trying desperately to keep my eyes open and my hands reached for Juniper because I wasn't sure what to do. My vision became thin and I saw spots in front of my eyes while the passengers that surrounded me began to scream and panic.

"Prepare for an emergency landing," was all the pilot said on the overhead and it was the last thing I heard before I felt our descent and everything faded to black.

"Viridian? Vee? Come on, Vee," I could hear someone distant calling for me through a mental fog. I slowly regained consciousness. I'm somewhere warm. Somewhere soft.

"Juniper?" I was able to speak. "Where are we?"

"We made it to my apartment actually. As soon as we landed I called my driver to come pick us up. Everyone on the plane made it safely."

"What...happened?"

He sighed. "No one knows for sure. Something strange was happening to the plane, like there was some sort of malfunction. So the pilot had to make an emergency landing."

I started to sit up and really took in my surroundings. I was in some sort of minimalist bedroom. Brick walls, gray bedding, black painted furniture, wooden floors. I had several blankets on top of me. Too many for southern California. This is why I felt so warm. Juniper was sitting in a chair near my bed, still in his clothes that he was wearing on the plane, covered in a bit of soot. I looked down at myself and noticed the same. There was blackness caked underneath my manicured nails.

"God, that was so scary. I'm so embarrassed."

"I didn't leave your side for a second. I knew you were going to be okay. As soon as we were granted permission to exit the plane I carried you to my car and my driver brought us straight home. I wanted to make you comfortable."

"That's not how it happens in the movies."

"What do you mean?"

"Like weren't there like detectives and stuff? Wanting statements and asking us a bunch of questions?"

He tried to be casual, "I'm kind of a big deal around here, I have some pull with the LAPD. I gave them a statement for the both of us and they sent us on our way. I do a lot of work for them. Besides, you were completely out of it. "

I was quiet. Not sure how to respond. It made sense with his company and what he does, he helps a lot of people. But I still had so many questions.

"You knew something was wrong, June. You knew and you jumped right into action. How did you know?"

He paused. "Sometimes I just get this feeling, Vee. I can't explain it. When someone isn't telling the whole truth, I just know it. Most of the time these feelings aren't that strong, but for some reason when I'm around you everything is just crystal clear."

Through my cloudy mind this all just seemed so familiar to me. People have said similar things to me before. I'm used to such hyperbole at this point. But could there be some merit to this?

I quieted this thought, "You realize how insane that sounds, right?"

"It's the truth. Test me."

"What?"

"Play two truths and a lie with me right now. I'll be able to tell you instantly which one is the lie."

"That's ridiculous because it's always easy to pinpoint the lie," I quipped.

"Humor me."

I began thinking, reluctantly thinking of how I want to approach this.

"One, I want to quit smoking. Two, I want to quit shoplifting. Three, I want to go home."

He smiled crookedly. "Oh, nice trick."

I was puzzled. "How so?"

"They're all lies. You're an addict. Psychologically you know you should quit smoking and shoplifting but part of you wants to keep holding on. And lastly, despite it all, the last place you want to be is back in Rock Island," he said smugly.

Maybe he knew me better than I knew myself. I was honestly speechless.

"That doesn't prove anything," I said, mostly for my own benefit.

"How can I prove it to you?"

"I have no idea."

"But when we were on that plane, as soon as you touched my hand this *feeling*, it got turned up to a thousand. I knew that the pilot was withholding information. I knew that it wasn't just turbulence. I knew that something was wrong and we needed to land if we wanted a fighting chance to make it out alive."

I scoffed. "This is too crazy. Juniper, I'd really like to be alone. Does that sound truthful enough to you?"

His face dropped, "It does," he said quietly. He got up from his chair and headed to the doorway. "I've never told anyone about this part of me. I didn't expect you to understand," he said with his back turned to me. "You have your own bathroom and it's stocked with towels and soap if you want to freshen up. Our luggage hasn't arrived yet but it's scheduled to be here by the end of the day," he turned to look at me, "I'll bring you a change of clothes."

He departed through the door and closed it softly behind him. I exhaled quietly.

There's just too much going on. I needed a minute. My logical brain didn't care for this much. At the same time, this very brain is working harder than ever before. So many things are familiar. Certain people are inexplicably drawn to me. And even little notions that *me just being around* was their key to success. Obviously not stated so plainly, things that were said in passing. Things that could be conceived as just compliments or comments. How I've perceived them my whole entire life.

I rubbed my eyes for a moment and made the decision to wash up and shower. I made my way out of the bed and headed to my modest ensuite bathroom. It contained a standing shower, toilet, and sink. On the rack there was a towel ready for me and the shower was stocked with luxury soaps that I had never heard of before.

I undressed myself in a slow manner, feeling unknowingly sore from this entire trip. I'm sure that the emergency landing that I was unconscious for wasn't the cleanest. Deep down I wish I could call my dad. I wish I could let him know that even though I survived this whirlwind disaster that I am okay. But now I don't have anyone to call. I don't have family to let know I'm fine. I suppose I could call Collin or Charlie. Then I remembered I still don't have a phone.

I stood before the mirror, seeing what I had become. I remember what I thought I looked like before. I was just a girl. Short, small, with long brown hair cascading down my back. I stared myself in the eyes. I have always been told that my eyes were large. My father honestly called them cow eyes much to my chagrin. They were deeply green, once bright and cheerful and now sunken into my face from the crying, drinking, and poor sleep quality.

I finished undressing and I got into the shower and washed this day off of me. I took a generous heaping of body wash and lathered. I went over my side with my hand and felt an intense pain. I look and from my thigh to my hip I have this rugged, patchy, purple bruise nearly taking up my whole side. I can only assume this is from the rough landing and I've always been easy to bruise. But this one looks scary.

I finished up the rest of my shower, quickly washing my hair and rinsing thoroughly. I knew I just wanted to get right back into bed. I was more tired than I thought I was. I stepped out and dried myself off and wrapped myself in a towel. When I exited the bathroom I noticed a pile of folded clothing on my bed. Some sweatpants and a large t-shirt. As I placed the clothes over my body I smelled Juniper. That faint smell of cloves, just like his jacket that I wore the day before. He even included a pair of black socks and I slipped them on over my feet.

My stomach was in knots so I headed out of my room to explore the rest of his apartment. Before me was a mostly open floor plan. A modest sized kitchen with granite counter tops and updated appliances. There was a living room with an

L-Shaped neutral colored sofa across from a flat screen with various gaming systems. And a small eating area, it was a high top with two chairs and a few pieces of clutter accumulated on the table top. What was most noticeable of all was the bay window that overlooked what appeared to be Little Tokyo, a neighborhood in LA. I saw little shops and plenty of red paper lanterns streamed down the street.

I could hear another shower going from a door at the end of the kitchen area. Juniper must be trying to wash these last 24-hours off of him as well.

I walked over to observe for a moment out of the bay window, and I noticed a small cafe serving sushi and ramen. People were smiling, people living their lives so deeply unaware of the absolute calamities of others. I envy them.

I ran my hands through my hair and tried to separate the soaked strands, speeding up the drying process a bit so I could look a little less like the girl from the Ring. I heard the shower come to a halt and I headed over to the kitchen and started looking around, seeing what he had available. I noticed the refrigerator dispensed water so I searched for a glass from one of the cupboards and helped myself to some water before opening the fridge to see it almost entirely bare, with the exception of two take-out containers, individual packs of soy sauce, some mustard, and a bottle of lime juice. I closed the door in resolve, knowing that I was not going to get any sort of nourishment from this refrigerator.

I took a seat at the little dining area and took a few sips from my glass of water. Upon finishing I placed the glass in the sink and I headed back to my room. I sat on my bed. Then I got under my covers and rested even though the daylight persisted through my window, where the happy people continued to live in bliss.

My attempts at sleep were short-lived because I was so tangled in my web of thoughts. Maybe I should have just stayed passed-out. I had come to the decision that I may have been too harsh on Juniper. He had just saved my life, and even before then, he gave me an escape from my trepidation at home. Even though I couldn't fully understand him, I had to give him some credit. So with this thought, I crawled out of my bed and headed to what I believed to be his room. I did knock on his door but there was no response heard. I took it upon myself to enter his room on my own.

He was asleep, breathing steady. Without thinking too hard, I slipped under the covers beside him. I didn't touch him—I just needed not to be alone. His bed was warmer, bigger, and felt safer than mine.

Through the silence I heard the rhythm of his breathing. It soothed me in a way I haven't felt since sharing a bed with Walter. The association made me uncomfortable, because I didn't want to be thinking of him right now. I tried to clear that from my mind and live in this very moment, just like the people outside our window.

I focused on his breathing, as well as my own, and was able to finally get some rest.

From across the room I spied Walter. He kept his distance from me and I was thankful for that. Him and his daughter, Winona just kept to themselves mostly. Connor, Collin, and Charlie stood near me as I greeted each guest at the door. Always loyal. Connor approached me and grabbed me by my hand.

"Charlie said she'd take over with the greeting. Let's step outside.

We could tell you could use a breather," He looked back at Colin and Charlie and they began heading over to where I was standing.

"Thanks, guys," I told them as they approached. I just put my father to rest, and now I had no choice but to celebrate his life with his employees, business partners, and friends.

"I love you," Charlie responded.

"Go take a little break," Collin said.

Connor began dragging me out the doorway, "I'll be back in ten!" I hollered.

We went out to our usual spot. We headed to the garden, currently encrusted with the January snow. But this time was different. I didn't even see them sneak out – but Walter and Winona stood there arguing behind the bushes that surrounded my garden. Winona, with her perfect strawberry blonde hair that cascaded down to her waist. Her glass skin, her slim frame.

Connor and I turned to each other. Without a word I put my finger to my lips indicating to be quiet and we were totally about to spy on them.

"Winona, I'm going to need you to stop," I heard Walter scold her as we got closer.

"Don't touch me, you're so disgusting."

"Why are you acting this way?"

"I didn't know you'd be working with that fake nobody." I felt my hands turn into fists.

"Winona, it's half her company now. What did you think was going to happen?"

Connor turned to me then, quite horrified and confused. I was equally devastated. He grabbed out his phone and we started inching further to their conversation. I watched as Connor opened up a voice recording application.

"It was for nothing, you know," Said Winona shortly.

"What are you talking about?" Whispered Walter angrily.

"I know about the affair, daddy. I know you've been sleeping with Gwenore."

I gasped. Connor turned to me in absolute horror.

"Winona."

I felt a tear trickle down my face.

"No, daddy. I can't believe that you were sleeping with a girl the same age as me. That's low. Even for you."

"Winona, it's so much more complicated than that. It's not that cut and dry," I could hear Winona begin trudging away from him. And Walter followed after her, calling her name. My heart was pounding.

Connor ended his recording and I gasped out a huge sob.

"Viridian this can't be true. There's no way...?"

I slunk to the ground, my legs just stopped working completely. Connor came down with me, holding me by my arms. "I never wanted you to find out. Not like this. Not ever, Connor," I just cried and blubbered away into my hands and Connor wrapped himself around me.

I shot awake this time, and I felt a cry escape my lips entirely involuntarily. I felt so cold, like I was still there. But Juniper was here and it took me a moment to get my bearings and fully recognize where I was. My eyes opened and the light that crept through the window was no longer there, I could see the red paper lanterns alight outside creating a warm glow with the sun rising behind them into the bedroom.

"Vee?" He spoke softly with concern.

He had shaken me awake. His hands still held my shoulders carefully. We made eye contact for a brief moment before I quickly looked down in embarrassment. Both of his hands left my shoulders and I felt his thumb lightly graze my cheek, wiping a tear I hadn't realized was there.

"Are you okay?"

I shook my head, " I just had a nightmare," I said roughly. My mouth felt dry. I felt a shiver shock down my back and it shook my entire body. Juniper was quick to notice and wrapped the covers around me.

"You're going to be okay," He reassured. He got up from the bed. "I'll be right back."

I stretched my arms out in front of me, orienting myself. But I couldn't help but remember my dream. Connor's recording was enough to ruin Walter Valentine. But I begged him to delete it. I never wanted anyone to know my shame. He fought me on it for weeks. Until eventually we just grew apart. And he killed himself.

Is it my fault that he did it? Because he just couldn't deal with my long affair with Walter? Was this why he couldn't love me? These were questions that had kept me up through countless nights.

He took my secret to the grave. A true, loyal friend.

I brought my hands to my face and rubbed my eyes, I must've been crying in my sleep. I took my sleeve and wiped my face with it, drying any remaining evidence of tears. In an attempt to assess how crazy I must look right now, I ran my hands through my hair. Snarl after snarl of course. I then began to finger comb through my hair trying to straighten it at least to an extent.

Part of myself felt so embarrassed to be seen this way. Baggy t-shirt, waking up with snarled and partially damp hair from falling asleep with it still wet. And best of all, crying. But

Juniper isn't someone that I was worried about. He's already seen me at my worst, hasn't he? How could this make much of a difference?

He came through the door with both a bottle of water and a mug of freshly brewed coffee. "I've been awake for a little while. Our baggage has been dropped off and I had some groceries delivered. I didn't anticipate any guests before I left so my fridge was pretty bare but it should be pretty much stocked now."

"I was really looking forward to making myself a mustard, soy sauce, and lime juice sandwich," I said jokingly.

"Ah, so you saw the fridge," he said, handing me the mug of coffee.

I took a sip, "What? No, not at all," I grinned. He set the bottle of water next to me on the bed and left the room and quickly came back with his own coffee mug. He sat down on the bed, leaving ample space between us.

"So at what point...did you end up in here?" He asked cautiously.

I thought about my answer, "I'm sorry," I started. "I wasn't trying to be weird. I–"

"No, don't apologize, I didn't take it as weird."

"Right, I just, I was thinking of you."

"You were thinking of me?"

God, I'm such a fucking idiot getting these words out he's going to get the wrong idea.

"I was thinking that I'm not the only one that's had a traumatic experience. I didn't want to be alone, and I didn't want you to be alone either."

He took a sip from his coffee and grinned. "I believe you. And again, you don't have to be sorry or anything. It was nice waking up and not being alone."

"Well, I couldn't lie to you, could I?"

"I suppose not."

A few days had passed and I was really quick to fall into a routine with Juniper. He worked remotely since I had arrived and I was able to get my hands on a keyboard once again. I had found that I was able to help Juniper with his program that he was using to find criminals and even missing people.

Juniper's software had promise, but the facial-recognition matching was clunky and way too slow. I rewrote a few key algorithms and streamlined the UI—cut out two unnecessary verification loops and integrated a better match index. Now it could ping footage from any unsecured IP camera and still recognize a face with 85% accuracy, even on grainy feeds. It wasn't clean, and it wasn't legal in all states, but it worked. It was honestly revolutionary. It kind of reminded me of my dad in a way, how he worked in home security, and then even surveillance for businesses and banks. We need to have this kind of program implemented over at V Corp. It would only give our company even more credibility and merit.

Each day, we have woken up together, drank coffee together, and gone to work together. The evenings vary on whether we decide to get drinks or not but be that as it may, we have consumed copious amounts of sushi in his neighborhood, and typically end up putting some old movies on the TV. We're akin to taking turns picking one of our favorites and putting it on. He showed me *Once*. It's actually a musical set in Ireland. It was charmingly romantic and I was so surprised to see that kind of thing interested him. Then I showed him *Natural Born*

Killers, some of Tarantino's early work.

I haven't had a phone, and I haven't touched social media. I'm going to make it a priority to get a new phone tomorrow. I need to check in with Collin and Charlie if I can. I mean, Collin for sure, but Charlie could be in South Africa for all I know. It's hard to keep a hold of that girl.

After finishing our movie of the night, together we settled into bed in Juniper's room. Deciding it was better than sleeping alone and we talked until we couldn't keep our eyes open any longer. We talked about everything and nothing all at the same time. He had the most genuine laugh, how he would often close his eyes and cover his face while laughing, like he couldn't possibly show any sign that he isn't as tough as he'd like to appear.

But it hasn't even been a week. And in this week I have fallen into the most strange but comfortable pattern. Every night now, Juniper and I go to our separate rooms, but once it is time to sleep, I wordlessly climb into bed with Juniper. We do not touch, and we only occupy our respective sides of our bed, and we enjoy not waking up alone. It's uncharted territory for both of us. I have feelings, so many feelings. Feelings for Walter, feelings for Connor, but I have feelings for Juniper. I don't know what to do with them. I'm being childish, I know I am. I am an adult, and this is probably confusing for him. But he's known me as a child, as a teenager, and now as an adult. He says things to me, like how he is drawn to me, or how I make things more clear for him, but that doesn't directly correlate to a romantic attraction, does it?

Today was the same as the days before it, but I felt differently. Our movie came to an end and we both headed to our respective rooms and began our nightly routines. I headed to the bathroom and brushed my teeth and groomed my hair, splashed some water on my face and headed to my suitcase to change into some sleeping clothes. I opted for some shorts and a large band tee-shirt I've had for years. The bruise on my thigh that led up to my hip was visible in these shorts, no longer purple but it transformed into a brown/bluish hue. It was healing at least. But still ugly.

I think tonight will be the night that I try to regain some normalcy. I don't want Juniper to get confused. I feel like deep down, I truly have feelings for him, but I'm such a complete and absolute wreck. How could I not have feelings for Juniper? He has saved my life, and allowed me a place to grieve and even feel normal and useful. He is just so safe to be around. I feel safe with him.

On that note, I left my door open just a crack so the light from the kitchen could come through, and I turned off my light and headed into my bed that I have neglected the majority of my stay here. It was honestly just as comfortable as Juniper's bed, maybe a little smaller.

But I settled in under the covers and closed my eyes, waiting for sleep to wash over me.

"Vee? Viridian!"

I felt myself gasping for air. I opened my eyes to a dark room, unable to see anything that was in front of me. But I could hear Juniper calling out to me, worried and afraid. I caught my breath and brought the covers up to my chest.

"I'm sorry. I'm so sorry," I said ashamedly. "I keep having these... Nightmares."

My eyes adjusted to the darkness and I could see Juniper

slipping closer to me. He reached out to me. And I jumped slightly when his fingertips lightly grazed my shoulder. I know he was trying to comfort me and I'm not sure why it shocked me like a hint of static electricity. But I did realize that while I have touched Juniper before... It's usually me doing the touching. It's me reaching out to him. He isn't usually the one to touch me first, with the exception of the last time he shook me awake from a nightmare. "I'm sorry," he quickly stated, almost like he was ashamed of himself for touching me unannounced. He began to get up from the bed and that brought me more panic.

"Wait, Juniper, please I'm sorry. Please stay," I said with uncomfortable tears in my eyes.

He paused. "Are you sure?"

"Yes, I'm sure, I'm sorry I feel so embarrassed right now," I finally felt as though I could catch my breath as I saw him slip into his side of the bed. Just like our routine. The comfortable one. The one that makes me feel so secure. To not be alone.

It was quiet for a moment. We had both settled into our respective sides of the bed, and I laid my head down on the pillow facing him, and he cautiously turned to face me.

"Vee, I'm sorry if this is a weird question, but you've been sleeping in my bed for a few nights now..."

"I know, I know, I..."

"Why didn't you just...?"

"I don't know. I guess... I was feeling confused. And I was worried you were also feeling confused. But I don't want you to think that..." I groaned audibly. God this is coming out so incredibly dumb.

"I get it, I'm just your friend," He said evenly. "When we sleep next to each other, it's not that deep."

My heart sank, "No, no, no that isn't what I was trying to

say," I wish I could fully recognize his facial expressions at this point. "I didn't want you to think that I didn't like it. Sleeping next to you. It actually um, means a lot to me," My heart was pounding. Between the nightmare of my fathers funeral and this I'm surprised I'm still breathing at this point.

He was completely still next to me, I didn't even hear him breathe. "It means a lot to me, too," he finally said. "Would it be alright, if tomorrow night, we just kind of like, go back to normal?"

I smiled, he couldn't see me smile, but I did. "I think that would be good," I settled in further into the comforter and pillow and felt more at ease that we were able to come to some sort of understanding.

"Vee?" he addressed me quietly.

"Yes?"

"Do you think I could touch you?"

"You want to touch me?"

"I wouldn't mind holding you, actually."

Butterflies erupted inside me like Mount Vesuvius. My mind began to race with all the possible implications of what this could possibly mean. Letting him be this close to me could be either really good for me, or really bad for me. I really do think I want him to. But keeping him at this comfortable distance has been so much... less scary? But really like he's already in my bed, it can't be that big of a difference?

I must've taken too long to respond because he hurriedly adds, "It's okay, Vee. I'm happy just being here."

Instinctively, I felt myself untangle from the comforter and slide over to be next to him. I turned my back to him and he slid his arm around my side. I felt warm. I was able to burrow myself in his embrace and he completely engulfed me. I took in his scent yet again, something that I have found so comforting and familiar. I felt the top of his head rest next to mine, and I imagined him taking in my scent in return. I wondered what he gathered from me. I kept moving myself closer and closer to him. The sensation of having a warm body next to mine soon became so urgent.

He cleared his throat kind of loudly and moved away from me and adjusted his position, "excuse me," he said uncomfortably. It was then when I realized what was happening.

I felt my face redden. "I'm sorry," I pleaded.

He chuckled, "No, uh, it's okay. You know. It happens. I literally asked if I could hold you. Should have known better."

I turned and flipped my body so it was facing his. I tried to make out his face in the darkness. His arm was still around me. I reached up with my hand to feel his face. I ran my fingers across the stubble on his face. And I carefully traced his lips. My finger tip lingered on his bottom lip for a moment. This urgent feeling taking over me. This feeling like I needed more of him. Him holding me wasn't enough. So I leaned in to him, and I pressed my lips into his.

I was a goner. I knew from that exact moment on that my feelings for him were incredibly real.

With urgency I felt him kiss me back. His hands gathered my face and held me closely. He was just as shaky as I was. Nervous, out of control. I pulled away for a moment so I could breathe. My brain felt so spacey, and my skin was completely humming. I was dizzy with ecstasy. And I suddenly felt so incredibly awake.

"Everything okay?"

I answered with a kiss. I began trailing them down his face, to his neck, and I lingered near his sharp collar bones. He shivered and breathed heavily and I felt his arms wrap around me and while his fingers trailed up and down my back.

But my wandering hands needed more, so I began tugging at the shirt that hung off of his body and began attempting to get it over his head. My lips set his collar bones free so he could complete the task. I began kissing him again, my lips to his. His lips were wet and warm and moved perfectly in the rhythm of mine. It has been nearly a year since I've kissed anyone. My hands trailed down his torso so I could learn every curve of his skin.

He then returned my fascination and I felt his fingers begin to lift my shirt as well. I stopped what I was doing and he helped me lift my shirt over my head. Instantly upon removal he scooped me up in his arms and flipped me onto my back so he could place kisses on my chest. I gasped and my breathing was strained. My collar bones and bust, and my navel; cold and exposed. But his hands also reached to feel me, sliding slowly down my sides making me shiver with anticipation, and his lips pressed lightly upon my nipple, where I felt all ten thousand nerve endings scream with excitement as he began to play with me with his tongue. I wrapped my fingers up in his hair, starting from the nape of his neck and pulled gently and I tried to stifle a moan from escaping my lips.

I suddenly felt him remove his hands from my torso and he gathered himself upward, keeping my nipple between his lips and as he moved upward it snapped back and the pressure of it returning to my body left a Instinctively through my body and I audibly gasped. He shook his head and shook my hands out of his hair where he thoughtfully grabbed my wrists and placed them over my head. His face came back down and began teasing my neck and I whimpered and writhed underneath his grasp.

"I need you to keep your hands up here until I say so," he whispered in my ear. "Do you understand?"

All I could do was gasp.

"I don't have anything to restrain you with and I need you to follow this instruction. Do you trust me?" he said in between kisses and teasing my neck with his tongue.

I swallowed quickly to lubricate my drying throat. "Yes, I trust you," I said. And he let go of my wrists, and obeying him I left my hands over my head and allowed him to explore my body. There was a quick second that I worried that maybe my touching him was bothering him, and that's why he asked me to keep my hands away. But those thoughts were quickly quieted as he trailed kisses down my torso, and began loosening my pants to remove them from my body.

I lay in front of Juniper completely bare. And he was so thoughtful, and so meticulous with every touch. So calculated. He ran his right pointer finger down my sternum, over my navel and without stopping took a little sample of the pool of desire I had been collecting for him as soon as he allowed me in his arms. He had placed one finger, shallowly inside me, just testing me, teasing me to no end. He moved it in a circular motion around my pussy like he just needed to know. I saw him move this finger up to his lips, to taste me for himself.

"So sweet," he said. "So sweet and just for me."

I whimpered. It was becoming so hard to keep my hands to myself. But I didn't dare break his rules.

He settled down lower on the bed and I felt his face get closer to my opening. He kissed the inside of my thighs, delicately and sensitively. Teasing me to absolutely no end. And his lips finally made it to my clit. He kissed it, and even tugged it lightly between his lips. My chest heaved up and down and I felt tears welling in my eyes. I found it so hard to stay still, my legs were shaking. His arms came around to hold them in place, breaking away to kiss each thigh once while doing so. He found the most perfect circular rhythm as he let go of one thigh, and placed one finger inside of me, applying pulsating upwards pressure. The tears escaped my eyes and I was failing to hide every moan that slipped out of my mouth.

"Wait," I whimpered.

He quickly stopped, entirely puzzled. "What is it? Are you okay?"

"I–I–" It was hard for me to get words out. I closed my eyes for a second to steady myself.

"You can use your hands, I'm sorry," he spoke very concernedly.

I gathered my hands together in front of me, and covered my eyes, almost like I was giving myself some privacy.

"No, I'm sorry, I just... don't want to cum yet," I removed my hands from over my eyes and began reaching for him.

"Vee, I've been listening to your body, and she seems to think you do," he nearly sounded... frustrated? Listening to my body, though? Excuse me?

"I want to cum..." I trailed on while running my fingers down his happy trail, "on your cock. Please. Let me see him. I don't want to cum without you," and with care, I placed my palm over him, throbbing and hard, dying for me to touch him.

"I should've made you keep your hands to yourself. You had me doubting my abilities for just one entire second," he said, almost sternly, but also with a sprinkle of elation. No one has ever spoken to me like he was right now. The confidence in his voice makes me melt, honestly.

But he grabbed each of my wrists in his hands and placed them over my head yet again. "This is for you. I need you to keep your hands over your head now. I'm going to let go. But you need to be strong and not let them leave this spot. Do you understand?"

"Yes," was all that could escape my lips.

He kicked off his pants and underwear and I was not able to fully see him in this dark room. When I felt him I got the faintest idea of what to expect but part of me feared what would be penetrating me. I was able to see him bring his hand to his mouth and lubricate it slightly. He brought his thumb down so he could stimulate my clitoris for a few moments, and watch me recoil beneath him. I spread my legs for him further, granting full access to my opening. I felt him place another finger inside me, testing me, making sure I've been teased enough. Making sure I wanted him enough. And slowly he positioned himself at my opening and slid in so cautiously and gentle.

I gasped followed by a moan. I did end up feeling the tiniest pinch of pain, he was so much more than I was used to. He began to edge even further, still thoughtfully stroking my clit and making me writhe underneath him. I felt myself form around him as his rhythm began to pick up some speed. His arms were dropped down and he brought his chest next to mine, one hand stabling himself, his other still motioning my sweet spot with his thumb. I felt so wet it pooled beneath me. He brought his mouth close to my ear and tugged at my earlobe with his teeth playfully. "Cum for me, baby," he whispered.

I whimpered and instantly felt myself getting close. The heat from his breath, and the sound of his voice was pushing me over the edge.

"I want to hear you cum for me," he whispered once more.

And before I could let out another sound I felt myself crumble into ecstasy. My chest heaved and I felt tears break from my eyes once again. He placed his hand over my mouth to muffle my euphoric cry. "God I love this sound," he said once again into my ear. He picked up the pace and and began fucking me harder than before while my mouth was still covered. "I'm getting close, baby," he drew himself up and quickly pulled out of me before grabbing both of my hands and pulling them down, only to flip me over and penetrate me deeper than before. He quickly grabbed both of my wrists and pinned them together behind my back. It nearly knocked the wind out of me and I could barely breathe at all with how hard he was fucking me. It hurt, but it hurt in the right way.

"C-cum with me," I struggled to get out words and before I knew it. I felt him rip out of me and complete his mission on my back. He let out a low, soft moan until he was completely spent.

I exhaled slowly, I couldn't move, for more reasons than one.

Juniper's body was different from Walter's. I felt some guilt comparing my only two lovers. There was something edgier about Juniper. While Walter was just so different. The sex that Walter and I shared wasn't very focused on my pleasure. He liked keeping me restrained, and couldn't climax unless he was choking me. There were frequent times where I had achieved completion but it was not as consistent as he did. But he had me trained not to touch him. That's all I knew. It's like Juniper knew that.

But Juniper loved so much differently. Almost with urgency.

It's all quite a blur, how this even got started. But once we did start, it was difficult to stop. The sex was full of fire and it was completely passionate. Every kiss followed a bite, every touch followed groomed fingernails marking the surface of the skin. Territory being claimed.

I think I might belong to him. He truly touched me in a way that I had never experienced before.

Moments had passed after the inevitable clean-up, I had rolled myself under the covers and onto my back, waiting for Juniper to emerge from my bathroom. The sun was actually rising through my window at this point.

He climbed into bed with me within moments. And I shyly slithered over to him and rested my head on his chest while he placed his arm over me.

"Nothing has to change between us," he stated evenly.

This took me aback and I turned to face him. "Juniper, *everything* has changed between us."

"But it doesn't have to. If you don't want-"

"I want this," I stated with conviction. "I've made up my mind about you the second I touched you."

He was quiet. He took several deep breaths and I felt his chest move up and down beneath me while I waited for his response. The silence worried me. Like was he really going to fuck me like that and say he only did it as a friend? Was this all a joke to him or something?

"I've wanted this for so long, I'm sorry, I'm acting like an idiot."

"How long?"

"What?" he asked.

"How long have you wanted this?"

"Just being with you? You potentially being mine? Since we were kids, Viridian. But you were always his."

This puzzled me. And I furrowed my eyebrows together in frustration. "His?"

"You know who. He always had an iron-clad hold on you. You couldn't break free if you tried."

Oh my God, "Are you talking about Connor?"

"Vee, I'm not the only person you know that has a strange and inexplicable heightened ability, okay. Connor was something else. He just had this way with people," he said defensively, "and with you especially and I never trusted it."

"Way with people?"

"He has like. Charisma."

"A lot of people have charisma, June, it doesn't mean he has super powers."

"And a lot of people know how to catch people in lies, but not like I do," he retorted.

"Listen, I humor you a lot. I really do. But this is like a mental illness," I said dismissing him. I turned away from him and out of his grasp. I could not handle hearing him talk about my friend like this. Connor is dead for Christ's sake. "What, were you just waiting for him to die so you could make your move?"

"Viridian, absolutely not," He said in horror. "Please don't think of me that way. I know I was being cruel about him but please believe me, my feelings for you are so incredibly genuine. I have been truly, completely drawn to you for as long as I've known you. I didn't mean to say the stupidest things so quickly. I promise, you'll never hear me talk ill of Connor again," he pleaded. "I know what he means to you."

I was quiet while I took in his response. I had to give him the benefit of the doubt. After the night we just shared together.

"But I'm being honest about my special talent, even if you don't want to believe that it's extraordinary in any way. How else do you think I could touch you exactly how you wanted?"

My breathing halted and just hearing him talk about it

swirled my head into a state of anxious excitement.

"I listened to your body. Do you remember when you stopped me and I was so confused? It's because I listened to how your skin hummed and it told me, Vee. It told me how you wanted to be fucked."

My mind raced as he stated his claims. Things were honestly making sense but it's not like I had the experience to fully support them. He is the only person I have ever been with other than Walter. Walter was capable of satisfying me in the past, it's part of what made our relationship worth it. But he was right. He knew exactly what I wanted.

"Juniper, I'm sorry. I'm sorry for doubting you. I still can't fully wrap my mind around this but can we please just rewind back to when I felt completely charmed by you. I need you to be holding me now."

"Please," He said while shifting, making room for me in his arms. I closed my eyes while the sun slowly rose outside through my window and I dozed off in my new, extraordinary lover's arms.

3

Villain Magnet

Viridian

Last night was full of discoveries. Honestly, there is so much to unpack. Okay so, one thing at a time. I have never in my life achieved that level of satisfaction. Juniper's claims could actually have some merit. I needed to look into this further and do my own research. People with… heightened abilities? It sounds completely absurd and I think I need to set aside my logic-brain for a moment and establish a suspension of disbelief. I have confirmed a point where I actually want to believe him.

But I'm struggling to shake all the things he said about Connor. I can't deny how I've felt about him nearly my entire life. Connor and Collin have been in nearly every childhood memory I have. No matter how bad things were, Connor had this way to make everything better. He always had the right thing to say to me. I've said this before. But never in my life had

I considered he had some sort of underlying ulterior motive. But with Juniper claiming he always can spot a lie, or he always knows what's true…To truly believe Juniper, I'd have to also believe what he was saying about Connor.

While I lay in bed in deep contemplation, Juniper rolled over in bed and wrapped his arms around my waist. I felt his face buried into my neck, breathing in deeply before planting a kiss.

I think he could be genuinely in love with me. And that seems so horribly terrifying. But if he knows the truth like he says he does, he must be fully aware of how big of a wreck I am.

I felt him pressing himself against me, grinding slightly, and an unsteady breath escaped him. I smiled, because it just felt so right to me. When we make love, have sex, my brain has to be quiet and it gives me a break from everything.

But his hands slithered down to both of my hips and I felt him grip them with confidence and he began grinding with more urgency.

A tear brimmed at my eyes, I had forgotten about the massive bruise I still had from before, and I cried out in pain. He let go immediately and set me free of his grasp.

"What's wrong? Did I hurt you?" he said, full of concern.

I tried to mask the pain in my voice, "I'm fine, it wasn't you."

And he pulled the covers off of me to reveal the scary contusion that painted my skin and gasped.

"Oh my God," he said. He immediately got up from the bed and put his face in his hands.

"It's not a big deal, I just bruise easily."

"You don't understand. I had no idea that was there, I had no idea that I did that to you," he said in misery.

"Juniper, you didn't. I've had this bruise for days, I promise," I reassured him.

"What?"

"I noticed it in the shower when I woke up in your apartment after the plane. I'm assuming the landing was just really rough. I wasn't awake, I don't remember. You don't need to worry, you haven't done anything," I kept comforting him. He was so concerned, so worried.

He came toward me, coming down to his knees and made himself eye level to the contusion before him. He gently grazed his fingers over the bruise, practically in disbelief that it was real. "I'm sorry," he said quietly.

"It's not like you gave me this bruise," I said. "You have nothing to be sorry about."

He was quiet. Looking down in shame.

"June, really. Even when you're with me," I said slowly, "your abilities have limitations," again, doing my best to give his claims merit. I knew this is what he was upset about. He always thinks that he knows everything. It must make him go insane when he finds out that he doesn't.

"And I have my whole life to determine what these limitations are."

I agreed, "You're right. Everything is okay. Let's go have some breakfast, okay? I have a bunch of things I'd like to accomplish today," my hand cupped his chin and guided it upwards so I could bring our lips together in a soft and reassuring kiss.

"Like what?" he questioned with a devious smile.

"I want to get to the computer, finish up some work I started yesterday," Not entirely true, but I wanted to use Juniper's resources to find out more about these alleged special abilities. "And I want to make sure I get a cell phone. I've gone almost a week without one, it's been great, but it's time. I want to be able to reach out to Collin and Charlie. Collin especially."

"I can help you with that, we can order one online and it will show up tomorrow."

"Ugh," I said. "I'm just not excited about being accessible to everyone 24/7 again. But this is just the world we live in now," I groaned.

"You don't have to get a cell phone," he said, "I like it better when I just have you all to myself anyway," he said with a grin.

I smiled back, "I'm sure you do. Now go get dressed, I'll make coffee for us."

"No, take your time, I'll make the coffee and get breakfast started," He said charmingly, He pressed his lips to my forehead.

I hope that this is another routine that we will fall into. Waking up together, he makes breakfast, I get forehead kisses, what more could a girl want?

Walter could never give me this. He never could.

After he departed from my room I got ready at a leisurely pace. I hopped right into the shower and cleaned myself thoroughly. I shaved and groomed myself, making my skin more touchable for him. I was able to blow dry my hair most of the way, leaving a little bit of dampness to where my hair would make some subtle natural waves and texture once it dried. Dressing myself I had decided to do something a little differently than I normally would. I put on a casual navy blue t-shirt dress and opted to skip the underwear in case I wanted to do something spontaneous later.

I took a second to contemplate. Juniper Proulx. A boy I have known for half of my life. We always attended the same private schools, wore the same uniforms, ate the same food, and shared so many memories together. He was always quiet when he was younger, a bit of a loner. But he fit right into our circle of friends. Connor and Collin obviously always paired together, then when they met me they joked that I was their triplet. Juniper started playing with us when he and Collin bonded over their love of "scary stories." I say this in quotes mostly because they were found in an elementary school's library. It turned into the four of us playing out the stories on the playground. Charlie actually approached all of us playing and she offered to be the monster that would chase us around. For some reason, Connor always wanted to be a dog.

But Juniper always wanted to be the hero in our sweet little make believe game. He never wanted to play the bad guy.

We all grew up in well-to-do households. Connor and Collin's parents were in real estate development, Charlie's parents owned a lifestyle brand that went viral before "going viral" was even a thing, and Juniper's parents were both patent attorneys.

In retrospect, I wonder why Juniper didn't get into law considering he seems to always know when something is true. But what he does now definitely allows him to be a hero, what he always wanted to be.

I made it out of my room and went right to the eating area near the kitchen. At the table a cup of black freshly dripped coffee waited for me. I grabbed it from the table and headed over to the kitchen where Juniper was tending to some scrambled eggs on his stove top. I set my coffee down on the counter and I came from behind Juniper and wrapped my arms around him, pressing my nose into his back and inhaling. He was dressed in some joggers and a cotton baby blue t-shirt. It felt soft against my face as I nuzzled into him. "Good morning," I said against his back.

"Good morning, gorgeous," he flipped off the stove and turned himself around and planted another kiss on top of my head. His careful hands grabbed me by my waist and lifted me up onto the counter top. He proceeded to pepper me with kisses onto my neck and I felt a giggle escape my lips, the small kisses left such a tickly sensation.

"You know," I started, "I feel pretty sore from last night."

He faced me then with a crooked smile, "I'll kiss it, make it better," he said deviously.

Parting my legs, he got down on his knees. He began trailing kisses from the inside of my ankle to up my thigh, lifting my dress gently to be pleasantly surprised by my lack of underwear.

"Oh, you are such a good girl," He said in between kisses. I instantly felt butterflies again and they coursed through my body, leaving an intense hum that radiated out of my torso and escaped from my fingertips. He disappeared underneath my dress. He finally met my opening and planted a kiss, so delicately it made me shiver, like a shock wave up my spine. His tongue began to make upward motions and I couldn't help but whimper and struggle to keep my legs still. Just like before he held both of my legs still underneath my dress, allowing him full control of my body.

I cleared my mind and allowed the pleasure to wash over me like a cool blanket. He teased me so incessantly. He varied back and forth between upward and circular motions, using nothing but his tongue, deciding which one made me squirm more.

He wasn't edging me on like last night, he was on an honest mission to bring me to climax as quickly and intensely as possible. He was staking a claim to my body, knowing exactly how to make me melt away into nothing. Ensuring that I was his. And it was working. He was *showing off*. I really didn't mind.

My hips buckled under his careful grasp and my body was freed into a euphoric release. I moaned so softly, trying to recover quickly from completely falling apart in front of him. He removed himself from underneath my dress and caressed the inside of my thighs. He wrapped his arms around me and I rested my head upon his shoulder to finish gathering myself.

"Did you like that?" He said slyly.

"Very much," I said catching my breath. I lifted my head from his shoulder and stepped down in front of him. He guided me with his arms still around me. I removed myself from his embrace and I straightened out my dress.

"Where were we now?" I said with a grin.

Juniper had left the apartment to grab more groceries. I started getting to work on my research. His desktop was quite impressive, located in a separate room off of the master bedroom. I believe it was intended to be some sort of luxury walk-in closet but he had repurposed it into a hacker's wet dream. It was quite admirable. Five monitors, two ergonomic keyboards, and three PC's mounted to the wall, clearly modified by Juniper himself. Separately, a lone gaming laptop set on the desk for leisure. LED lights were strung to the corners of the ceiling giving it an ambient light in this windowless room. I can see why he works remotely.

Using the databases at hand I was able to type in keywords. I wasn't sure where to start. But I started by just typing in "Juniper Proulx."

Among the search results we got a basic background check from a few different sources. I clicked the first one, it was a database used by the LAPD. I scanned the site and only saw that he was currently being contracted for them and there truly wasn't any other things noted which I thought was really suspicious. It didn't list his age, or address, or license plate number... all the usual things that these kinds of things would typically contain. I moved back to my search and clicked on the next link. Each site that typically would contain some sort of record for him had been completely wiped.

But I scrolled down to the bottom of the search results in the database and finally found something incredibly familiar. It was called "The Domain." That was the company that Collin and Connor's parents founded. Their company was known for developing real estate, and had honestly nothing to do with Juniper in any way. I clicked on the site anyway and it just brought up a homepage for their site, again, something I have witnessed before. It was describing their values as a company and how they have been an established company since 1948. I needed to hack into their mainframe if I was going to get to the bottom of this.

Hastily, I clicked into their employee portal and pulled up the HTML dialog box. I was able to switch some code around and find myself a way in.

My face turned completely white. I've seen stuff like this before... but only in college. I just didn't know that I would happen upon this in my lifetime. Before me was a perfectly filed database, including pictures, of every person that seemed to be a person of their interest.

It was sorted in alphabetical order and it had hundreds of people from all over the world. I scrolled right down to P to see if I was going to find Juniper. My heart dropped when I saw none other than both Connor, followed by Collin in this list. My mouse lingered over Connor's picture, wondering if I dared to click on it. Do I want to know?

With my eyes closed I quickly clicked on it to reveal a long history of none other than espionage. It included his name, his age, his height, eye color, and something new that I had never heard of. métier was what they called it. And next to the word métier, was the singular word: "Charisma."

I felt my stomach drop and I felt so sick. I quickly clicked away from the page. I had to satisfy my curiosity and I clicked on Collin's profile. His métier was listed as: "Adept." But I saw a new category for Collin, one that I didn't notice for Connor as I searched his profile in a fog. But his profile had a category called "Status" and next to it said, "Living and Active." I quickly went back to Connor's profile and it was also "Living and Active." That didn't make any sense.

I was literally at his funeral. Maybe whoever runs this database is bad at updating it. He has a bit of a history, recording different missions I can assume, all using code words and his last sighting was a day before he passed.

I continued my search and I soberly did find Juniper. My eyes skipped to his status and métier. He was only listed as "Living" in his profile, and his métier was known as "Intuition," which makes sense, I feel like whatever this ability is, it is more specific than that though. My heart was absolutely pounding, and my hands were shaking. I scrolled through his information listing his name and age, stuff I already knew but then I saw his history. His history was so different from Collin and Connor's. His were more like sightings. He had a sighting dated a week ago and included a JPEG file. I clicked on the file and downloaded it and it revealed Juniper getting out of a car.

With panic, I closed the picture. I tried so hard to determine what this means.

What about me? Am I in this?

I closed out of Juniper's listing and headed back to the search results and headed right to the letter V. And without fail there I was, with a picture of myself attached to my profile, it was an old social media profile picture. Gwenore Renee Viridian. Age 24. Rock Island, NY address. métier, amplitude. Status, unknown.

Unknown? I'm unknown? What does that even mean?

"Vee?" I heard Juniper call from the front door.

"I–I'm in here," I stammered. As fast as I could I exited out of every window and cleared the search history while popping up an HTML dialog box, making it look as if I was actually working on his program. I got up from the chair and I met him at the doorway of his little hacker hideaway. I tried to appear normal like I didn't just find out that Santa Claus is real.

I didn't know how effectively I could keep this from Juniper, but I'd be damned if I didn't at least try. I have too many questions unanswered.

"Hey," He started. "I ordered your phone for you so we'll be able to set it up first thing tomorrow."

"Thank you, that was really sweet of you. I really need a cigarette, will you join me?" I then began to shuffle passed him through the doorway and headed to my bedroom where I kept all of my things. I really need to be careful of what I say to him. But at the same time, I'm not sure why I'm trying to keep all of this from him. I'm just going to try to be normal.

I grabbed my cigarettes with haste and I lingered at the apartment entrance and waited for him so we could walk out together.

It was time for me to go home. I've just seen too many things that make absolutely no sense at all. Staying here with Juniper would definitely be the easier thing. But I have this underlying feeling that if I stay here I would be completely in danger. The Domain has their eye on Juniper and I don't think it's just because of his métier. There's something else going on. So on the stoop of his apartment entrance, I inhaled my cigarette and exhaled slowly, and let him know, "Tomorrow, I will be heading back to Rock Island."

He was entirely taken aback. "What?"

"I can't stay here." I said truthfully, avoiding his eye contact.

He was quiet for a minute, assessing what I just said, scanning his mind for some sort of falsehood to what I stated.

"Did something happen?"

Again, I am completely unable to lie, "Something did happen, June," I said with a somber tone. "But I don't understand what it means beyond me needing to go home. I just have this feeling deep in my gut that staying here any longer could be bad," bad wasn't the right word, dangerous is what I was thinking.

He threw his cigarette butt into the street. "Was it something I did? Did I do something wrong?"

"No," I said quickly. "I just can't stay here and continue to avoid the world. It's been so good for me. You gave me something that no one has ever been able to give me, June," I crushed my cigarette under the heel of my shoe.

"If that is true... I'm sorry I just don't get it."

"Juniper, I was always going to have to go back home eventually."

"I knew that. But... between last night and this morning I just thought..." he continued to trail off in disbelief.

I turned to him and came closer. I brought my hands up to his face to look him deeply in the eyes. His eyes, so dark, so brooding. "And it was beautiful," and I brought his face down to kiss me. He pulled away, tortured.

His eyes closed, like it could no longer take the intensity of my gaze, "Don't kiss me and tell me you have to go."

I was quiet for a moment. "I'm sorry," I said with a knot in my throat.

We made it back upstairs after a few moments passed by us. The silence between us was deafening. He was calculating, trying desperately to get a read from me. His thick brows were tense, his stance was rigid and unsure. In the kitchen I noticed that there was still some coffee brewed from earlier and I helped myself to a cup.

"There's something I need to tell you," he started quietly. "But I didn't even want to mention it unless I was sure."

I looked up from my mug of coffee and made eye contact with him intently. "What is it?"

"So my ability. It's usually limited. Typically, I can only determine the truth if it is spoken out loud. Any publications or even body language... I don't usually get like... a signal."

"So you do know how your ability works."

"Being around you helped me understand it more. But when I'm around you, everything is heightened. I can read things and know what's true and what isn't. That is very rare for me. But when I was making love to you, every sound that escaped your lips told me what you wanted from me. It wasn't just words any more. Sounds alone gave me everything..."

A shiver ran up my spine just thinking about the way he could touch me, "I get it," I said with a shaky breath.

"But since being around you, with you every day, some things have come to light. And I really don't know how to tell you this. Viridian... I'm just so scared to lose you."

He sounded so helpless. I set down my coffee mug on the counter and came closer to him. "June, you're scaring me. Can you please just talk to me? Please tell me what's going on."

He groaned and he put his hands over his eyes. "Fuck," He said with his voice cracking, completely broken. "I think Connor is still alive."

My heart instantly dropped into my stomach. "What?" I whispered.

"I saw his obituary recently and it just wasn't reading as true to me. And then I thought back to our time at Presley's Diner and how Collin had us step outside before he broke the news to Charlie about Connor. I know that's just a coincidence but I think Collin knew that he couldn't talk about it in front of me. That is just a hunch, but I really think-" he stopped suddenly when he saw I couldn't take anymore. I honestly felt completely numb.

His careful hands made their way to my face, wiping tears that I didn't feel escape my eyes. It was quiet. I stood like a stone. His hands began stroking up and down my arms, trying desperately to comfort me. My vision was becoming incredibly narrow. I closed my eyes and tried to shake my head into reality.

I cleared my throat before opening my eyes. "How long have you known?"

Quietly, almost in a whisper he spoke, "a few days."

"A few days?" I said with anger peppering my voice.

"I had to be sure. I kept checking other things to see-"

"But you waited to tell me," I said with my jaw clenched.

"Vee, you have to understand, I wasn't going to keep this from you."

"But you did, didn't you?" I jerked myself away from his touch. "I'm completely disgusted right now."

"*Viridian,*" he cried.

"Here's the universe I live in, June. I'm just going to spell it out for you. Nothing to decode, completely blunt and unadulterated. The universe I live in, you would have done anything to get to me. I'm still accepting this concept of having special abilities. Because I would do anything to believe that he isn't gone. But it also means that you would know and keep the truth from me. I can't stay here another fucking minute."

"Vee, please," he pleaded.

"I'm fucking gone," I turned my back to him and darted to my room to gather my things. I headed to the bathroom first to throw everything in my toiletry bag.

"Fuck!" I heard him yell, still in the kitchen.

The tears were running freely down my face now, and I had a massive knot in my throat trying to keep it together so I could get out of here. I've fainted before when I'm under too much stress but I can't just faint every time shit hits the fan. I needed to be fully aware of my surroundings. I fumbled all of my toiletries and they scattered all across the bathroom floor. I fell to the floor with them, frustrated, struggling to keep my eyes open and my vision blurring again.

Instantaneously, Juniper had appeared in my bathroom doorway, aflame with concern. "Vee?"

I gave him a blank stare. And then I turned in front of me and gathered my things that scattered in front of me and placed each thing in my bag. I was fully aware of how cold I was being to Juniper. But he has no idea what he has done.

I thought back to earlier today, The Domain had Connor listed as "Living and Active." They knew he was still alive. It wasn't a mistake. And that means Juniper is telling the truth. And he probably knew for days before he got me to sleep with him. I feel so ashamed.

Maybe he didn't have a chance. Since I'm just appearing to be a super villain magnet... he probably had no choice but to lust for me this much. And how powerful I make him?

I know that he was being selfish, but did he deserve all the blame? But I have spent all this time... with no idea. Completely ignorant to my own métier. Walter probably has a métier too. I'll have to think on that one more later. But my point is, do I accept some responsibility for this?

I picked myself up off the ground and steadied myself. Juniper still stood in the doorway, completely devastated. I pushed myself past him, without a single word. Now would have been such a good time to have a cell phone.

I need to find Connor. If he is out there, and alive... Part of me wants to say I will never forgive him. But then the more truthful part of me knows that once I see him I'll never let him go.

I set my stuff in my bag and began gathering all my other items.

"So this is it?" He said with remorse. I ignored him and continued packing.

"And you're ignoring me?" He continued.

I stuffed the last of my clothes into my bag and began shoving it down to force my bag to zip. With some effort I was able to zip it closed. I slung the bag over my shoulder and made eye contact with Juniper. I didn't have anything to say to him right now. The fact that he just stood there in agony and watched me finish packing said so much to me at that moment. I turned to the doorway and began heading to his front door. He trailed behind me.

I undid his deadbolt and turned the door knob. With one foot out the door he called out to me, "I knew you were never mine. But I wanted you more than anything, Viridian. Can you blame me?"

With my back still turned, I replied, "No," reluctantly, almost in a whisper. And I made it through his entry, closing the door behind me.

While I didn't have a cellphone, that would make life obnoxiously more simple than it is now, I still had my wallet, ID, and credit cards. I would make my way to the nearest bus station, and begin my journey back to Rock Island and search for Connor.

Connor is alive. I am alive. I have super powers. Superpowers that don't benefit me in any way at all, so that is super fun. Only me, existing in a universe where people can have heightened abilities, would I have a power that only helps other people. Essentially, super villains. I am a super villain magnet.

Walter had to have some sort of ability. He talked about being drawn to me just like Juniper did. God, I need to see that database again. I am so sure that Walter is included and has his own little fact sheet. I didn't even bring my own laptop with me to LA. I feel so disconnected. This entire week it felt so freeing but now that I feel strong enough to face the world this entire thing is daunting.

And this morning I felt as though I could really be falling in love with Juniper. Everything changed so quickly. I don't think Juniper is a bad person. But one of the last things he said to me resounded over and over in my head since he said it. "I knew you were never mine," he had said. God, but I really could have been completely his. I wanted to be.

Am I a bad person? The second I was told Connor was still alive, all bets were off. Juniper was just dismissed entirely. I was able to shake off the thought all together.

Logically I knew that when I arrived at the bus station, it would be days before I am back in Rock Island if I truly wanted to make this journey on the road. Do I have days to spare? Do I have it in me to make it to the airport? I felt so indecisive.

Upon my journey I witnessed the most curious thing. It was a payphone.

I haven't seen one in years. It had been tagged by multiple street artists. I walked up to it and pulled the phone off the hook and found that it was still in working condition. This has to be the last payphone in Los Angeles. I set the phone back on the hook and considered who I should call. There were five phone numbers I knew by heart. The first being 911. Of course, there is nothing that the law enforcement could offer me. Next would be my dad's phone number. Unfortunately, where he is he wouldn't be able to answer. Connor is out of the question for now as well. But Collin... kind of pissed at him recently. Connor's funeral makes so much more sense now. Collin barely even looked sad. He was more worried for me the entire time. He was definitely in on this. Which left me one more person... and hopefully she hasn't changed her number since I've heard from her last.

I dug into the side pocket of my bag where I kept my wallet and dug out three quarters. I dropped them through the slot and began dialing her number and waited for the phone to ring.

Charlie didn't answer. I could have misremembered the number. But I left a voicemail. "Hey, it's Vee. I know I'm probably calling from a weird number but I'm in LA and I'm about to get on a bus to head home now. It'll probably be a few days," there was honestly so much I wanted to tell her. So much I wanted to say. "I don't know. But I love you. I'll see you soon, I hope. Bye."

I hung up the phone on the receiver and walked away from the phone booth and continued my trek to Union Station.

It had been just over a week since I first touched LA soil. Being this close to the Pacific was so different from being on the Atlantic. There was something special about the air.

Arriving at the bus station I soon came to find out what journey I would have to endure in order to arrive in Rock Island by bus. Four and a half days and countless layovers in flyover states. I can't do four days. I just can't. So I took this opportunity at the bus station to find a bus route that would drop me off at the airport. I didn't have time to be so afraid to get back on a plane.

It seemed like an easy decision, likely I would be back home by the end of the night.

My bus stopped right at the airport departure gate and I felt so numb. I looked around at surroundings wondering if I dared get back on a plane, also knowing it was my best chance of getting home and confronting Collin as fast as possible. I just know it to my core that he was a part of this.

My back was turned to the world when I faced the automatic doors to the building, ready to purchase my ticket and begin my journey. I took one last look around, seeing people from all walks of life gathering their luggage out of the vehicles and saying goodbye to loved ones. I took a deep breath and made it through the threshold.

Before I had made it through the door I was abruptly stopped by a tug at my luggage I was carting behind me.

"*Viridian,*" this pleading voice belonged to Juniper. His face was riddled with distress.

"Juniper," I said shortly, "What are you doing here?" We made it into the breezeway and he pulled me aside.

"I'm not letting you go. I can't."

"That isn't up to you," I tried to speak calmly.

"I'm coming with you. If you're going back to Rock Island let me come with you. Give me a chance to explain."

"There's nothing to explain, June."

"Then give me a chance to prove to you that I never meant to hurt you."

I thought for a moment. His eyes were so full of sadness. He looked like he was ready to fall apart any moment now.

I was quiet for a painfully long time. I thought about what I saw on the computer, how he knew about Connor probably from the get-go, but also I thought about *how he is* with me. I thought about how he listens to my body. He could very possibly be my arch nemesis. But maybe every man I have ever grown to have feelings for could easily use their powers to end me.

This morning I was falling for him, and the butterflies are still erupting inside of me. Despite all of the betrayal. But someone is out there keeping surveillance on him.

I broke the silence, and my voice softened, "Make me one promise."

"Anything," he pleaded.

"No more secrets."

His stance relaxed and he smiled in relief, finally exhaling he said, "Nothing but the truth," he edged closer to me and he grabbed my left hand in his light grasp. "It's kind of my thing."

I wish the butterflies in my stomach would slow down for

two seconds so I could stay mad at him, keep my guard up, but there was a part of me that didn't want to.

I wanted him to be real. This little universe that we've been living in the past few days seemed too perfect, but I wanted to believe we could exist in the real world too.

"We have a plane to catch."

The seats on the plane were almost fully booked so Juniper and I were seated apart this time. Juniper put up a fight with the attendant at the ticket desk but with his insight being more in tune than usual he knew that it wasn't in their ability to change seats around to get us together. I had a huge knot in my throat finding my seat and seeing that Juniper was seated so far away from me. I think he could tell how uneasy I felt. Uneasy being a light way of putting it. But I sensed that he could be just as anxious as me. He probably wanted to be near me just as much as I wanted to be near him.

We just reconciled. So many emotions swirled around us from the perfect morning we shared to the afternoon of discoveries, feelings of betrayal and then...now. We felt slightly pieced back together before we got on this plane. Not fully mended but perhaps taped back in place so we can make it through until we can make-up for real later. We were under such a constraint. I was somewhere between dangling above a seemingly limitless chasm and drowning in an endless sea. It just didn't seem like I had the tools to get myself out of this.

Being seated alone gave me more time alone in my thoughts, realizing how I was being worn thin. My thoughts were blending together until they drifted back to a different time. I gazed out my plane window and recounted the evening that

Walter and I had first...connected. I had known him for most of my life, but it was the first time we had a moment where it was only the two of us.

It was cold, the night of my last coronation ball. I felt frustrated. These events used to bring me so much joy. It made me feel so connected to my mother. The stories I heard about her always included an elegant event in which she seemed to be the belle of the ball. Both of my parents, social butterflies, always the life of the party. But ever since turning sixteen, the winter before, I had felt lost. The event was going as expected, I played my part, I danced, I curtsied, I held up my proverbial pinky as I drank sparkling cider.

In my angsty way I steered out of there undetected, leaving my poor and unknowing escort in the dust. But I didn't have anywhere to go.

That's when I saw Mr. Valentine. Or rather, Mr. Valentine saw me. He stopped me and asked me where I was going, and I told him that I didn't know.

We were in the parking lot outside the venue. He had been leaning up next to his car, enjoying the silence and discreetly taking drags from his cigarette.

"Gwenore," he started. "Do you need a ride home?"

I thought internally, I really didn't know what I was doing and I didn't have a destination in mind.

He continued, "I'd just feel better knowing you made it home safely."

I changed trajectory and just started heading to his car. He had walked around the front of his car and opened up his passenger door, helping me get in, as my ball gown was bulky and difficult to sit in. I made a silent vow to never wear this much crinoline again.

Nevertheless I sat and gathered all of my dress inside, and he shut the door carefully once I was in the clear.

I saw him ditch his half smoked cigarette in the parking lot. And he got into his vehicle and began to drive. The journey from the venue to my home was not far, but with the Rock Island traffic, it doubled our travel time.

"What were you doing out there?" He asked. "What made you want to leave?"

I thought about what I was going to say. "I just felt like a phony. I finally realized that none of this was me, as I never aspired to be this type of lady. I just wanted to feel closer to my mom."

He nodded, "She really shined the brightest when it came to lavish events. But wanting to be closer to her doesn't make you a phony, Gwenore."

I sighed, "Don't call me Gwenore."

"Well, why not? That's your name."

"It doesn't suit me. I just go by Viridian."

"Your last name?"

"I look like a Viridian, don't I?"

"It's the color of your eyes."

I smiled softly, "It is, isn't it?" I got my eyes from my mother even though the last name was from my father. Seemed like they were meant to be somehow.

Without fail we ended up in a traffic jam, a complete stand still. He reached into his inner pocket and pulled out a cigarette.

"Do you mind?" Referring to the cigarette.

"Can I have one of those?" I spoke, he contemplated for a moment and I lied through my teeth, "I smoke all the time."

He put his cigarette in his mouth and lit it and then handed it to me. I took it from his hands and held it between my fingers. I pressed it to my lips and inhaled slowly, trying to appear like a pro.

It tasted absolutely disgusting.

He lit his own cigarette and rolled down both of our windows as we sat, nearly parked in his car.

"You better not tell my dad."

"The thought hadn't occurred to me," he said nonchalantly.

"Aren't you Winona's ride home too?"

"I'll go back and get her once I know you've made it home."

I nodded, it made sense.

"Wait, wasn't Victor supposed to be there?" he asked, referring to my dad. Parents usually make it to these types of events.

"He couldn't make it. He got caught up at the office, I suppose."

The traffic cleared and he crept forward until he was able to drive again. At the stop light we both ditched our cigarettes and he rolled up both of our windows.

The rest of the car ride was mostly silent. As we pulled up to my home Walter turned to me. "Viridian, I'm glad that I caught you before you took off into the night. Promise me you won't make a routine of that?"

"I would have been fine."

"I admire the confidence. But if you must storm away from some sort of sartorial ceremony again, please just call me and I'll make sure you make it home safe. I won't tell your dad. It can just be our secret."

I smiled lightly. "It won't become a habit." I stepped out of his vehicle and with one hand ready to close the door behind me I bid farewell, "Good night, Mr. Valentine."

He smiled crookedly, "Call me Walter."

The plane landed with ease this time. Thankfully I had the most uncomfortable memory to occupy my brain while I faced being in the air again. Nevertheless my hands were unsteady, unclipping my seat belt from its holster, and I wrung my hands together in my lap mindlessly until it was time to exit the plane.

Juniper was there in the tunnel waiting for me and he saw me quivering. His face softened and he came close to me. I reached out to him and he wrapped his arms around me.

"Shh," he soothed, "We made it, you don't have to be scared."

"I know," I said weakly, trying my best to stay strong. I nuzzled up to his clavicle for a moment and allowed me to ground myself. His scent surrounded me.

"We're going to head to your place and drop off our stuff and then we'll head straight to Collin. I'm not going to stop until we get to the bottom of this. I have this feeling deep in my gut that Connor is still out there and I promise you, even if it's the last thing I do, we will find him," he spoke softly into my ear with my face still buried.

My face lifted from his shoulder and looked at him, so torn. Juniper was here picking up my pieces. "I'm sorry," I said. It just slipped out. I wasn't even sure why I was saying it. It felt right. "I–"

"I'd give anything to live last night over again. Even this morning. But LA wasn't real. I mean it wasn't the real world. You can't be sorry about something that wasn't real," his last sentence came out woefully.

"Juniper," I started, "It was real for me," I reached up to his face. I felt hurt by his words. I have so many emotions dizzying around inside of me it wasn't even fair. First I'm angry at him for keeping something from me, and now I feel guilty because I know he could be right. My hand caressed his face and his eyes slowly closed. I know he was just taking a beat. His hand went over mine and took my hand in his. He brought my hand to his lips and kissed it softly.

"Can I just say one more thing?" he asked softly.

"What, June?"

"This morning when I told you about Connor, I just wanted you to know that I was always going to help you find out the truth. I was never going to stop you. I had been selfish waiting to tell you. And I own that. I know that..." I watched him trail off, completely tortured behind his eyes, avoiding eye contact with me in our close proximity. "And I know we're both operating on my own hunch right now, but I feel so certain that he's out there, Vee."

"I really, really believe that you could be right."

"Let's get out of here," he said with an even tone.

We then carted out of the tunnel hand-in-hand and headed into the airport. But as soon as we turned the corner we encountered an armada of men in SWAT gear.

Before I had a second to question why they could be there, they all targeted Juniper and I. "There they are!" one of them shouted.

It all happened so quickly. Juniper's hand was painfully ripped out of mine and I heard him shout my name, "Viridian!"

"June!" I shouted in desperation, I tried to reach back out for him as he struggled from their grasp, three men in SWAT gear, trying to carry him away from me. Two men were holding me back from him as I watched him get inched away from me through his struggle. It was at that moment I realized they weren't coming for me. They had come for Juniper. What has he done? My mind flashed back to this morning at his desktop, witnessing The Domain's database and their surveillance photos of him. He was being watched.

My fearful face dropped, numbly. And felt my lip quiver.

Juniper saw me and screamed, "I'll get this sorted out! There's nothing to worry about, Vee!"

Sorted out? Nothing to worry about?

"They think I'm-" one of them slammed him so hard into the rough airport ground and began cuffing him.

I felt like the wind had been knocked out of me. They think he's what? And who? Who is they? The men holding me back noticed I was no longer fighting them and slowly let me go. Through the barricade of SWAT men came an older gentleman, dressed formally under a brown trench coat.

"Gwenore Viridian, will you follow me, please?" he spoke.

I felt like I was in a trance going from one trauma to the next. I followed him across the airport into a conference room that overlooked the planes taking off and coming home. The sun was setting now, and through the large window of a wall I could see the horizon fading into pinks and purples. As I entered the room fully, the man closed the conference door behind me and I saw Collin sitting there at the head of the table.

"Collin?" was all I could get out. I was mystified. He rushed up from his seat and ran to me and put his arms around me.

"Oh my God," he said. He squeezed me so tight it almost hurt. I hugged him back because while I'm so incredibly fucking confused... I missed him.

"I thought you were dead," he sounded so tortured.

I quickly pulled away, in shock, "What? Why?"

"The plane! The plane to LA! God, Vee, it had an emergency landing and you weren't recorded on the scene! You weren't *in* any of the reports; you were completely missing!"

My stomach dropped. I knew that didn't seem right.

"My God," he continued, "and no one was able to get ahold

of you for days and until you left that voicemail for Charlie and got on this plane-"

"Collin," I interrupted. "Can you please just stop for a second," I said it almost in a whisper.

His eyes widened realizing that I was being overloaded. "Here Vee, sit down for a minute. I'm going to grab you something to drink. There's a kiosk not far from here," he guided me to the conference table and pulled out a chair for me to sit in, facing the view of the planes gliding effortlessly. Wordlessly he left the room, closing the door behind him. I brought my hands up to my face and felt a warm dampness cover my cheeks. Tears. I had been crying and I was too stunned to acknowledge it. My body recognized how stiff my throat felt, making sense as to why my words came out like a whisper.

Zero answers upon arrival and at least fifty new questions.

4

Métier

Viridian

ollin came up slowly behind me and I felt his presence. I felt like stone. I stared blankly out the window watching the planes passing by through the night sky. The sun had gone down hours ago, as winter was just around the corner, and the days were getting shorter. Without turning his direction I began speaking.

"I know that a lot has happened, but can you please just take me home," my voice was hoarse as my throat was strained holding back tears.

He wordlessly accommodated. I heard him leave the conference room with intention. My eyes never left the scenery in front of me. I tried so hard to just focus on the planes. Planes full of people with places to go and people to see. Meanwhile the people I have left are dwindling away before my eyes. I audibly wince and tear myself out of that thought because I know where that road is heading.

Only a few moments passed and Collin was guiding me through the airport and we headed straight for the pick-up area. There a car was waiting for us and we both sat in the back seat as the driver drove us away.

Juniper. I wasn't strong enough not to think about him. Where did they take him? Is he hurt? Is he in danger? Was he trying to hurt me this entire time? Is he my enemy? Is that why he's been taken away? I wasn't strong enough to ask any of this out loud. But I was weak enough to let these questions swirl around my brain like a hurricane. I wasn't ready for any of the answers to these questions. I just need to be numb.

Moments ago I was ready to find Collin and confront him. But now Juniper has been torn away from me. First Connor, now Juniper. And I never would have felt this way, but Collin was the one that pushed me to go with him. The feeling settled in. Like my blood was running cold. It felt in that moment that this was all his fault.

I broke the silence in the car. "Did you know this was going to happen?" I said without turning to Collin. I stared numbly out of my window.

He shifted next to me. "What?"

I thought for a moment on how to word this. I turned to him and my eyes pierced into his. The silence in the car was honestly deafening. "Did you *know*, Collin?"

He looked at me incredulously. His mouth opened, but had no idea what to say.

I started again, my voice increasing in volume, "Collin, did you know that this was going to happen?"

"I–I..." He looked at me so tortured. "I... what are you talking about?"

My heart sank. He might not know everything but he definitely knows *something*. I know this for certain. He just doesn't want to give it away. I smirked with my eyes still brimming with tears and shook my head.

"I know about Connor," I said to him.

"He's dead, Vee."

"Oh, so that's how we're playing this, huh?"

"Vee," he tried to settle me down. He gestured not-so-subtly to the driver of the vehicle.

"And I know about The Domain, and I know about métier. I know fucking everything, Collin," I spat the words out angrily. I knew that I didn't know everything. I just needed him to think I did.

"Vee!" He said stressfully with his eyes wide. His hands rose up to his head and gathered his hair in his fists. "Jesus Christ. Okay, well, fuck."

The way he reacted confirmed for me that I was about to get all of the answers I needed. Collin must've been hiding things from me for a very long time. I also have a feeling that what I know now is just the tip of the fucking iceberg.

These thoughts made my skin crawl. My body was signaling me that maybe Collin wasn't someone I could trust. And maybe Juniper was the only one I could trust all along. And he knew he had to get Juniper away from me so he could continue to lie to me.

Or, Juniper was responsible for that plane to LA going down. There's a reason why he made sure neither of us were in the police report. He needed me to be missing.

Two valid working theories.

"Where are we going?" I asked tensely.

"Relax, Vee. We're going to my place."

"What? Why aren't you taking me home?"

He sighed, "Because I promised Charlie I would bring you straight here so she can meet us there. She's been worried sick about you. You'd think you'd respond to any of our forms of contact, Viridian. Honestly..." he mumbled the last word under his breath. Technically speaking, his apartment was way closer to the airport and more centrally located versus my childhood home that was all the way across town and would probably take an hour to get to with traffic.

"I don't have a phone," I responded.

"You never got a phone?"

"I haven't had a phone since before Connor's funeral."

He groaned. "We're getting you a phone. This is fucking stupid."

I was shocked by his sudden anger. "Excuse me?"

"I thought you were dead. And we couldn't find you ultimately because you didn't have a phone. If you had a phone you would know that we thought you were missing, and you would have been able to answer any of our calls, texts, emails, fucking DMs...fuck. We're getting you a phone. I'm over this."

"You are not allowed to be *mad* at *me*," I said. "None of this is my fault," I concluded with conviction.

The car pulled into the parking garage of Collin's penthouse. The driver parked and we both got out of the car so quickly, closing the doors behind us nearly in sync. I popped the trunk and gathered my belongings from the airplane and followed Collin over to the elevator.

I hesitated before stepping in. I knew I must have taken this elevator earlier this week, but I was completely blacked out then. Collin didn't notice my hesitation. I just swallowed hard and held onto my anger, using it as fuel. I stepped inside and the doors closed behind me.

"Adept," I broke the silence after the doors closed in front of us. "That's what it said about you. You're 'adept.'"

He grabbed his own phone out of his pocket and began typing up a message. Completely ignoring me. His demeanor was absolutely fuming and in turn, unproductively pissed me off. What gave him the right to be pissed off at me?

The elevator opened up its doors and we quickly made it into his apartment. I dropped my things at the entrance and quickly locked myself in Collin's bedroom. My brain was over-stimulated and I was turning off. I climbed into his bed, where I had once found myself with both Charlie and Juniper, and pulled the covers over my eyes. The sun was long gone and night surrounded us.

My eyes closed but I don't think I am capable of sleeping no matter how hard I try.

A few knocks were made at the door, and more frantically once Collin realized that the door was locked. He called my name through the door but I didn't respond. He stopped eventually and I was swallowed by silence.

A light emerged in my peripherals, a soft yellow light from Collin's night stand, and I felt someone climb into bed next to me. I was nearly asleep, but I feel like not much time had passed.

"Vee?" a soft and sweet voice spoke.

"Charlie?" I turned over and saw her facing me. I had only seen her a week ago and her hair was already a different color. Her eyes were decorated in black eyeliner with small hearts printed in the corners of her brown eyes.

My body reacted before I could and I quickly embraced her next to me. My heart felt like it was being squeezed in a fist.

"We were so worried, Vee," she said into my hair.

I pulled away so I could see her face again. "I missed you so much," we laid next to each other, mere inches between each other's faces.

She looked so sad, "I missed you too," she said, "So much."

I wondered how she knew I was here and then I remember, "Did Collin-"

"Collin texted me once you guys got here."

"How did you get in?"

"Collin has a key to his own bedroom, silly."

I chewed on that statement for a second, "Yeah, that makes sense," I said, "But why didn't he let himself in?"

"He's... trying to be respectful. He knows what you're going through."

That sentence made me want to laugh. "Oh, he knows what I'm going through?"

She was quiet. And the silence felt so painful. This was supposed to be a happy reunion and I know my own poor mood was ruining it, "I'm sorry," I said, "I'm so happy to see you."

"Where were you the past couple days?"

"I was with Juniper in his apartment. We hung out in Little Tokyo, grabbed sushi, but we never really left the neighborhood," I considered telling her about the romance between June and I but now didn't really seem like the time. "Honestly, other than the plane's emergency landing... It was pretty laid back," as in me, on my back. Damn, I suck.

"Juniper's... apartment?"

"Yeah."

"We're actually surrounded by idiots."

"What do you mean?"

"There's no record of Juniper having an apartment."

I thought back to this very morning, the quick scanning of data I had done was practically fresh in my mind, "Juniper wiped everything he could," thinking of the FBI database where I couldn't find any basic information on him there.

"What do you mean?"

"God, Charlie, I don't even know where to begin with this shit. And it might even be dangerous for me to know let alone tell you. But I know Collin probably knows all about it. This has the Parrish's and *The Domain*," I emphasized, "all over it."

She rose up from the bed, "I'm going to get Collin. I'll be right back."

"What?" I muttered out. Ugh. It's probably well after midnight.

She exited the room with the door partially ajar. I sat up in the bed and straightened my clothes and hair. Collin entered in with Charlie behind him. He was bearing a mug of coffee.

"Peace offering," he muttered trying to be sincere. And handed me the mug.

I took a sip, it was truthfully delicious. "Thanks."

"Okay. It's time to talk," Charlie declared. She took a seat beside me in the bed while Collin pulled up a chair to the end of the bed.

Collin groaned and sighed. "What... Do you *think* you know?" he said to me.

I took another sip of coffee before I spoke, giving myself another moment to gather my thoughts. "Here's what I know for sure, Juniper is not listed in any database, he has been completely wiped. The only database I could find him in was for The Domain, *your family's* business. I was in there, you were in there, Connor was included, and of course Juniper. What I saw—"

"You got in? To the mainframe?"

"What, like it's hard?"

Collin groaned and rubbed his eyes dramatically, "Alright, continue. What did you see?"

"None of what I saw made any sense."

"Like it was encrypted?"

"No, I was able to decrypt it just fine."

"God, wow. Okay."

"Collin, are you going to give me anything to go on here or do I need to make things up?" I said with frustration.

"Okay - how do you want it? You want me to just spit it out? Plain and simple?"

"Please."

He got up from his seat and started to pace about. "This isn't how things were supposed to go, and you were never supposed to know about this. I know it looks bad. But we were all trying to protect you."

We, that's the word I got hung up on. What does he mean 'We were all'?

"Charlie?" I said turning to her. "Do you know what's going on?"

Her face dropped, like she suddenly realized that she wasn't off the hook. "Vee, it's just me, Collin, and Connor. Outside of the three of us... I mean there's more people like us out there... But you didn't need to know."

"You've got to be shitting me. The three of you, my best friends on the planet. You have been keeping a secret from me?"

"We're spies," Collin finally spitted it out.

I scoffed in amusement. "Excuse me?"

"Actually, I'm more of a freelance gal. My métier is weirdly specific and I'm not super useful," Charlie tried to add in casually.

"Okay we're not entirely spies, but that's how Connor saw us. My parents' real estate development company is just a front. For generations the Parrish's have been working with the CIA to find other people with enhanced abilities and... recruit them. So they can reach their full potential, and find their place in society," Collin tried to explain.

"And you've known that I have...MET-tee-ay," I tried saying the word out loud.

"Since we were kids, Vee. You're the reason we're together, you know?" Charlie spoke.

I tried to fully digest that last sentence. My whole life leading up to this moment. Every time someone said that they were drawn to me so inexplicably. Well, it's so easy to explain now. It's been narrowed down that I just simply have super powers. And I'm the exact super villain magnet I've accused myself of being.

"But in addition to being so drawn to me... I also make you more powerful? That's a fun and useless power. I just stand here and make other people better?"

"You got it, kid," Charlie tried to say lightly.

"It's why we were trying to protect you. It was better if you didn't know. The less people that knew about your power the better. We didn't want the wrong person to find out and... We didn't want you to be in danger."

"Hah," I chortled. "My plane had to have an emergency landing and I was MIA for days. Nice job trying to protect *me*, buddy," I was trying to remain level headed, but this was so hard.

"We thought you would be safe with Juniper," Charlie said with disappointment.

"Oh, so you were in on it? You told Collin to convince me to leave?"

She was silent, but I knew that meant I was right. "And Connor? Tell me he isn't dead. Tell me that Juniper was telling me the truth," I pleaded.

Collin was quiet, but he quietly moved back to the chair next to the bed and took a seat. He took a moment before making eye contact with me, "He's alive, Vee," He whispered. "Juniper was telling the truth."

Two thoughts fought with each other instantly. One, I need to see Connor, now. So I can hug him and then murder him. Two, I need to see Juniper. There has to be some sort of misunderstanding. I don't know where he is right now, but based on how I last saw him, I'm sure it's not a high-rise penthouse apartment in the Rock Island garden district. I know that his thing is knowing the truth, so he'd have absolutely no reason to lie to me. I don't think he has ever lied to my face.

"Where is he?"

Collin sighed, "I don't know."

"Nice try."

"No, Vee. He really didn't tell me. He didn't tell anyone, I swear. Last I heard he was chasing a lead in DC or maybe Russia. He's on a mission right now that he said he needed to completely disappear. He said it was the only way. We fought about it for weeks on end."

"Weeks? He was planning his death for...for weeks?" I said incredulously.

"I couldn't stop him," He said forlornly. "He said this was the only way."

"You know I'll stop at nothing to find him." I said that like I was stating a fact.

"I know."

"He has been there for me through everything, and I'm not giving up on him. I won't. I won't let him be dead."

"I'm sure he'll resurface, Vee. It's just a matter of time," Charlie said, trying to sooth me.

"Did you know?"

"I was in Peru when all of this was happening. I didn't know anything until Collin told me at Presley's Diner."

That sparked a memory. "Juniper," I said. "That was one of his hunches. He knew Collin couldn't lie in front of Juniper, especially with me standing right next to him. He had Juniper and I go outside right before he told you."

"And that's also when I told Collin we needed you to get out of Rock Island for a little while," Charlie stated. "I suggested it because you being here was starting to get dangerous. Not that there was impending danger, more that you had become so vulnerable, and we wanted you to be as far away from Walter Valentine as possible."

My eyebrows furrowed together. "Walter? What does he have to do with anything?" Other than being my secret lover, and essentially faking all affection for me to convince me to hand over my father's company to him. But they couldn't possibly know about that. Connor swore he would never tell anyone.

"We've been following some leads, and Walter could be up to more than we think he is," Collin informed.

"He's a super villain, isn't he?" I asked.

"We do think he has some sort of ability but we're not sure what it is, or... what his limits are."

"And The Domain is convinced that Juniper is working with him," added Charlie.

I set down my coffee mug on the night stand beside me, "What?"

"They think that Juniper and Walter worked together somehow to bring your plane down."

"Um, no. Juniper saved us on that plane. I would be dead if it wasn't for him."

"Okay, but then you went missing immediately after that," continued Charlie.

"Because I didn't have a cellphone. It was a personal choice that I accept all consequences for. That doesn't have anything to do with June," I defended. "Where is he?"

"He's in a holding cell in The Domain. He's being held for questioning. He got himself in a lot of trouble."

"But he didn't do anything wrong!"

"We don't know that for sure," Collin quipped.

"I KNOW THAT FOR SURE!" I shouted. "Take me to him," I said, settling down my voice. Both of them were stone, completely taken aback by my outburst. I don't lose my shit like that often.

"Vee..." Collin said slowly. "It's past midnight."

"So? It's your family's fake business. Pull some fucking strings."

"Vee," He pleaded.

"We're getting him out of there. Tonight," I said with finality.

Collin was beside himself, I could honestly see him cycling through scenarios in his head. He was determining if there was a way he could possibly get out of this. He knew even if he refused, he'd have to literally lock me in a cage in order to keep me from marching up there by myself, causing a scene, and threatening to release their entire database Wiki Leaks style. I watched him struggle with all of the possible worst case scenarios. Him, knowing what I'm capable of, knowing how fucking impossible I can be.

"Can you just... give me a moment? I'll be right back," he spoke, his fingers clenching the bridge of his nose briefly and then standing up from his chair. He was out of the door before Charlie or I could even respond.

Charlie and I looked at each other, briefly, and shared nearly a comical glance, because we both witnessed the same thing. Charlie and I shared that glance and knew I was about to completely get my way.

Collin emerged through his bedroom doorway holding an iPhone box and held it out to me.

"Here," he said simply.

My mouth gaped open in surprise, "Collin!" I took the box from his hands.

"I picked it up on my way over," admitted Charlie.

"Charlie!" I exclaimed, turning to her.

"We're not about to have another week like our last one," Charlie said.

I opened the box and grinned, somehow it was already completely set up. My old background still as my lock screen, all of my apps where they used to be.

"All of this, but no otterbox?" I quipped jokingly.

"That's exactly what I said," Charlie said slyly, looking over at Collin.

"What if I promised you that he's completely fine?" Collin

said, changing the subject.

"Collin-" I started.

"Vee, please," Charlie said, trying to sooth me. "Collin, can you give us a minute?"

He made a face like he wanted to object, but he agreed to leave the room, closing the door behind him. We both sat up in Collin's bed. Just like we were a week earlier, but last time Juniper wasn't here with us.

She wrung her hands in her lap, anxiously. "When we were kids... we didn't know about any of this stuff. We just knew that being around you made us feel better. We didn't think much of it. We all had our own métier. Our own affinities that for the longest time were just kept to ourselves. Collin was kind of just naturally good at everything. Connor was great at making new friends. You... again as kids we just knew we wanted to be around you, never questioning it. But then there was me," she paused. She looked down at her hands. She was finally going to tell me what her métier is.

"I had this wildly specific knowledge. I just know when people are dead. It's not exceptionally helpful. But when there's a missing person, I can at least help narrow down if they're alive or not."

My mind was taken back to my conversation with Juniper. His suspicion that Collin couldn't lie in front of him to Charlie went so much deeper. It wasn't just that Collin couldn't lie in front of Juniper. It's that Charlie would know if Connor wasn't dead.

"How does it work?" I asked carefully, not sure how to even word my question.

"If I personally know the person I can know instantly. Other-wise if it's a person I don't know like that, usually just a picture of them is all it takes to know for sure."

"Do you ever feel scared?" I slipped out, "It seems like it could be scary."

She shook her head, "No, I never felt bothered by it. I could see if I just suddenly had this ability it could be scary but it's my version of normal."

"When did you realize you were different?"

"It was before I even met you. I was really little. I mostly kept it to myself. But you know me, really connected to spirituality. Being close to you heightens my ability. Sometimes I can get a vibe about the person, it's rarely super helpful. But if I'm around you for long enough, I can not only find out if they're alive, but also how they are feeling, like emotionally. Like if they feel scared or stressed or calm. But there are times where the Domain has me verify things for them."

This felt so unsettling to me. My best friend, finally coming clean to me after all these years. I felt like such a terrible friend. But then in the same way, I felt a sting of betrayal. Because they knew something about me for so long and never told me. Granted, I had my own secrets. They never knew about Walter.

"When did you figure out that I was different?"

"I didn't, actually. It was Connor. He figured it out about you, told Collin and I. And we knew we needed to protect you. It was senior year of high school, I was just starting to learn about The Domain. The real Domain. And Connor was adamant on keeping you out of this."

"None of you thought I'd be the least bit helpful?"

"Vee, that isn't it at all," she said softly.

"Then what? What is it?"

I watched her pick her words carefully for her reply, "Not all of us are heroes, Vee. People like us... People that have métier, we're not all looking to make the world a better place. There are people out there that are filled with.... darkness. There are people that could really hurt you. Especially if they knew... how powerful you are."

"I don't feel protected, Charlie. I feel... I feel left out on decisions that directly affect my life. How is it that the only person in the world that was honest with me... is behind bars now. It doesn't seem right."

"None of this seems right. And I'm really sorry that we kept this from you for so long."

I sighed, "I know that you only thought you were protecting me. I know that there is no malicious intent, but I feel so fucking hurt right now. And I can't just turn it off. I don't know what it will take to make that feeling go away."

Charlie's voice cracked, "I know. And I promise I won't be keeping anything from you ever again," she was fighting back tears.

"I want to see Juniper."

"I know you do."

"Then let's go."

"I don't think that's a good idea, Vee."

"Why?"

"Because..." she trailed off, trying to determine the right wording, "We aren't sure about him. Not like you are."

"Collin let me leave with him, Char. Not even a week ago. He insisted upon it."

She cringed and her body stiffened, "I know. I know he did," she said with discomfort.

"Char! You just said!"

"Collin was keeping an eye on Valentine, with you being out of town making sure that you would be safe. It's all part of the mission, Vee."

I felt so incredibly helpless. And sure, I've gotten some answers but now even more questions. How much of my life has been completely manipulated by the people I have trusted the most? With that thought...

"I'm gonna go smoke a cigarette," I said abruptly, getting out of Collin's bed heading to my bag that was still next to the entrance of the door. The side pocket that contained my cigarettes and lighter were just where I left them.

"Yeah, I'm bumming one," Charlie announced with certainty.

"You don't smoke," I said, about to put my cigarette pack back into my bag.

"Only on special occasions."

"What are we celebrating?"

"That you're still alive," She said flatly.

With every thought racing through my brain, it had forgotten to register the week that Charlie just had. I had just spent a week thinking Connor is dead. She had just spent a week thinking her best friend is missing.

"I'm sorry," I apologized. I snatched another cigarette out of the pack and put it back in my bag."But it's not like you thought I was dead," I added, trying to joke.

She revealed a small smile my way, "I just made that abundantly clear, didn't I?"

We headed out the patio door revealing Collin's terrace. We both lit our cigarettes and I watched how Charlie took her first drag. Seemingly in pain, she coughed violently.

"This is disgusting!" She said through a coughing fit.

I couldn't help but laugh. "I know."

"You should quit!"

"I should quit? Maybe you should quit." I joked.

"I will!" and she threw her cigarette dramatically over the balcony.

"What a waste of a perfectly good cigarette," I said, feigning disapproval.

I continued to pull drags off of my cigarette, shaking my head at what just happened. Another question popped into my head just then.

"Are there more people out there? That have a métier?"

Charlie recounted out loud, "Well there's Collin and Connor, there's me and you, Juniper, Walter Valentine, and oh..."

"What?"

"Winona."

"Winona?"

"Yeah, Winona has a métier too."

"What is it?"

"Okay, so I have to be honest. We don't know the full extent to everyone's métier. Because we don't even think Winona knows. But all we know is that she makes some of our abilities... not work. Like for example I could not tell you if Winona is alive or dead right now."

"That's so weird."

"I mean, I'm sure she's alive and well out there... but it's like... I can get a read on anyone on the planet, right now, but not her."

"But some people... with abilities... still work?"

"She literally dated Connor so you know his charisma still worked on her."

I thought about that for a second. They didn't date long, only a few months. And she really seemed completely smitten by him. But everyone likes Connor.

5

Hero Repellent

Winona

I couldn't fucking stand him. Connor Parrish. Girls always falling for him, boys following him around like a lost puppy, teachers bending to his will. I could never understand it. It had always been that way. In eleventh grade algebra, we had been sat next to each other and my hatred for him intensified. He was such a loser and somehow I was the only person who could see it and it drove me absolutely insane.

The teacher passed back a simple homework assignment and I couldn't help but notice he got all sorts of red exes on his paper but on the top a smiley face signed with "Great Effort!" and an A plus. I looked down at my own paper and saw my own work that made it back completely unscathed. I got an A as well, but where was my smiley face? It was that day in class I had had enough.

Furiously, I scribbled down on a piece of paper, "*I can see right through you,"* and folded it and passed it to him.

He opened it carefully, not to be caught with it, and saw my words and his demeanor instantly changed. He didn't seem so happy-go-lucky as he usually did.

He didn't write to me back, but he stayed completely silent for the rest of class, not daring to look my way. But after school that day he had approached me.

I was by myself, not in a hurry to get home that day. I was sitting outside the school on the steps, organizing a few things in my bag and flipping through my phone.

"Winona?" He had asked me, "What did that note mean?" He seemed genuine but that's all just part of his act, I was just so sure of it.

"It means I'm sick of your shit, Parrish."

He almost laughed, "What does that even mean? Have we ever even interacted before?"

"I see how everyone treats you like you're hot shit, and I honestly just don't get it."

His eyebrows pulled together slightly, with a puzzled look on his face. Like he couldn't believe I wasn't completely enchanted by him.

"That isn't true."

"Sure," I said plainly. I zipped up my bag and got up from the steps. I began to head for my car and he started following me.

"Get out of here, Parrish. Stay out of my way." I said without turning my back. And it was after that very moment that Connor Parrish was completely obsessed with me.

A lot of people forget about this moment of time, because Connor and I's love story was short winded. Maybe a few months at most. We were young. Young love is fleeting.

Connor went so far out of his way to impress me, to get in my good graces. I think it started in that math class. He started actually trying and his papers were no longer "Fake A's" they were genuine. Then he'd leave flowers in my locker, much to my chagrin. I didn't even question how he got them in there. He had the vice principal in his back pocket, and he was literally class president. But for me what finally won me over was when I saw him use his powers for good. This weird influence he had.

In high school, I wasn't as much popular as I was well-known and feared. People knew who I was because they knew I came from money. My circle was small. The company that I kept were the other kids in the French Club. To someone on the outside, they would say I was snobby, uppity even. But they just didn't understand how angry I was with the world. No particular reason back then.

But I saw Connor do something important. It was such a small thing but it made a huge impact. There was a new guy in school that was having a rough time. A few people were making fun of the shoes he was wearing. The next day, Connor arrived at school wearing the exact shoes he was wearing, made it a huge trend, and gave the new kid all the credit. Of course, they were Crocs. Connor was stuck wearing Crocs every day for the rest of the semester and in turn, everyone at our high school started wearing them.

He didn't do that one just to impress me, at least I don't think that one was for me.

I went up to him that day, and I told him that I knew what he was doing. And he smiled this crooked smile and I suddenly felt that charm that everyone else seemed to notice except for me.

Before I knew it I was telling him about my dreams, and he

showed me all his favorite places in Rock Island. We both loved to ice skate. Before the winter came and froze the ground, we would skate together at the arena. No one knew us there, and it felt like an escape.

November was rolling in and we walked hand and hand at the pumpkin patch, the tail end of the season. This is where he asked me to be his girlfriend. He told me he's never asked a girl to be his girlfriend before. And I had never had a boyfriend either. We joked about being new to this kind of thing. I had kissed boys before. And I knew that he had kissed other girls before me. But we kissed for the first time then. And it felt kind of like magic. But it was kind of scary too. I had never felt this way before.

Right as I thought that to myself, out loud he says, "I have never felt like this before." And his eyes just beamed into mine. And again, we shared another kiss. The awkward, teenaged kind, that only happens once in a lifetime. We were in love.

No one really knew about us until after we made everything official. His friends didn't understand me. I want to say that maybe there was this big misunderstanding between Gwenore and I, but really she just hated my guts and always did.

Gwenore was Connor's next door neighbor and practically his shadow. Everyone knew that she had feelings for Connor. But that wasn't really that deep. A lot of people had crushes on him, I didn't think it was that big of a deal until Connor and I started dating.

But Gwenore and I grew up together. Our fathers were partners at V Corp, this home security company that blew up when we were toddlers. We had essentially the same up-bringing, but that still wasn't enough for us to find any common ground. I liked being a girl, she liked... I don't even know what to call it. Being dirty? But not even in an out-doorsy way. She was edgier. Less clean cut, more smudged eyeliner, less skirts, more high top converse.

Her distaste for me was only intensified by me dating Connor, and I don't think she ever recovered from that.

Connor and I had this sweet moment in time that felt like this perfect little universe that only him and I existed in and nothing could taint it, no impurities could infect it. It only belonged to us and in that time that's all that mattered.

It seemed to end all on its own, but I'm sure that between Gwenore, Connor's twin brother Collin, and that insane chick Charlie Locke, they had something to do with it. Which is weird... considering everything I found out about Gwenore later.

I catch myself recounting these times while I sit here, at a church pew, at none other than Connor Parrish's funeral. It had been years since we had our moment in time. We both went away to college. I studied abroad in Paris, he stayed in Rock Island and went to RIU, only to go work for his father at the Domain. Our paths never really crossed again. We only saw each other in passing.

I made it up to the front of the congregation. It was that time where everyone had their opportunity to share things about him. I looked around and saw Gwenore Viridian dash out through the back like a crazy person. I shook my head to myself. What in God's name allowed *her* to be so insane? She had been fucking my dad for years.

But that's a different story.

I stood there for a moment and I considered relaying the love story we shared. But I remember it had only belonged to the two of us and I intended to keep it that way. And instead I talked about how Connor got everyone in our school to wear Crocs for an entire semester. I could tell some people in the crowd remembered this as well. Like they hadn't thought about that moment in time in years and they were glad to look back on that memory. It felt good to share. I stepped down and went back to my seat and noticed that Collin, Connor's brother, was missing from the congregation. Probably trying to settle Gwenore down. She was wildly selfish.

That night I went home to my apartment. Nothing overly lavish, but also plenty of distance from my father who I hadn't spoken to in almost a year. Not since I finally confronted him. About sleeping with a girl the same age as me. His business partner's own daughter nevertheless. He disgusted me.

I want to blame Gwenore, every fiber of my being wants to blame her. But I can't. Because my father should have known better. It was definitely all him. She was just a fucking kid.

It's a miracle that my father and I haven't had to speak a word to each other considering we both work at V Corp. I was hired after college in the International Relations office. My office was on the third floor, his was on the top.

After reading a few emails on my phone I stepped out of my apartment and decided to enjoy the crisp October air. Today was about Connor after all, and this time of year reminded me of him. I considered stepping into Presley's diner as I walked by, but in the window I saw Connor's old crew together. Collin, Gwenore, and even Charlie who wasn't at the funeral. She looked different than the last time I had encountered her but she was always the type to change her appearance drastically. There was also a fourth person who definitely looked familiar. They sat together and I observed briefly. It seemed tense.

Gwenore stepped out with the mystery guy and began smoking together. The way she smoked made me want to chain smoke one hundred cigarettes.

I turned the other direction, these people weren't my friends. Hardly even acquaintances. They lived in a completely different universe that I was not a part of.

I strolled further, and found myself at a hole-in-the-wall cocktail bar. It was my particular haunt, they knew me there. They knew my order right as they saw me. I took my usual seat at the bar and the mixologist brought me my usual, an Aviation with Empress Gin served on the rocks.

I had offered my card to start a tab and the barkeep refused. They pointed behind them and said "That guy over there insisted on buying your round."

I looked and an undistinguished figure sat in the back booth by himself, too dark to make him out from here. My curiosity got the best of me. I thanked the bartender for the drink and I took a sip. I gathered my things and I began heading over there.

I got closer and he removed his hood slowly, revealing those warm brown eyes that I had once known to love. He stood up from the booth and he looked at me, afraid.

I nearly dropped my drink out of my hand, I felt so startled. He rushed over and grabbed my drink out of my hands and set it on the table.

"Winona,"he started.

"You're..."

"I know."

"You're supposed to be dead," I said in a daze.

"I know."

"I was at your funeral. Today. It was today, Connor."

He cradled me while I worked myself out of my daze. I felt

so fucking stunned. I didn't know what to fucking think at this point.

"You're the only person I can trust, Nona. That's why I'm here," God I hate being called Nona. I regret ever letting him call me that. I almost winced when I heard it.

"What?"

"No one can know that I'm here."

"Are you a ghost?"

"Winona, I'm not actually dead."

"What *is* this?"

He sighed. "Please, sit down. Drink a little more. I can explain."

He guided me into one side of the booth and he got on the other side. He scooched the drink closer to me.

"Trying to get me drunk, huh?"

"What?"

"I can't fucking stand you, Parrish."

He looked like a scared little kid across the table from me. I had just noticed he dyed his hair, formerly a sandy blond, now his hair was a deep brunette, almost black. It fell into his eyes.

"I'm sorry that I've put you in this situation, Nona. But there's no one else I can ask for help."

"Why did you... fake your death?" I can't believe that sentence slipped out of my mouth.

"I can't tell you."

"Fuck you, Connor. You want my help, you have to answer my questions," I say in a harsh whisper, to not attract attention to us.

"I can tell you as much as I can but... everything is highly confidential. I'm all tied up here."

"Then talk to me."

"What if I just begged you to come away with me?" his eyes beamed at me, pleading.

"I'd say 'fuck you,'" I spat at him incredulously.

With that he annoyingly smiled, classic Connor. "God, I missed you."

"What?"

"Nothing. Just. I can't explain this all to you right now. I just knew I'd find you here. Thought I'd be able to butter you up a little. Will you please come with me? I will explain everything to you when we get there."

"Where?"

"Just this spot across town, we won't even leave city limits, "he tried to sound convincing.

"You can't just buy me a drink and expect me to go to some undefinable location? Do you think I was born yesterday?" I said with disgust. I haven't even had time to collect my thoughts.

He smiled, in a tired way. "You're the only one that can help me. You have to know that you're...special. That you've always been different than everyone else."

I rolled my eyes at him. And him witnessing it seemed to only make him smile more. God, he pisses me off. "What are you so happy about?" I hissed at him.

"Some things never change," he said, softening his apparent glee. "Please, come with me. I have a car outside waiting for us."

I grabbed my drink and I slammed the remaining contents. I tried to consider what all of this could mean. My first boyfriend has faked his death and swears that I am the only person who can help him. He's never lied to me before, why would he start now?

We arrived outside an older office building. Street lights illuminated the building revealing the sign. The Domain. I knew this to be the name of the Parrish family real-estate development company. But this isn't a location I knew about. It was much smaller than the one we had visited when we were kids. In middle school, Connor's parents allowed the students to tour that facility, like a job-shadow opportunity.

Connor saw me look around and he answered my question before I could ask it.

"This was our first location. Not many people know that it's still here. Just hidden in plain sight."

Connor approached the entrance and lifted up a latch revealing a fingerprint scanner. He pressed his pointer finger on the scanner and it unlatched the front door lock. He then opened the door and I followed him inside.

The lights turned on automatically revealing a small reception area with a desk, a few chairs in a waiting area, and an elevator. Everything was outdated. The walls were wood paneling and the seats on the chairs were a neon orange. But the elevator had the same latch next to it requiring a fingerprint for entry. Connor went right up to it and scanned his finger again. The doors opened to the elevator and he stepped inside and I followed suit.

Instantly modern, the ceiling was affixed with fluorescent lights and we stood inside a chrome box. The elevator had many buttons and I saw him press several of them in a sequential order. My gut spasmed and I suddenly felt like I wasn't safe anymore and everything was about to change. The elevator began to descend.

I wanted to speak but I wasn't sure what I was supposed to ask, what I was supposed to say. How I was supposed to respond to everything that was happening.

I looked at Connor. Wearing some casual jeans, a larger black hoodie, with a button down flannel underneath and some canvas sneakers. It seemed abnormal to him. He typically dressed more intentionally, more clean cut and pressed. I guess he is trying to be in a disguise and be more unrecognizable.

I must have looked concerned. Connor turned to me, "Hey, I just want to prepare you. This is probably going to be a little overwhelming for you, but I promise I will explain everything. Everything is going to make sense."

"Connor," I said quietly, "I have a feeling that none of this-"

The elevator door opened and bright, piercing-white fluorescent lights invaded my retinas, "...Will make sense," I finished.

When my vision returned to me the setting before me began to form.

Something beyond my own imagination. The room before me, if you can even call it a room, was vast. Something close to an entire football stadium, enclosed in cement. No windows in sight. Sterile, scientific, almost militant in a way. There were multiple tiers that could all be viewed from our position above.

I stepped from the elevator and examined further, in wide-eyed silence. I walked right up to the white-painted metal railing. The floor below us beeped with machinery, and the floor below that seemed to be some sort of command center with multiple monitors; some with data, some with camera footage, perhaps it was being streamed live. I had no way of knowing for sure. Every floor seemed to serve its own purpose and have its own assignments. There must have been more than a dozen floors below us.

Connor watched me take it in with awe. I had never seen anything like it. I snapped back to the present and I turned to him.

"Connor, what is this place?" I said in nearly a whisper.

"The Domain," he said evenly.

I shook my head. "No, I've been to The Domain. I know what it looks like. This isn't anything like what I've seen."

"This is the real Domain, Nona. I know this is a lot, but you had to see this place. It's the only way I can get you to listen."

I tried to fully digest and understand what he was telling me. I almost felt dizzy. I looked him into the eyes and I said, "Your parents aren't real estate developers, are they?"

He laughed, "Well, they do that too, technically. But no. We're much more than that."

I turned back to the facility before me. My mind still wouldn't let me process it. I desperately tried to determine what this could all mean. Nothing has prepared me for this. I almost felt embarrassed, but emphatically vulnerable. I was scared. Everything in me was telling me to leave.

"Come with me. I want you to meet someone," Connor said. He held out his hand to me, and my hand trembled as I extended out to hold it.

He noticed, "Don't be scared," he tried to assure me. But I think my face was giving me away.

He guided me down to the level below us where all the machines beeped and the noises echoed in every corner. People in lab coats tended to their different stations of interest. Past their stations there were multiple doors leading into private offices. He led us to door 221, and knocked before opening the door and letting us in.

Before us was a tall man with a dark mullet, he stood with his back to us, aggressively writing math equations on a white board.

Connor was full of glee, "Beck, there's someone I want you to meet."

Beck was startled as he turned around, "Jesus fucking Christ, Connor, you can't do that to people," his voice was surprisingly feminine for a man of his stature. He wore glasses and had a five-o-clock shadow with an overgrown mustache.

"This is Winona."

Beck looked angry, "You can't just bring random hot girls down here, are you fucking kidding me?"

"Hey dude," Connor said, instantly defensive, "She has métier, she isn't just a random hot girl."

Métier?

I took french, years of french, I've lived in fucking France. I know what this word means. It's usually used to describe someone's job or expertise or something. I have never heard it used this way in English.

"Prove it."

"Easy," Connor said. He stepped up to the white board and began erasing a corner of what Beck had been working on.

"Hey!"

"Oh please, like you wouldn't be able to do this again in 5 seconds..." Connor said dismissing him. Beck then stepped aside from the board. "Winona, write down a math equation. Literally anything you can think of."

"What? Why?" I said incredulously.

Connor sighed, "Just trust me."

I felt so uncomfortable in my skin it felt like I was going to shake apart. I walked up to the board and steadied my hand while lifting up a black dry-erase marker and wrote carefully. I wrote the simple equation of 144 divided by 12.

"Okay, now stay right here," Connor instructed. "And

Beckett, come over here and try to solve this."

"It's literally twelve," Beck spat angrily.

"Come over here and say that, champ," Connor asserted.

I stood right where Connor told me to without moving. I briefly thought about how strange this was. It's the middle of the night and I'm forcing this punk scientist to do equations the day of Connor's fake funeral. This was not on my fucking bingo card. I wish I had drank more before this.

Beck knelt down and looked at the equation at eye level. I witnessed him begin to set up the equation like he was going to do long-division. He put the 144 in a bracket with the 12 to the left of it. He stared at it and began crossing off numbers and just stopped. The silence in the room was unsettling.

Beck set the marker down and put his thumb and pointer finger over the bridge of his nose and closed his eyes tightly. "I...can't solve it," he said with defeat.

"What the fuck?" I accidentally said out loud.

Connor was grinning, "Okay Nona, get away from him, We're done torturing him."

As soon as I stood back with Connor, Beck stood up from his crouch and just erased the equation all together and just started rewriting the section the Connor had originally erased.

"Okay, now that the universe has been restored to its normal equilibrium... What the actual fuck?"

"Just testing a theory, and I was completely right," Connor said smugly.

"Connor, nothing about this night has made any sense," I said tensely.

Connor just looks at me, beaming with excitement. Seemingly out of nowhere Connor just takes both of my hands in his and brings them up to his lips and kisses them. I gasp and wriggle them out of his, justifiably repulsed by this gesture from a man I haven't seen in years, a man I had thought to be dead.

Instead of responding to me he does one last quip to Beck, "Alright buddy, we're out of here. You've been a great help!" And Connor leads us out of the office and back into the noise of whirling machinery.

As soon as the door shuts behind us my fear fades and I am seething with anger. "I'm leaving. Everything is just a fucking game to you. I'm not playing," I turn my back to him and begin heading for the exit.

He grabbed my hand to stop me. "This isn't a game, Nona. I promise. I wasn't sure before but I'm going to tell you everything. I owe that to you," He said it to me like he was trying to gather all that charisma that usually works on everyone else. Everyone but me. I can see through him. I always have.

"You're used to getting everything you want, ghost boy," I said acidly. "But I'm not going to be manipulated by you. No fucking way," I ripped my hand out of his.

He groaned. "You're right! You're right, okay. I am used to getting whatever I want but that's why... Just give me a chance. Please. Let me sit you down and explain everything," he pleaded.

"Give me one good reason, Connor."

"Because... I can't complete this mission without you."

I groaned. "You're practically speaking in code with me right now."

"Please, just let me take you to one more place here, and I'll explain absolutely everything."

I contemplated for a moment. I am so sick of everything

tonight. Waking up ready to mourn this man. Finding out he's alive. Arriving at this strange, seemingly militant facility, and then that weird greasy scientist nerd that suddenly can't do simple long division in front of me?

I have no reason to give Connor a chance to explain anything. But I couldn't help but remember our three-month, unspeakable union. If it had happened to anyone else I would have scoffed in disgust. But I was the one living it. We were there together in that moment in time. And he has never done anything to me to make me think he was anything but genuine. Even after then.

I guess that gives me one reason. One reason to give him a chance.

"This is your last chance, Parrish. I swear to God."

He smiled. "Follow me."

We sped past every station, giving me no time to analyze what they were trying to accomplish. We headed down a flight of stairs and he led me to another elevator. We stepped inside and he lifted up a panel that scanned his finger. The doors closed and I felt it rise. This felt so strange. We went down a flight of stairs to go up an elevator?

He could sense my confusion. "This is the only way to get to my office. It's where I'm staying while I maintain my... leave of absence... from society."

I scoffed.

The doors opened to a seemingly normal apartment? He just called it his office but it looked like a studio apartment. It was an open concept, large tinted windows on three of the four walls that enclosed us. A modest queen sized bed to the left of us pushed into a corner, with a sectional couch next to that. A large desk directly in the middle facing us. And a small kitchen area to the right. no counter space, but let's be real, Connor doesn't cook. In the top right corner we can see an entry to what I would assume to be a bathroom.

"Must be a bitch to get Postmates to deliver here," I quipped jokingly.

"I have people for that," he said, taking a load off on his plush couch.

I sat in the other corner, still not comfortable enough with him to sit any closer. I kicked my shoes off and brought my feet up into a cross-legged position, making myself comfortable.

"So, why did you fake your death?" I said starting off strong.

"Whoa, whoa whoa, I can't start there."

"Why not?"

"Because there's-"

"You promised."

He paused. "Because of Walter Valentine."

I was taken aback. "Excuse me?"

"He's at the center of this."

"Wow, excuse me again, can you vague that up for me?" I'm starting to feel offended by all the efforts he's making to keep me in the dark.

"A couple months ago... After Victor died, I took a position at V Corp to get closer to Walt."

"I literally work at V Corp, how did I not hear about this?" I questioned with annoyance.

"I was in a secret sector, no one knew about it."

"What was it?"

"Research and Development."

"Shut up."

"I'm serious."

"R&D isn't a secret sector, it's literally just the entire 5th floor."

"Have you ever been there?"

"No, only people with specific clearance are allowed-"

"Exactly."

"Fine, continue," I said reluctantly through my teeth.

"Your father was spearheading a new type of tech. Something dangerous, Nona. Right before Viridian's dad mysteriously passed I got word of it. Then Victor just dies? No one thought anything of it?"

I thought for a moment and I was brought back to that time. I knew exactly what he was talking about. It was Victor that introduced the development of the new quantum technology that was on a timeline to be released two years later. I don't know much about technology. Not like that. Most of that discussion was lost on me. But I remember how my father had acted during that time. He was distant and cold, stressed to say the least.

Connor continued, "A quantum computer. Something that is so far beyond a typical American's comprehension," Connor began speaking faster, more zealous, "This computer is different. While the concept of quantum computer has been around for decades, it's just given scientists and engineers more time to play God. V Corp designed its own quantum computer, something that works nearly 5000 times faster than a normal computer. I'm not talking about loading Minecraft without lagging, I'm talking about a computer that can break any encryption of any server, a computer that can be used to weaponize technology to create *untraceable* cyber weapons."

"Okay, I'm listening. Very dangerous stuff. But what does that have to do with my dad? And you? And you faking your death."

"I found Walter's plans," he said gravely. "That's exactly what he was going to do, Winona. He was going to create that exact tech. And sell it. To very dangerous and powerful people. He knew I was getting too close, but he didn't know how close I was. I was on his hit list. Just like Victor was. The only way I was going to be able to stop him was to remove myself from the equation."

I sat there awestruck. So much information. So much to process. Not even a quantum computer could break down everything I just heard.

"You think my father... Killed Victor Viridian?"

"I think he had a hand in it. Yeah."

"Victor Viridian was killed by an elevator accident. My dad doesn't...there's no way," I said in disbelief.

Everyone knows what happened to Gwenore's dad but no one speaks of it. He was at the top floor of V Corp. Using the elevator like he usually does, when the elevator failed and it suddenly collapsed and he fell 22 floors to his death.

"Yeah, the day after a scheduled elevator maintenance? V Corp ended up suing that company for his death. The maintenance man said he checked that elevator and swore it was working correctly. Nothing was out of place, it was a perfectly maintained elevator. It had no reason to fail," Connor reasoned.

"That doesn't make any sense. Victor was his best friend."

"Brutus literally stabbed Caesar."

"Jesus Christ, no Shakespeare comparisons," I said in disgust.

"My guess is that Victor didn't want any part of Walt's plans."

I needed to move on from this topic. "And so what happens

when you bring my dad to justice, huh? You're just gonna resurrect yourself? Come back from the fucking dead like nothing ever happened?"

"The work that I do... I don't have to be a real person."

That just pissed me off, "What the fuck does that even mean?"

"Society doesn't recognize people like me."

"You know how fucking stupid that sounds?" I got up and took a look at his modest collection of finer whiskeys and started to help myself to some Laphroaig, a spirit that I would normally savor, but in this case, was being gulped. "You throw away your entire actual society-recognized life. For what?"

"It's worth it if it means I can stop Walter, and the people *I care about* are safe."

I sipped some more whiskey before sitting back down on the sofa where I was before. The people he cares about. Okay. I get it now.

"Oh," I scoffed. "This is about Gwenore," I snorted. "Of course it is."

He was quiet. Calculating in his mind how to possibly respond to this knowing I was completely fucking right. Be so fucking for real, Connor. I can see right fucking through you, and I always have.

"She's in the most danger right now. She's like us, Nona."

"God, I fucking hate being called Nona," I said dismissing him.

"She has métier. Just like me. Just like you."

"That sentence doesn't make any sense and I'm fluent in French."

"It's the word we use to describe our special affinities. I know you noticed it. How easy it is for me to charm people? You think that's normal?"

"No, it's fucking infuriating. But some people just have charisma, not that I could ever understand it."

"You're the only one on the planet that can call me out on my bullshit, Winona. That's why I need you. You have métier too. Something so important that I've kept it to myself all this time. The Domain, Collin, your father... they have no idea."

"Oh yeah, what's this great power I have?"

"It's quite brilliant actually. You make every métier within proximity of you cease to work. I couldn't charm you if I tried."

"I could have told you that," I continued to scoff.

"That's why Beck suddenly couldn't solve that equation," Connor finished, "His affinity for mathematics is part of his métier. He has this ability where he's presented a problem and he always finds the solution. That man could solve the Navier-Stokes equation in his sleep but then couldn't do basic long-division."

"So in short, I'm like pure, unadulterated hero repellent?" I asked flatly.

Connor didn't know how to respond because he knew I was right.

I sat there a while, finishing my last sip of scotch. Feeling the alcohol enter my bloodstream so I could possibly deal with all this information.

Connor broke my concentration. "Do you want a cigarette?"

"I don't smoke."

"Do you want to join me outside?"

"Not really," I said, knowing I'd be trailing behind him anyway. There was a door past the living space that seemed really out of place but it led to a very unremarkable terrace. It hasn't seen the touch of a woman, that's for sure. It was mostly just a concrete slab, a single plastic yard chair, and cigarettes littered everywhere. There was no view, the small space was nearly boxed in by grey concrete brick walls, and the only light we had came from a small wall sconce near his doorway. This space didn't make sense. But I looked above me and noticed the stars shining down on us.

He saw me scanning the area and laughed. "Would you like to take a seat?"

I rolled my eyes and I obliged. He lit his black American Spirit cigarette facing away from me and the wind.

I thought back to when we were kids. I had been reminiscing all morning, thinking he was fucking dead, so it's all fresh in my mind. If what he's saying about me is true, it unfortunately makes complete sense.

"I changed my mind. Give me one of those," I said to him. He got another cigarette out of his pack and handed it to me along with his lighter.

It's been years since I've done this. What's a little nicotine buzz?

I lit my cigarette and did a shallow inhale, tasting it. God, this was fucking disgusting.

"How have you been?" Connor said, uninspired, unsure of what to say. After all, we're strangers now.

I struggled to come up with something. But I wanted to say something that I haven't had anyone to confide in about. "I haven't spoken to my dad since Victor's funeral."

His interest was instantly piqued. "Did something happen?"

I was instantly brought back to my feelings of absolute disgust. I remember finding out about his affair with Gwenore. I was in his room. I wanted to find something of my mothers so I was in the very back of his closet where I found a strange, unlabeled box. I had assumed it would have been full of my mothers things. But I was wrong. I found years of memorabilia, chronically his perverse relationship with a girl only weeks older than me. Letters, old receipts, photographs, disgusting naked Polaroids... I was horrified. I didn't blame Gwenore. How could I? She was just a kid. But that doesn't excuse all of my other reservations towards her.

"My father's greed... I found proof of how far he was willing to go," which also somehow validates everything Connor had told me. He would do anything to have Gwenore's half of the company. "I found it to be unforgivable. And to be honest, it makes whatever you tell me about him...completely believable," I took a long drag from this rancid cigarette and exhaled.

"I found out a lot about your father, but I need help piecing more of it together."

"What's in it for me?"

He shook his head. "I don't know how to answer that in a way that would satisfy you. What's in it for you, Winona Valentine? A safer world. Your father will be brought to justice. You can be a part of something bigger than yourself."

"That sounds very, very *kumbaya* of you."

"Would you do it for me? Just because I asked?"

"I'm not one of your brainless followers, Connor."

"I know you aren't— but after everything we went through together—"

"We were kids! We're strangers!" I said incredulously. "Besides, I already know you're just doing this for Gwenore," I said acidly.

He sighed through his cigarette. "Nona, honestly. This is so much bigger than your beef with Vee. Did this start as a mission for her? Sure. But this-"

"So you admit it."

"Admit what?"

"You have feelings for her. You always have. Even when we were together."

"It's very very complicated, Winona. I don't even know how to explain my relationship with Viridian."

"She's in love with you. Surely, you know that," I said sternly.

He audibly groaned. "It isn't... I have feelings for her, I will admit it. Deep, strong feelings. But I'll never know if it's our métier working simultaneously together or if it's real. That's what makes you and me different. We had something, and I never had the ability to charm you. You genuinely hate my guts 90% of the time and look at you. Here. Smoking my cigarettes, drinking my scotch, listening to my mission... You and I? We're real. We have the real thing. It's right here in front of us whether you want to admit it or not."

I ditched my cigarette to the ground and stood up and stomped on it. I got really close to him. I stared deeply into his eyes. "I'm leaving," was all I said.

I paused there. Fuming. But something in me wouldn't let me walk away no matter how badly my body was screaming to leave.

I watched a series of emotions cycle behind his eyes. He dropped his own cigarette to the concrete ground. His hands reached up to my face and his eyes burned into mine for a moment that felt like an eternity. He brought his lips to mine slowly, and as our lips touched it was like a peak of a crescendo. Like the moment I woke up this morning was all leading up to this very moment. And I thought to myself it's just like Connor said, *some things never change.*

6

Moscow, Iowa

Winona

everish. That was the best word I could use to describe us. The kissing led to touching, the touching led to holding, and the holding led to our clothes thrown about on the floor.

Having sex with the newly deceased Connor Parrish was not on my bingo card this morning.

Was it the alcohol? Was it my frustration? Was it nostalgia? What brought me here? Being pressed against a wall by a man I can barely stand?

He had one hand to my neck, and one hand inside me, slamming into me rhythmically, curling with precision, perfectly hitting my sweet spot. With his lips to my shoulder he bit into my flesh, causing me to lose control of my volume. I couldn't muffle the sounds escaping my mouth. He wouldn't even let me touch him, he just wanted me to suffer in my pleasure. And he was feeding off of it. I could feel his annoyingly smug smile against my skin. I hated how much I was enjoying myself. I didn't want him to get the satisfaction.

I felt my pussy contract around his rough but precise touch. I turned away as I felt like I couldn't face him. I couldn't let him see this look in my face when I was about to cum so hard in the palm of his fucking hand.

My body writhed beneath his touch, still against the wall, and my pool of desire overflowed over his fingers. I cried out in pure euphoric misery.

I didn't want him to know that I came for him so easily like that. I couldn't let him know. Luckily all of my moans blended in with that one. And he continued to finger me, unstoppable as it seemed. My hands went to his chest and I tried to shove him away. I wish I didn't love this so much.

He felt what I was doing and he lifted his fingers out of me causing me to let out a broken whimper. His hand lifted his grip over my neck and his teeth let go of my flesh.

"Get on the bed. I want to fuck you," He said in a low guttural tone.

I did as he said to do and I laid on top of his bed, my breathing still uneven and my brain practically shattered from the orgasm I just withstood.

He was quick to get on top of me and instantly grabbed my wrists to pin them down over my head. In a swift, and primal motion he inserted himself inside me, instantly hitting a metaphorical back wall within myself. I cried out in pain.

"Hey, bad. Bad pain," I couldn't make out more syllables.

"Sorry, am I too big for you?" He readjusted his position so that he was no longer hurting me while openly chuckling at his own one-liner.

I groaned. "Oh my God..." I rolled my eyes.

In a weird way, this is exactly how I always thought this would go for us. Our first time having sex. I had a feeling he'd be exactly like this. So fucking smug. And unfortunately *rightfully* confident in his abilities.

"God, you are so wet, Nona," he said in between thrusts. My pussy tightened around his length. I tried so hard not to look at him. I didn't want to like him this much. I didn't want to enjoy being fucked by him this much.

"I want to taste you," he slowed down his thrusts, and slid into me gently, turning my involuntary moans into nothing but whines. It allowed me a moment to not just focus on the pulsating movements of his cock, but also how each part of him felt as he entered me deeper and deeper. I was able to catch my breath a little when he pulled out of me without any warning. He let go of my wrists and made his way down to my center. I was dripping.

He brushed his hair off of his forehead and studied it for a moment. Looked her dead in the eye, before placing a finger inside and learning me. His lips went straight to my trigger and placed a kiss before he began teasing it lightly with his tongue while his finger searched around inside me. He would slowly exit and re-enter me. Teasing me to no end. My hands were balled into fists in the comforter below us and my heavy breathing turned into moans.

He stopped for a moment and lifted his finger out of me and brushed it across his own tongue. Finally, a break from all this deeply enjoyable insane sexual torture. He wrapped his lips around his forefinger, and removed it from his mouth. That smug smile came back and I had a front row seat to see his shit-eating grin.

I wonder what my face looked like as he stared at me like this. Hopefully, I looked apathetic.

Then in turn, he added his middle finger into the mix, two fingers inside me, curling up and hitting my G spot so precisely. And his tongue picked up the pace, beginning a new flow that I have yet to experience. A shock went through my body like an electrical current. I tried to keep my mouth closed to not give him that satisfaction. I didn't want him to know how good he was. He's too powerful.

I just fucking came, there's no way I'm about to cum again? Be so fucking for real.

But I felt it build again. The pressure built up inside me and my pussy squeezed around his fingers, nearly forcing them out of me, resulting in another bone-chilling orgasm that I had to keep a secret. His tongue just continued to dance around my clit and I did my best to contain my moans, but there was no hiding the actual, literal tears dripping out of the corners of my eyes. I freed my own hands from the fists I had them in and quickly put them over my face and rubbed the tears away from my eyes.

He continued to tease me and my body was screaming at me. I was deeply overstimulated but I wasn't going to let him know that he was making me cum. I was not going to admit it if my life depended on it.

He was having his fun, watching me writhe, beneath his mouth, around his grasp that he had over my womanhood. And I let him indulge in me. I let him make me his own personal playground. After all, I am indulging too. What kind of person would I be to deny myself this kind of pleasure?

His fingers exited my opening. He stopped again to taste me for himself.

His hands grabbed me by my waist, "Flip over," he asserted. And he did the work himself. He flipped me over like it was nothing. I went face first into his pillows and I turned my head to breathe. He moved my hair over my shoulder and off of my back and grabbed both of my hands, and into one of his to hold them together behind my back. I was just grateful I didn't have to make eye contact with him, to face him.

I felt his free hand glide up my waist, over my torso and gently grasp my neck while he hovered over top of me. He wasn't inside of me yet, and I wanted more of him.

"How do you want me to fuck you, Winona?" He whispered in my ear. "Do you want me to fuck you hard? Or do you want me to take it easy on you?"

I swallowed hard. This sounded like a challenge.

I opened my eyes slowly to see his grinning face almost touching mine.

"I fucking hate you," I said while my eyes beamed into his.

He laughed in my face. "What?" He laughed again. "No one has ever said that to me before," he was deeply amused by my exhausted contempt.

"Hard. Fuck me hard, Parrish," I said ignoring his neurotic laughter.

I was prepared for the most force and instead he took the head of his cock and teased me incessantly against my entry and my clit. My body reacted so dramatically. My body just betrayed me to his touch. Completely giving me away. He's going to know I'm completely fucking enjoying myself.

He stopped teasing and I braced myself again for his forceful motions. But he stayed still.

"I changed my mind," he said.

"What?" I croaked out, my throat fully dry.

"Turn over."

I paused slightly and internally I screamed, I didn't want to face him. But he got out from in between my legs and allowed me to turn myself over. And I faced him. I allowed myself to look at his body. Milky white skin stretched over his toned and muscular form. He had a crooked smile as he gazed at my bare form below him.

In a fluid motion, he entered me. I turned my face away and closed my eyes while exhaling. Taking in his length, feeling each part of him become one with myself. His dick surged slowly inside me. His breathing became labored with each motion.

I can't keep doing this. I know I said I wouldn't deny myself, but unbeknownst to him, I've already orgasmed twice.

"I-I...want you to cum," I plead in a whisper. Still not facing him.

He brought his hand down to my face and forced me to look at him.

"Look at me. Look at me in the eyes."

Like I had a choice.

He brought his body closer to mine and we began to breathe together in sync. His eyes, before, so eager and enthusiastic and smug, now showed something different. Is he showing weakness? Is that what that is? Vulnerability, even?

His mouth connected to mine and shared a slow passionate kiss while continuing his momentum with his cock, building in speed. I moaned in between each kiss we shared.

His body became rigid over me as I watched a shock wave tear through his body. A final labored sigh escaped his lips and he ripped himself out of me and a cry came from his mouth. With his cock in his hand, I watched him bust. Leaving a pool of our sins over my torso. His eyes were clenched shut and his breathing began to slow.

He reached across me to his night stand and grabbed something to wipe up the mess and then without skipping a beat, crashed next to me.

My own breathing slowed, but my heart continued to race. I had this urge to put my hand over my opening to metaphorically protect it from any more stimulation. My back turned to him.

This mother fucker was supposed to be dead.

He turned to me and cradled around me. Such a softy. He exhaled with such satisfied contentment with his nose in my hair.

"Did you cum?" He asked.

I wanted to snort, I wanted to scoff in derision. But I couldn't lie to him as well as I wanted. So I just said through my teeth, "Maybe."

He chuckled. "Yeah, okay."

He couldn't see my face, which was my preference. But I frowned. I really really didn't want to like him. I wanted it to be bad. After years of witnessing people bend to his will. He would manipulate, charm, and practically hypnotize people.

The sex was so good, I'm practically having an existential crisis. I'm so tired.

"Can I sleep here?"

"What?" He questioned.

"Like... is it safe here?" I mean, how safe could it be hanging out with a guy that is pretending to be dead?

He tightened his arm around me. "Do you feel safe?"

No. I laughed internally. I feel so far out of my comfort zone my bones want to jump out of my skin. I decided to answer by settling in closer to him. Feeling our skin connect, somehow in a deeper way than we just were. I felt that he was waiting for a verbal response from me. But I couldn't give him one.

I rose from the bed and I looked around, my head foggy from pounding all that scotch, and Connor was not in bed next to me. It left me feeling stupid. Disappointed in myself for wanting him near me at all.

I laid back down and pulled the covers over my face and internally groaned at myself.

Before I could collect myself, Connor stealthily snuck back into bed next to me. Like he was going to pretend he never left my side. He let out this contented sigh and wrapped an arm around me. My gut opposed this significantly but my body was drawn to his warmth.

"Winona," he said quietly, calling out to me to wake me up gently.

"Hmm?" I responded, pretending to be just waking up.

"I'm fueling up the jet right now. We're leaving for DC. You and me."

My eyes flung open. "Excuse me?"

"This mission. The one I can't do without you."

"Did it not occur to you that I, I don't know, have a job?"

"Tell them you're...mourning."

"Oh yes, my high school boyfriend. Of course. His death threw me off so much that I need to take the rest of the week off? Are you fucking kidding me?" I questioned him sarcastically.

"Luckily you're the daughter of the CEO and you're untouchable. What are they going to do? Fire you?"

This argument is futile. It solves nothing. "You really

haven't been specific as to why I, Winona Valentine, have to be the one to accompany you on this mission. I'm super hero repellent, remember?"

"You're more than super hero repellent, Nona. You think everyone with métier is a hero? I don't need my métier to complete this mission. No one has to like me or inexplicably trust me. But you can, however, stop anyone that tries to stop me."

"And what exactly does this have to do with the District of Columbia?"

"I got word this morning. Your father is keeping something really important to my mission in a place called the homeland. The only thing that could be is the Department of Homeland Security in DC. It's just a hunch because it doesn't completely make sense. There were a lot of mentions of Moscow too."

With the mention of Moscow my stomach dropped. But he continued to ramble on, "And if it isn't in DC I guess our next stop will be in Russia. But it doesn't matter, I have the rest of my life to stop him from—"

"Connor, stop. Whatever my father is hiding? It's not in DC," I finally turned my body to face him and I let him continue to cradle me.

"What are you talking about?"

"Homeland? That's what my father always refers to as his childhood home. In Moscow. Moscow, *Iowa*."

"Holy shit, are you kidding me?"

"Miles and miles of cornfields. I used to visit my grandfather's farm every summer."

He quickly gathered my face into his hands and pulled me into a frantic and excited kiss. "God, this is why I need you, Nona," he said with gratitude while pulling away. He jumped out of bed and quickly began dressing himself. He turned to look at me, who still hasn't moved from the bed, and quickly pulled a shirt over his head and put his arms through the holes. He stood next to my horizontal form and knelt down to my eye level.

"I'm serious, Winona. I can't do this without you," his eyes beamed into mine earnestly. "If anyone is going to know where to go, it'll be you. Please," he pleaded with me.

I weighed the options. He's right. I could take the rest of this week off of work. I haven't taken a personal day in months. He didn't know that about me, but perhaps he did, since he's been at V Corp for months and I had no idea about it.

But if I didn't take this leap, what then? I go back to my apartment and start getting ready for work? I pretend that none of this ever happened? I have no way of reaching him, if I don't do this, I'll probably never see him again.

Part of me loves that concept.

But...no. I'll spend the rest of my life wondering, and I can't live like that.

I won't live like that.

We were in the air before the clock could even strike noon. The inside of his jet was small but still had a hint of luxury. Something about a milky off-white interior with leather seats gives off the impression of lavishness. This was nowhere near my first go on a private plane, but this one did seem to have the quietest cabin. A pin could drop and the sound would startle me at this point. But perhaps it's because I've been on edge since I arrived at the tarmac and boarded the plane.

I was able to make a quick trip home to pack but that was

done in a daze. Connor told me that even though my father and I have been out of touch for nearly a year, he was definitely still keeping tabs on me.

My father. The last person I wanted to be thinking of. Deep down I had always known how twisted he was, but I never could have imagined it was to this extent. Growing up I remember the fights my parents would get into.

It's fucked up. My father worked more than anything. It made me jealous of Gwenore because it seemed like her and her father had such a great relationship. But her mom dipped on them really early on in her childhood. I think we were around seven or eight years old. Kendall Viridian was never heard from again after that.

This was back during a time Gwen and I really got along. Back when she still let people call her Gwen. It's my fault that we fell off. My mom contracted a rare cancer when we turned nine, leading to her death before we even reached the age of ten. I refused to go to school and was home schooled the rest of the year. When I finally decided to come back, she wasn't Gwen anymore. She only wanted to be called Vee, or Viridian, and had a new group of friends that didn't want to come anywhere near me.

It was probably my very fun hero repellent quirk that seems to only attract smug jocks like Connor.

My father stayed distant after my mother's death. I don't even think he knew anything about me. We weren't the type of family to eat dinner together. He instilled a certain independence in me that stuck with me into my adulthood. I didn't make friends, I maintained networks of like-minded, career-driven individuals that enjoyed expensive wine and letting loose with some uppers. But I struggled to find the intimacies of true friendship in these peers. They didn't know about my childhood. I don't even think they knew my favorite color.

Therapy was forced upon me in my youth following my mother's passing. But no therapist could give me the tools to break down a few walls and experience true intimacy. Things would have been different, I think, if I had just allowed Gwen to be my friend when I needed her back then.

"Someone's deep in thought," Connor teased, breaking me out of my trance while I did nothing but stare out my window.

"I'm just thinking about my dad. How all the things led up to this, I guess. I wish I was more surprised that things turned out this way," I said, laced with disappointment, not turning to face him.

"Hey," he started, taking the seat next to mine. "You know I couldn't do this without you right?"

"That is what's been alleged," I said bleakly, continuing my stare through the clouds.

"I would be in DC chasing a dead lead right now, Nona."

"Who gave you that bad lead?" I questioned.

"My brother. He's been doing everything he can to help me. To help Viridian. To protect the Domain. We think that in addition to this super computer Walter built... He's figured out about The Domain."

"Knowing my dad, he definitely knows about the Domain already, Connor," I said, shaking my head.

That took Connor aback, "What? What makes you say that? We're a highly confidential and underground organization. The President of the United States doesn't even know about us."

I snorted. "My dad has a quantum computer and an incredibly powerful home security company. He probably has access to every camera in existence. Who knows what his limitations are. I know I don't."

"I've considered that, Nona, do not get me wrong. But there's no way. I've spent months in R&D and none of my investigation led me to believing our cover had been blown," Connor argued in disbelief.

I shrugged. I finally turned to him. "I hope you're right."

"Okay, so once we get to the airport do you know exactly where we're going?" Connor asked.

"Pretty much. But where we're going is going to be a bit of a drive from the nearest airport. This might be overwhelming to you how rural this area is. I'm not sure if you've seen anything like it," I warned.

Connor leaned back into his seat and shook his head with his smug grin. "You realize I'm literally an international super spy? I mean, cue the music. You wouldn't believe the things I've seen."

My eyes narrowed at him, "Yes, I'm sure your ability to persuade masses of people to wear Crocs really made you a valuable asset against the drug trafficking pandemic."

His eyes lit up for a moment. "You remembered that?"

"Connor, everyone remembered that. It was the memory I shared at your funeral."

"I kind of wish I could have been there."

"Yeah, Gwenore was ballistic. Collin was doting over her the whole time. Knowing what I know now, everything makes sense."

He frowned and then he snapped at me, "Dude, what is it with you and Vee? Why do you treat her like she's your worst enemy?"

My eyebrows furrowed together. "I don't treat her like my

worst enemy. You have this completely wrong. She isn't my worst enemy. I'm *her* worst enemy," I said with finality. "And she'd never let me forget. She couldn't even give me grace at your funeral. She saw me go up to the podium to share my memory and stormed out of there with Collin following behind her."

He continued to frown, no longer looking my way, just tilted his head down and stared into his lap like he'd find the answers if he just stared down hard enough. "I knew this would be hard on her, but this is how it had to be. Even if she never forgives me for this, at least she'll be safe."

I sighed softly and turned back to the window. No further discussion occurred for the duration that we remained in the clouds.

I might have him right now. But no matter what I do, he is always going to be hers. Something I've accepted a long time ago. I couldn't even tell if this was what I wanted or I was just too afraid of the possibility of regret. Either way, it doesn't change the fact that this is where I am now, and this is the path that I have chosen. It doesn't matter if I've lost all sense of self, because I just have to continue on.

"I want a Tesla."

"No."

"Come on, it'll be cool."

"You're the worst spy that ever existed."

"Let me have my fun."

"Oh, and when it runs out of gas-"

"It doesn't take gas."

"-where are you going to charge the car? Are you going to

plug it into a grain silo?"

We continued like that for a few more moments. I swear to God, did I die? Because this is hell. I'm in hell.

Finally I talked him into renting something more sensible and less suspicious looking. Plus, we're dealing with gravel roads. And I know how easy it is for gravel to get kicked up by the speed and crack a windshield. I mean, fuck an extra expense. It just makes us look poor as fuck. But also, maybe that'd be a good thing so we could blend in even further.

We sped off from the airport in our modest mid-sized sedan and began our journey to Moscow, Iowa.

The drive was mostly quiet between us, and I allowed Connor to control the music. He wanted to be ironic, or perhaps unironic, and played mostly country music from the 1970s to get into the spirit of driving through BFE. This is a trip I had made with my father every summer. There was one summer Gwen came with us. It was such a wonderful summer. Back when all of our parents were still around and got along and we were excited to play make-believe together. I remember never feeling bored.

An hour or so passed, we turned onto 330th Street and passed the old bridge where my grandfather and I would tirelessly go fishing to no avail. We made it miles down this street, no houses in sight, until finally over the horizon I could see my grandfather's homestead. The Homeland as my father would call it. A modest sized farm house, where the shadows of grain silos would prevent the home from getting almost any direct sunlight. A large red barn that once housed his combine harvester tractor. A piece of equipment that was the first to be sold after my grandfather passed. And a chicken coop to the other side. A coop that we had painted yellow, the summer that we were all together like one big family. Victor, Kendall, Gwen, Me, Mom, Dad, and Grandpa. Grandpa had let me pick the color, it was my favorite color at the time.

We pulled down the driveway and Connor turned to me from the passenger seat. "Do you have a key to this place or like..?"

"They don't lock the house. Never have," I answered with a laugh. "People don't lock their doors out here."

"That...makes sense I guess."

I parked close to the back door of the home and saw the backyard had stayed mostly the same. A pool made from an old stock tank, a rope swing, a sand box, it all stayed there untouched by time. My father must have been paying someone to maintain the yard.

We both exited the car and took in everything that surrounded us. I could feel the culture shock setting in. This morning we woke up in one of the most busy cities in the world, and now the sun is starting to set and we're in the sleepiest of towns.

I led us up to the back door and saw something new. Something I haven't seen before. A keypad on the door. Shit.

"No one locks doors out here, huh?" Connor teased.

"Don't," I snapped back at him. I hit the enter button to see if the code was just a ruse but it beeped angrily at me. I groaned.

"Try your birthday," Connor suggested.

I did as he suggested. The keypad suggested it would be a 4 digit password so I entered in 2, for February, 9, for the 9th, and 01, for 2001. It beeped angrily at me.

"That wasn't it."

"What about his birthday? Your mom's birthday?" Connor continued to give me ideas.

I tried both and they both failed.

I thought for a moment and I groaned at myself for even thinking of it. But I went for it, what's the worst that could happen?

I entered 1-9-0-1.

I was granted access. And I felt overwhelmed with anger.

"Was that…?" Connor asked carefully, he could see how tense that made me.

I slammed down the door handle and I entered my grandfather's home.

"Gwenore's birthday," I said in a low, and disgusted voice. "Don't ask," I am not going to even begin to explain my fathers sordid affair with a teenage girl. Let alone with fucking golden child Gwenore.

I heard him behind me exhale a long breath. The house had been closed for months. I instantly started opening the windows in the kitchen and I ran through the kitchen to the living room to open the front door and get some airflow. The house was exactly how my grandfather had always had it. Every detail. The floral curtains in the kitchen window above the sink, living room furniture that has never left their spot. A large monstrosity of a TV across from the sofa with an obnoxious antenna, and a DVD player/VCR combo on top of it. He had never thought to upgrade to the flat screen TV's. He just wanted to watch sports, and pretend he could still see the screen.

Grandfather had passed the year we graduated high school. He died alone. Not here, not where he had raised his family or lived his life. But in a retirement community in a nearby town.

I feel so disgusted thinking this. But something tells me that this was one of the places my father and Gwenore would hide and… yeah, no thanks I don't even want to say it. It would further explain why the key code on the door was her birthday.

I have no proof. But this would be the perfect spot for a tryst. No place like the middle of nowhere.

"Hey," Connor began, knocking me out of my train of thought. "I...I have to tell you something."

"Okay," I said hesitantly. I was still going around the house and opening windows to air out the home. The air I let into the home was crisp, as an Iowa autumn usually is.

"I know about Walter and Viridian. And I know you do too. And I can tell that you're really struggling with it. So I just wanted you to know that I know about it, in case you wanted to talk about it," He said each word so hesitantly and with so much care. Like he didn't know how to communicate. He's not used to using any sort of extenuation with people. He's used to people just adoring him for no reason.

But my blood ran cold. I could blow up on him. I could lose my mind that he would even suggest that I would want to talk about this. But what drove me the most crazy is that he spent this entire time knowing about this. Who knows how long he knew about their disgusting affair? And he's just going to love her anyway. And feel bad for me?

"I don't need your pity. And I have nothing to talk about," I tried to keep my tone even. He followed up the stairs. I opened the window at the top of the stairs and began to open every door upstairs along with their windows. "I'm sorry, I know it's cold. I just need to do this for a few minutes to get the house back to its normal homeostasis. My grandfather would have never let his home get this stuffy."

"I don't care about the cold," he said. I still haven't made eye contact with him. I was in my grandfather's room, the master bedroom, and I had just finished ripping his window open when I turned around to Connor perfectly behind me. Forcing me to make eye contact with him for the first time since we arrived. "I care about you," he finished his thought.

He reached his hand up to my face, and caught a tear that had fallen from my eye. "You don't have to be so strong all the time, Nona."

I frowned. "I'm not crying, it's just really stuffy in here and it's triggering my allergies," I stepped away from him and began heading down stairs and headed straight to the kitchen. He was not far behind me. "And mind your business!" I shouted back at him.

I opened the refrigerator and grinned. I pulled out two Pabst Blue Ribbon premium American lager cans. Beer doesn't expire. Grandpa has never failed me.

He whipped down the stairs and I threw a can into his hands. "Want to shotgun these?" I asked him.

"What? No. Not really."

I scoffed at him. "You're no fun."

I cracked open my PBR as normal and took a seat at the dining room table.

"Aren't we going to be looking for something?"

"Do we even know what we're looking for?" I said before taking a huge gulp from the can. He took a seat across from me.

"I just know it's important to Walt's scheme. It could be anything. For all I know, he could have a quantum computer hidden here."

I snorted. "Yeah, right."

"We don't know, is all I'm saying," Connor defended.

He cracked open his beer finally and started drinking with me. We shared a moment of silence between us, the only sounds came from the window, the wind whipping through. That's one thing I remember about Iowa. There was nothing stopping that wind. A good gust could knock you right off your feet.

I slammed another sip from the PBR, nearly finishing it. "I'm sorry, I just needed a second."

"I get it. I really do. I'll unload the car. What room do you want to stay in? I was going to take the guest room at the top of the stairs."

It had just occurred to me that we wouldn't be sharing a room. That makes sense. Yeah he may have fucked me last night, but it's not like that was some sort of promise.

"I'll take my grandfather's room. The big one."

"I figured as much," he took a large sip from his own can and set it down on the table and he did as he said he would. By the time he was done unloading our stuff I had finished my beer. A younger version of myself would have drank it like a shot. And it was now time to close the windows in the house, it had been aired out to my desired air quality. It felt normal here again. Like my grandfather was going to be stepping in from tending his garden any second.

When I was a kid this farm had horses, but as his sight began to fade, my father made him sell them. Spending time with my grandfather was so precious to me. He would tell me that I was his best friend. And we'd spend hours circling the property, riding horses. He told me that we were the same and we were so much alike, and I prided myself on being so much like him. Until I grew up and everything felt different. After my mom died I was different. The things I used to look forward to I didn't feel connected to anymore.

When his kidneys failed my sophomore year of high school, I was going to give him my kidney if I was a match. My dad got himself tested as well. Neither of us were able to be a viable donor. So Grandpa spent the last measly years of his life on dialysis. And then he died. Alone.

I don't think I ever forgave myself for letting him die that way. It's really hard for me to let that go.

Once I finished closing all the windows I spotted Connor at the dining table fiddling with his phone. He groaned and he set his phone down.

"What?" I wondered what the problem was.

"No signal," he said distantly.

"That's... kind of to be expected, don't you think? Look where we are," I said unsurprisingly.

"It's just annoying. Collin won't have a way to reach me. I doubt your grandfather had–"

"WiFi? You can't even get WiFi out here. I do remember him having some sort of like... hot spot box that he would use to check his email. But that was so long ago. Even if I could find it... there's no way it still had service."

"Right. That makes sense," he said unmoved.

A moment had passed us by and then he stood up to turn around and face me, who was still standing in the doorway between the kitchen and the living room. "You hungry?"

We arrived at The Cove. The only establishment Moscow, Iowa had other than its post office. What made it so memorable was the life size dinosaur statue that seemed to be there for no reason at all. It was a diner known for their sour cream and raisin pie, another thing that seemed to exist for no reason at all. The locals however, swore by it. It was even advertised on their marquee.

Stepping through the doors with Connor felt like walking

into a time capsule. This place was untouched by time. Their menu has stayed the same, as did their tables, chairs, place mats, and floral curtains.

We were seated and presented menus, that of course, doubled as the place mats.

"Can I get you something to drink?" Asked our server, a short and stout woman probably in her late 50s. She had probably been working here our whole lives.

"Coffee. Black," Connor spoke up.

"The sun just went down, you're drinking coffee?" I objected.

He ignored me, "And a water please," he told the server.

"And for you, Hon?"

"Just water," I answered.

As the server walked away to begin gathering our drinks Connor turned to me, "So, what are you going to get?"

My eyes scanned the menu. "Looks like they have a Cobb Salad, I'll probably just go with that."

"Booooo," He chided. "Boring. I'm going to get The Cove Burger. With a side of onion rings."

"You're not going to try the famous sour cream and raisin pie?" I teased.

"I'll see if I have room after my entree," he smirked.

A minute had passed us by and the waitress set down our drinks and took our order. Before she could walk away Connor couldn't help himself. "So, tell me about this sour cream and raisin pie? It's been a hot topic of conversation."

She began explaining the pie to us when another server approached our table. She was tall and carried by a very thin frame, with dark hair cut short that framed her sharp features. She took off her glasses and began inspecting me. "I know you," she said, her voice shrill.

"You do?" I asked confusedly.

"I haven't seen you since you were knee-high to a pig's eye!" Our original server walked away to place our order and the new server continued to speak while I tried to assess who this person was to me, "I'm Lisa. Wally's neighbor."

"Wally?" Connor whispered to me, questioning.

"My grandpa," I answered, finally remembering. She's the pie lady.

"I knew it was you!" She said excitedly. "We really miss old Wally around here. He ate breakfast with us nearly every day for... well, it must've been 30 years. Or even longer!"

"He really loved this place." I said with a small smile. It was nice meeting someone who loved him. Nice knowing that he was being remembered.

"And your daddy...I saw him here not too long ago! It was early this year."

Connor straightened in his seat.

"My dad? Did he say why?"

"He just made it sound like he was getting some affairs in order, doing some work on the old Homeland as he and Wally would always call it. He said he was only in town for a few days, but that was the only time I saw him."

Connor and I looked at each other uncomfortably. We didn't want to seem suspicious.

"Hmm, he didn't tell me he was going home for a few days. But hey, it was nice to see you again, Lisa." I paused, "You're the one that makes the pies around here, aren't you?" I was pretty sure I remembered that about her.

"Yes! Sweetie, you are correct. I made a pie with you once when you were nothing but a toddler." I did remember that correctly. I can't believe that I remembered that.

"Can you please get my friend here a slice of the classic, Midwest, sour cream and raisin pie?"

"They use the word 'neighbor' real liberally down here," said Connor as he closed his door behind him when we arrived back at my grandfather's farm. "The closest house to this one is over a mile away. But yeah, Lisa, totally neighbors."

"Okay, but luckily no one can mind their business, either. She ratted out my dad so fast. I wonder what he could be doing here."

The Midwest wind whipped around us and I ran to the house and began entering in the key code so we could be granted entry.

"It's not what he's doing, Nona. It's what he's *hiding*," Connor responded.

I groaned as Gwenore's birthday granted me access to my grandfather's home. It just pisses me off every time. I look forward to the day where it no longer feels like Gwenore Viridian doesn't destroy everything that is mine.

"I know we haven't looked in the house at all... but I just highly doubt whatever it is you are looking for is in here. I know where all the good hiding spots are, Connor."

"We'll start turning this place upside down tomorrow," Connor decided. "I'm pretty wiped from traveling all day. Kinda want to hit the shower and go to bed."

"That's a good idea," I agreed.

"Do you want to shower first, or...?"

"You can shower first, I don't mind. Just don't use all the hot water."

"Or you can join me?" He said with a coy smile.

I began calculating this in my head. He had already seen me naked, what did I really have to lose? I didn't feel fully at ease with this however. I have never showered with someone before. What does this implicate? Does this mean we're going to have sex? Or is this just purely for the sake of sanitation?

He watched me work this out in my head. "Hey, I know a no when I see one. Not that it happens to me, ever. But like, I've watched a lot of TV," Connor joked.

I pulled off a half smile and shined it at him, "I'll meet you in there. Just give me like 3 minutes."

He beamed at me and turned towards the bathroom. I headed upstairs and straight to my room. I pulled my hair into a high bun in an attempt to keep it from getting submerged in water, today is not a wash day. Plus, I knew this was well water that we were dealing with, and I've spent too much money on my hair to put my hair through such abuse unless I had absolutely no choice.

I stared at myself in the mirror above the dresser and thought about this for one second. I decided this shower didn't have to mean anything. I set out a matching PJ set on my bed so I can quickly change into it when I get out of the shower. Then I headed back down the stairs and straight to the bathroom.

I opened the door without knocking, Connor was already in the shower.

"Hey, stranger." Connor greeted me as he heard me enter the bathroom.

"I'll be right there." I said with a little smile, undressing myself as quickly and efficiently as possible.

I pulled back the shower curtain and entered behind him and instantly felt freezing, little goosebumps beginning to arise over the surface of my skin. Why do people do this?

He turned around and smiled at my naked form. He wrapped his arms around me and I pressed my body against his, I told myself it was mostly for warmth. His chin rested at the top of my head, and he maneuvered us around so my back was in the water, getting all of the warmth, putting himself in the cold air. I exhaled and untangled myself from him and spun around, letting the water coat my skin and cascade down my shoulders and over my torso. I felt his hands grab at my hips, bringing my body close to his again. I granted him overwhelming consent to keep touching me, but I did my best to remain apathetic. I reached for some body wash and began lathering myself in it. It smelled like fresh fruit.

He couldn't be bothered by me trying to wash myself, he was kissing my neck as the suds finished rinsing down the drain. Still standing behind me, his hand over my throat, and his lips trailing up my shoulder and to my neck, while his other hand held my hip firmly, so he could grind his hardness against me.

I felt like I must be blushing. But can he see? Through the steam? I don't want him to know. It goes against everything I believe in to let him have that satisfaction.

Part of me believed that he was only doing this to keep himself warm.

But then the hand that was holding my hip in place began to trail to my opening, and teased me lightly, gently grazing thousands of nerve endings, making my body jolt involuntarily.

"You like that?" he asked wickedly.

"Yes," I wanted to sound reluctant, but I know I only came across desperate.

He chuckled and I frowned. He couldn't see it, thankfully, as my back was still turned to him. But I was so defenseless when it came to him. I didn't want to like him this much.

He turned me to face him. His hand had let go of his light grasp around my throat and held me by one teasing finger inside of me. He forced me to make eye contact with him. I don't even want to imagine the face I was making. I'm sure I looked absolutely frazzled and pathetic.

"You are so sexy," he said looking over my body.

Well, apparently he is really attracted to frazzled and pathetic?

I rolled my eyes at him and shook my head. He began lowering himself, making himself eye-level to my pussy. I moved forward slightly, so he wouldn't have to experience Chinese water torture while doing what I think he's about to do. And he did. His tongue gently made contact with me and my knees just felt weak. Like they would give out at any second.

Like a true gentleman, he made sure I reached completion. I allowed him to know how much pleasure I was in. I let each breath and moan escape my lips freely. And when he turned me around and pushed me against the wall of the shower, and entered me like he owned me, I let him know how amazing it felt. With my face pressed against the wall, and his cock slamming into me, I didn't bother gathering myself, I just let go.

So this is why people do this. I get it now.

As the sun broke over the horizon, Connor and I woke up together. It was silly to think we would be sleeping separately. But you won't catch me admitting it's because I can't resist him. It's simply because he's obsessed with me. That was the only explanation.

I didn't want to consider for a second what this was. Just two old friends catching up. That's all this is. Two old friends, catching up, fucking sporadically, and saving the world, maybe?

He rose out of bed before me. He left my door open as he exited to his room, where all of his clothes were gathered. I assumed he was getting dressed. I decided I would do the same.

I pulled on some warmer attire. A long sleeved top with a vest and some tailored jeans with thick socks. I pulled my hair into a single braid that hung down to my waist. I didn't bother with any make up, but I did do a quick skin care routine in the mirror that sat above the dresser. When I finished my skin glistened slightly. I made a beeline to the bathroom downstairs, the only bathroom this old farmhouse had, and brushed my teeth.

Before I knew it Connor was behind me with his tooth brush and scooched me over to the side so I would share the small bathroom sink with him.

I finished rinsing and he was finishing up himself when I said, "There's no food here, do you want to grab a quick bite at The Cove and then start our adventure?"

He spit into the sink. "We can't go on an adventure on an empty stomach, can we?"

I smiled. "Sounds good." I stepped outside to warm up the car and the cold hit me so hard. How can it be this cold with no snow on the ground? I hate it. I knew nothing about Iowa Autumns. I only knew about the summer.

It's crazy to think this is where my dad grew up. Thinking of who he is now, you'd have no idea that he was out here tending to chickens and horses all day. Helping Grandpa rotate crops. Braving every type of weather. The current version of Walter Valentine? He would never. This man was pampered and wouldn't be caught dead in a place like Moscow, Iowa.

Breakfast was brief at The Cove with no run-ins with neighbor Lisa again. I guess even she needs a day off every now and then. Connor continued to mess with his phone to no avail. He was able to get enough of a signal to get a text to deliver, but neither of us were able to receive anything. I think he was just trying to reach his brother. No one directly explained how The Domain worked... But I have found that Connor and Collin seemed to be the ones in charge. Their parents were nowhere to be seen. You'd think that they would be more involved but maybe they really were developing real estate.

I let Connor drive us home from The Cove. And it gave me the opportunity to gaze at him uninterrupted. There was something sexy about the way he drove. It's something I would never admit. His hand barely touched the steering wheel and drove mostly with his knees, but his eyes focused on the road and his mind was always calculating. His hands were too busy protecting my thigh, gripping it preciously. And me, still trying to appear disinterested. I fought him so hard, but I'm pretty sure it only makes him want me more.

The sun was in our eyes at this point. Nothing would shield us, protect us from its rays.

We pulled down the long driveway and Connor shut off the car.

"Where do you think we should start?" He said, turning to me.

"I'm not sure. I think we should split up actually. Again, I don't think there's much to find in the house. Whatever my father is hiding it isn't going to be in there."

He looked out in front of him at the extent of the old chicken coup to the left of the property and to the machine shed to the far right end, with nothing but a vast field of dirt and unharvested corn in the middle.

"Okay, I'll start over there at that yellow building-"

"The chicken coop," I added.

"And why don't you check out that barn and we'll holler if we have found anything."

"Do you think we'll find something big?" I asked, almost worriedly.

"I think it could be. This property is huge."

We both stepped out of the car and made our way to the opposite points of The Homeland. I made my way over to the machine shed. Past the tree with the rope swing, the sandbox, and over the rusted wire fence. I had only been in this barn a handful of times. Grandfather didn't like me coming in here. He told me this equipment was just too dangerous for a little girl like me to be around. He'd turn in his grave if he knew I was following around a spy that is pretending to be dead. Talk about dangerous. And definitely a bit stupid of me.

The barn's red paint was cracked and peeling off. Like this place could fall down at a moment's notice. It was predominantly empty now. The turbine that used to dominate this place had been sold for years, and now there were a few work benches with tools scattered about and a concrete floor, dusty, covered in random hay, and with several cracks blemishing it. I left the door open to let the light in, and I pulled my phone out of my back pocket, ready to be my flashlight if I needed it.

I took a few steps inside and I felt a shift almost immediately. Like there was a low continuous sound that had been occurring this whole time, but it suddenly went away when I walked in. I didn't notice it until it was gone. I tried taking a few steps out of the barn to see if it would come back, but to no avail. I brushed it off and I went back in to investigate some more.

I began circling the room, studying each nook and cranny, trying to find something out of place. I picked things up, wrenches, wood scraps, old plans for a new barn build, only to set them back down. But I spotted with my eyes something on the tool bench. A very large hard copy of the holy bible. Now, that was strange. My grandfather, nor my father, regularly practiced any sort of faith. But I was drawn to this, wondering why in the world it would be placed in this barn, next to all of this old debris and rusted tools.

I touched the cover and slid a finger over it, caked in sawdust, leaving a line behind it. I came down and looked at it at eye level, and heavily breathed air over it trying to clear the cover. There was an inscription on the cover. It was personalized with my father and grandfather's name. W. Valentine, was what it read in the bottom right hand corner.

I lifted the bible open only to find it was false. It was glued down to the table. Inside the book was a large black button.

With the book still open I began to look around me, goose-bumps erupting over every inch of my skin. A deep feeling of if I hit this button, everything is going to change.

"Winona!" Connor came bursting through the doorway. "Did you hear that sound?"

I jumped out of my skin, completely startled, "What?"

"Well, more like lack of sound. Like something changed a couple minutes ago. I didn't find anything but I felt something. Something is off. So I came running over to you as soon as I realized it," he explained, catching his breath while coming closer to me.

"I found something. Look." I said solemnly with an edge of

fear.

He only looked at it for one second and I saw a glint in his eyes. Before I could take another breath he slammed his hand down on the mysterious button.

"Connor!"

"What?" he tried to say innocently.

"We don't know what that *does*!" I screamed at him in fear.

There was a large sound coming from beneath us, louder than the hum that was there before. And one of the cracks in the concrete had begun slowly descending, mechanically, revealing a spiral staircase.

I stood there with my jaw to the floor and my heart pounding.

"We do now," he said with a crooked grin.

7

The Other Side of the Mirror

Winona

We couldn't see where we were. Simultaneously we both reached for our phones to illuminate our flashlights. Standing back to back, even with the room now flooded with light, I didn't want to process what I was seeing.

My father's inner sanctum. I wondered how long this was here. I have been so far removed from reality. I never thought for a second that a place like this could exist. Maybe this is why my dad was in town a few months ago. This is the only thing that would make sense.

When Connor and I carefully stepped down through the crack in the concrete, down an iron spiraling staircase that led to a mysterious elevator, we discovered none other than my father's secret lair. He really was some sort of super villain.

Connor, braver than me, began to scan all around the mid

sized room, covered in black monitors, computer towers, various buttons, dials, knobs, and a desk chair pointed at it all. Each wall of the room lined with other types of tech. Wires, unkempt, everywhere. Me, frozen to the floor. I wasn't even sure if I was breathing.

To the corner of the room stood a tower of technology I didn't have a name for. If I had to describe it, it looked like something Nikola Tesla would have invented if he were canonically a villain. Honestly, it looked like some sort of futuristic chandelier.

Connor stared at it with me and he shifted towards me. "Nona, do you know what that is?"

I was quiet for a moment. "No," I said without emotion and shook my head.

"That's a quantum computer, babe. It's right fucking here."

"What does this mean?" I asked in nearly a whisper, fear lacing my throat.

"What do you mean, 'what does this mean'?! Winona. We can stop Walter right here, right now. We can use this to figure out what he's planning."

"I thought you already knew what he was planning," I said in confusion, my brain buzzing.

"Cyber weapons could just be the beginning," He said without a hint of comedy. He turned to face me and put both of his hands on my shoulders. "This computer makes him more powerful than we can even imagine," he spoke gravely.

I took a second to consider what he was saying. I never took the time to consider my father to be powerful. But I thought about him, how I've seen him, his strengths, his weaknesses. What he could be capable of.

"He has métier, doesn't he?" I said fearfully. Connor would

know. And he wouldn't lie to me. Not after the last few days we've spent together.

"I've had no way to put it to the test, but I think he does. There's so many layers to this. There could be a reason why you personally had never noticed him be extraordinary-"

"I'm hero repellent," I interrupted. Shaking my head and shrugging.

He finally removed his hands from my shoulders. "Okay but also, I suspect that's why he pursued Viridian. Her métier... it makes other people with métier even stronger. I think he knew that being around her made him more powerful."

I wanted to gag. "What do you think his métier is?"

"Definitely something with tech. I couldn't tell you exactly what."

I stewed on that for one moment. Of course Gwen has this special ability that makes other people around her more powerful. God, they're probably completely drawn to her. They're drawn to her, but they're repelled by me. Maybe we were destined to be enemies. Maybe that was just always in the cards for us. Fate decided.

I finally moved from my spot in the room and put my phone away in my back pocket.

"Let's get out of here. Let's go find a lantern or something so we can look around some more, maybe figure out how to turn everything on in here," I suggested. Connor just nodded in response.

I began heading back up the stairway that led to the ladder with Connor trailing behind me.

My eyes squinted as they adjusted to the daylight coming through the machine shed, I climbed up the ladder and reached my foot to the concrete floor of the barn.

Connor made his way up the ladder next and I waited for him at the top, reaching out a hand to help him further. He grabbed it, not like he really needed it, and stood next to me next to the entry.

"I can tell that you're really struggling, Nona," Connor said quietly, looking my way, but I didn't want to make eye contact with him.

"What do you mean?" I said turned away from him.

"You can talk to me. I can't imagine what you're going through. I can't imagine for a second that it's easy to pretend nothing bothers you all the time," his hands reached out for me, trying to comfort me by brushing my arms lightly.

I exhaled and my breath left fog in the air. I finally turned to him, my eyebrows furrowed together, feeling slightly agitated, frustrated, and scared, if I'm being frank. I said nothing, but the look I gave him was enough for him to continue.

"You don't have to be so strong all the time."

I shook my head at him and just started to walk towards the exit. Besides, now that we found my dad's secret lair of doom we had our work cut out for us.

Before I felt the pain, I heard a very distinct *pop* sound as my foot was impaled by an old nail through my boot.

I screamed out in pain, "*Fuck!*"

Connor rushed to my side, "What's wrong?"

My knees buckled and I would have fallen to the ground if Connor wasn't there to catch me. He lifted me up instantly and I screamed. "Put me down! There's something in my fucking foot! Fuck!"

"Let me get you out of here first," He said, getting us through the doorway, me flailing in pain, completely freaking out. He was quick to get us over the wiry fence and to the concrete porch stairs and set me down. I laid my foot out and he looked to the bottom.

"Yeah, it's a nail. You stepped on a nail. We need to get to the hospital."

"No!" I shrieked. "Just take it out!"

"No can do, babe. You could bleed out. Also, you probably need a tetanus shot."

"Fuck! Fuck, you're right! Fuck this hurts!" I said. I took a big deep breath and tried to calm myself down. I shook my head and brought my hands into my hair, trying to grasp ahold of the tiniest shred of sanity I had left.

"Do you know where the nearest hospital is?"

I began to explain the directions to where we would need to go while trying to stand up and walk on my own and quickly fell down on the small path to the driveway. Connor picked me up again and opened up the back seat and set me down.

"Okay, keep your foot elevated, I got this. You're going to be okay."

I breathed heavily. "Fuck. This is so annoying. Okay."

He peeled out of the driveway and furiously made his depar-ture down the road trying to get us to the hospital as quickly as possible.

"This is so embarrassing," I said in pain, with so much disappointment.

"No, it's not, this could have happened to anyone, Nona."

I tried desperately to control my breathing, wanting to focus on anything besides the throbbing pain in my left foot. "Distract me, do anything," I pleaded from the back seat.

He made a quick glance behind him so he could make eye contact with me, see my face. He was quiet for a second.

Of course this motherfucker started singing. "*Eight'o'clock,*

Monday night, and I'm waitin'...to finally talk to a girl a little cooler than me."

"Connor, nooooo," I pleaded, my eyes closed, my thumb and my forefinger clenching the bridge of my nose.

"*Her name is NONA, she's a rocker with a nose ring, she wears a two-way but I'm not quite sure what it means,*" He sang my name so loudly, and head banged wildly while he sang horribly.

"*And when she walks...all the wind blows and the angels sing, she doesn't notice meeeeeeeeeeee.*"

"You can't be serious! I am dying right now!" I hollered at him.

"*SHE'S WATCHIN' WRESTLIN', CREAMIN' OVER TOUGH GUYS, LISTENIN' TO RAP METAL, TURN-TABLES IN MY EYES.*"

"Connor, please," I sighed.

"*It's like a bad movie, she's lookin' through me, if you were me then you'd be, screamin' someone shoot me, as I failed miserably, tryna get—* Take it away, Nonaaaa!"

I cried out in full, embarrassed misery, "*Trying to get the girl all the bad guys want.*"

"*SHE'S THE GIRL ALL THE BAD GUYS WANT.*"

He continued to sing the song all the way to the hospital, there was no stopping him. It did distract me from the pain, but this singing was so unforgivable. Even if I did chime in during the chorus occasionally.

When we were teenagers he'd always play this song when we were together. Always said that that song was our song, even when I did not fit this description of the girl Bowling For Soup is describing at all. But the nickname I despised, the name I allowed Connor to call me, was proudly sung in the song, and back then I loved seeing the joy it brought him.

By some weird miracle...I guess it wasn't exactly a miracle,

I was screaming and red in the face, I was able to go back to a hospital room, and sit patiently on an exam table and writhe accordingly almost immediately upon arrival.

The doctor gave Connor a proverbial pat on the back for not removing the nail from my foot before they got there. Petting his ego, let him know how inherently correct he was that removing it from me before they got there could increase complications. But the doctor told me I was lucky. The nail didn't go through anything too important and they were able to save my boot along with my foot. Removing the nail was agonizing of course, but the team of doctors worked together to remove it quickly and apply pressure over the wound before cleaning it and bandaging it up.

They said I'd have difficulty walking on my own for a few days but I'll be almost back to normal by the end of the week. Just in time for me to re-enter the real world again. I didn't like thinking about it. How can I just go back to work after everything I have seen?

It was just Connor and I in the hospital room, the nurses and doctor left, and said that one of them would be returning shortly to give me a fucking tetanus shot. So that will be fun.

"I can't believe they wouldn't let me keep the nail," Connor said jokingly, standing next to me and wrapped his arm over my shoulders as I sat on the exam table. He pressed his lips to my forehead and I gave him a soft smile. The best I could muster.

"Of course they wouldn't," I laughed.

"See? That wasn't so bad. Was it? They got you all fixed up," Connor reassured.

"Yeah, except now your secret weapon is busted," I said, referring to myself.

"That isn't true. Because you were here, the doctors didn't let me keep that rusty little nail. If you weren't here, they wouldn't've been able to resist me. It feels so good to be normal." He said while releasing me from his side-hug and going over to the chair to take a seat. I saw him pull out his phone and his eyes widened instantly.

"Oh my God. My phone is working."

I pulled out my phone and I saw all my usual emails from work were there, not that I was missing them. We finally have a signal. I had a few texts but none of them were important. After a few moments I looked up from my phone to see Connor completely pale.

"Everything okay?" I asked.

"Um," was all he said and he got up from his seat and went for the door. "I'll be right back, excuse me."

He made a phone call, to I assume Collin, and he didn't know, but I could hear every word he said through the door.

"You're a fucking idiot," he sounded so tense, and I felt my stomach drop to the floor. "No really, an actual fucking idiot. You let her leave?" Gwenore, of course.

"With fucking Juniper?" Who?

"Where has he even been all this time? You realize he's my actual arch nemesis, right? And now he's with Viridian and he's more powerful than ever? She could literally be fucking dead right now. She has been completely MIA. Her fucking plane did an emergency landing and she wasn't documented on the scene. I went over every case file and there's no record of any of her statements in the system. I cannot believe how fucking stupid you are."

Oh my God, Gwen. Jesus fucking Christ. She's missing?

With a startling amount of noise, Connor burst through the

door, visibly fuming, but I could tell he was trying to stay composed.

"Okay, we're on a deadline."

"She's missing?" I said softly, he knew who I was talking about.

"You could hear me?"

"Crystal clear," I sighed.

"I was going to tell you, I wasn't trying to hide anything from you, I just know how you feel about her."

He is always going to be hers, this thought repeated in my mind.

"But now I have to find her. She's in danger. God, if she's even...alive," I saw him crumple up his body and run both of his hands through his hair.

"What did Collin say?"

"Fucker didn't even answer. I was just leaving a voicemail." He said tensely.

That was one hell of a voicemail.

I felt angry too. I couldn't pinpoint why. But I felt my blood growing warmer underneath my skin. He was right, hearing about Gwenore did something to me. I didn't like hearing about her. But this situation made me feel too many things at once. This was a girl that used to be like family to me. I'll always have a soft spot for her, I'll probably always care about her deep down. That's why everything hurts so much. But I can't help but blame her so deeply for everything that she has taken from me.

Great, she didn't mean to? What everyone will say. They'll say she didn't mean to. But she did. Like she's taking Connor from me right now. Even though I never wanted to care about him in the first place, here we are.

It was jealousy. I'm jealous of a girl that goes missing the day after Connor fakes his death. God, this girl is so fucking dramatic.

The nurse came in to give me my stupid tetanus shot and then they let us leave. She sent us off with nothing but a little ibuprofen for the pain that still throbbed away deep inside my foot.

I made my way to the car slowly, declining any help from Connor. I stumbled and limped the whole way, but it let me grasp my last shred of dignity.

"Do you want to try to call him again? Before we lose signal again?" I suggested.

"No," He said more calmly than before, but was still speaking through his teeth. "He's avoiding me now. Guaranteed."

"Who's Juniper?" I asked after a moment of silence.

"Old schoolyard friend. He was... great at first. When we were younger. But... I don't know, as we got through middle school a lot of things changed."

"Oh, Juniper Proulx, that one skinny weirdo," I said remembering. "I thought everyone loved you."

"It's complicated. While Juniper can still be... Charmed by me... he has a very specific skill that kind of works against me."

"Well, what is it?" I asked confusedly.

"I don't want to admit this." He said, with a tone of shame.

"Connor," I chided.

"He knows when I'm lying, okay. He knows every half-truth, white lie, and fib. He's a bullshit detector." He said throwing up his hands in frustration and immediately returning them to the steering wheel.

I snorted. "He sounds amazing."

He scoffed in disgust. "God, he'd make me feel like everything that came out of my mouth was bullshit."

"I guess he would know," I wittingly added.

He rolled his eyes. "I was so relieved when he moved away. I don't even know what he was doing in town. How he got to Vee," he exhaled.

"You died, remember?" I laughed again. "He was probably in town for your funeral, idiot. You just said you guys were friends."

I knew I was right. I saw the old gang together at Presley's before I arrived at my usual cocktail bar where Connor found me.

"It's complicated," he repeated.

"Why?"

"It just fucking is," he said in defeat.

I knew I wasn't going to get any more out of him. I looked at the horizon in front of us. Already surrounded by nothing but gravel roads and cornfields. The sun was beginning to lower in the sky. My little injury wasted so much daylight.

"I'm sorry," I said. Filling the silence of the car.

"Don't apologize, Winona. I'm happy you're going to be okay." He rested his hand on my knee and gave it a light squeeze in reassurance.

I didn't want his reassurance. I wanted to not be broken.

He had me set up in the living room. He found a channel that seemed to work on the TV while he made me elevate my foot on the worn couch that still stood in the living room. He brought me blankets and pillows, too many. Convinced that I needed this many to be comfortable.

"I'll find a way for you to help, I promise. I know this is

probably killing you. I'm going to go back to the... what are we calling that?"

"I've been calling it the lair in my head, I'm not going to lie."

"Fitting," he agreed. "Yes, okay, I'm taking the headlamp that we found and I am going to go try to get everything to turn on. This is huge, Nona."

I sighed. "That technology is out of my skill set anyway. Even if I was down there with you, I don't know how much help I would be," I reluctantly admitted.

"That's the spirit, babe," he encouraged. "Now just stay here. And stay off that foot or you're never going to recover."

I sighed again and he exited my grandfather's home.

Of course, the only channel that would come in properly was the local news channel. I guess the temperatures are going to drop tomorrow, as reported by the nerdy weather guy. I considered pulling out my phone and organizing all my apps by color, since it being without WiFi or data it's basically an eight hundred dollar paper weight. But the TV piqued my attention when Gwenore's plane made national news.

No mention of her specifically, which left me feeling uneasy. But the reporter was interviewing the pilot of the plane. He explained that he had to do an emergency landing due to some sort of technical malfunction. He was getting alerts of engine failure. The thing is, he knew they weren't failing. For some reason, the engine failure light was lit up on his ECAM, but everything was fine. The plane was going through some rough air and spooked one of his passengers, but upon inspection upon landing, both engines were running perfectly. He just got a faulty notification. His interview ended and we got to see some footage of the scene. No one was hurt. And it was reported that there was now an ongoing investigation on the airline.

I looked at my arm and it was covered in goosebumps. I should have just organized my apps on my phone by color. I sighed as they moved on to the next segment. I've been sighing like it was going out of style.

God, Gwen, where the fuck are you?

I wish I could just call her. I wonder if she has the same number? It's been years since I've had to communicate anything to her. She was supposedly my boss at V Corp, right? But she pretty much just let my dad take over after her dad died. She just didn't have it in her to step up and run everything. I don't blame her. She'd attend a few meetings a week but she did not put in what my dad did. I'm not saying she couldn't do it, but she just wouldn't. How can you work in a place that killed your dad?

I hate that she has me caring about her this much. This is the most I've thought about her in fucking years.

I heard a loud clatter behind me. It was Connor entering the house. He was carrying a large white archive box that was practically overflowing with papers. He dropped it on the floor next to the couch.

"One sec," he muttered.

He went into the kitchen and dragged out a kitchen chair and set it next to me and set the file box on top of it.

"Here you go. Something to do. Go through these files."

"Um?"

"Come on, I know you want to be useful. This is all the paperwork I could find in there. Something in there has to be important."

"My father with hard copies? Unlikely. I'm sure none of this means anything," I dismissed him.

"It was important enough for him to keep in a secret lair underground in Moscow, Iowa," he said while shrugging.

I groaned at him and lifted the lid off of the archive box. "I wildly dislike you," I told him.

"I know," he said with a smirk.

"I saw Gwen's plane on the news. It was like... a notification error. The plane was completely fine, and it ended up landing for no reason. Everyone on the plane was fine. No injuries or anything."

I looked at Connor and he was like stone, seemingly calculating what I just told him.

"Wherever she is, she's okay," I tried to reassure him, much to my reluctance to do so. Very out of my character to provide him any sort of comfort.

"Yeah..." he said, trailing off uncertainly. "Yeah, I don't know. This is more complicated than that, Winona."

"Why?"

"Don't make me do this," he pleaded agitatedly. "You don't want to hear it, anyway. I know you don't."

He was kind of right. I can imagine what he's thinking. He literally faked suicide to keep that girl safe, and what does she do in return?

"You're right," I huffed. "I don't need the whole spiel. Get back to work. I have files to... examine."

He turned to leave and quickly turned back around and bee lined it back to me. He left another kiss on my forehead. I feel like this kiss was supposed to say something. Like some sort of statement like, he loved her, but he cares about me too? So fun, being second best. I shoved that thought away from me. "Thank you," he said sincerely. Then he ran out the front door, with the door closing behind him.

I reached the end table behind me and turned on the lamp so I could see. I just began picking up documents one at a time.

None of this was relevant to anything in the last year. It all seemed to pertain to my grandfather's medical records and nothing more. All stuff I already knew about.

But then I came across something with my name on it. It was the test results, back when I wanted to give Grandpa my kidney. Both me and my father were on this sheet. It listed our results and some other contributing factors, like our blood types. Mine, AB negative, circled with a question mark next to it in red pen. Well, I didn't like the looks of that.

The following sheets of paper, showed multiple tests being done, on my blood alone... to verify that was my blood type. I had never given my blood type any thought before. I've never considered donating or anything, I've had no major surgeries... nothing that would require...? This is so weird.

The bottom of this particular stack held a sheet of paper that made my stomach drop to the ground.

A paternity test.

What?

Excuse me, *what?*

I furiously scanned the paper in front of me. Reading it over and over and over. Reading it, but not processing what it was saying.

Walter Valentine wasn't my father.

Victor Viridian is.

"Winona? Winona!" I could hear Connor through my existential daze but at this point I had lost myself so far I didn't know where I even was anymore.

I remember the numbness I felt at first. I had gotten up from the couch, a place that was supposed to represent safety and comfort. I had stumbled my way to the bathroom and looked at myself in the mirror. I examined my face, a face that no longer resembled my father. I used to be able to look at myself and see him staring back at me. And now I look at myself and I don't know who she is.

But I don't see Victor, either. I just see Gwen. Arguably, my arch nemesis. And now she's my blood?

I kept looking into the mirror and decided to splash my face with some water. I began running the sink and cupped my hands full of water and splashed it over my skin, trying to wake myself up. But it didn't. I looked back up at the mirror, grabbed the soap dish, and slammed it into the mirror.

I don't know her. I don't know who she is. I don't fucking know her. That girl in the mirror? A fucking stranger.

I threw everything off the sink and watched it splatter across the bathroom floor.

I wept and I didn't even know I was weeping.

I started destroying everything in my reach, until my foot just hurt too much to stand and my back slid back against the wall and I put my head in my hands. Before I knew it I was just splayed on the floor, pathetically, a mess, a lost cause.

Which is when Connor found me. The sobbing didn't fade. I think he tried to talk to me but I wasn't there. I could not come to the phone. I felt him pick me up off the floor. He was trying to talk to me. Trying to get me to tell him what was wrong. But I couldn't get any words out. But he held me there for a moment. For a minute he just allowed the tears to flow freely.

I think this was it. My breaking point. Like I couldn't possibly handle one more thing.

Faking a death? Reasonable. Existence of super powers? No big deal, honestly just made a lot of things make sense. My dad's a super villain? That tracks. Nail to the foot? Must be a Tuesday.

But finding out that... the only family you have left isn't even... I couldn't even get myself to finish thinking about the sentence.

The tears never stopped, but I was able to calm down enough to let the agonized wailing subside. Connor got up, lifted me, and carried me to bed. At this point he had stopped trying to get answers out of me. I wouldn't look at him, I didn't want to see whatever look he had on his face.

But as the sobs still quaked through my body, he held me as he lay next to me in our bed. He allowed me to curl up into him, and cry myself to sleep.

8

Hypothesis

Viridian

Shockingly, Collin burst through his sliding door, increasingly upset. I nearly jumped out of my skin in surprise.

"Collin, what's wrong?" Charlie said surprisedly.

He audibly gulped, his eyes tired, "Juniper is missing. He escaped from The Domain. Nobody saw where he went, he's just gone."

My ears immediately started ringing and all I could hear was the deafening silence. I ditched my cigarette over his balcony. I tried to process what Collin said. And I tried to quickly compile everything I know so far. Juniper is a skilled computer engineer, and has the ability to know the truth no matter what.

Collin stared at both of us momentarily and pushed himself back into his penthouse apartment, ejecting himself from his doorway and immediately began pacing.

"This is all my fault. This was my responsibility and I should have been there to keep an eye on him."

"Vee needed you here, Collin," Charlie reassured him. "You couldn't have been there."

They went back and forth like that a few times. My mind was blanking, incapable of staying present knowing someone I trust is now gone. This was my chance to save him, return the favor, and now he's just alone. Why do I feel like this is all my fault?

Did Juniper run away because he's guilty? Or did he run away because he's innocent?

"I need to go home," I said, interrupting them. I need to get to my computer. I made my way out the sliding doors and Charlie was quick to follow after me.

"Viridian," Collin started.

"Don't talk me out of this. I'm going to have an Uber pick me up and take me back to my house. I just want to be alone," I said coldly.

I grabbed my new phone and slid it into the side pocket of my bag. I gathered any of my other things and took one last sip of my coffee.

Perhaps storming out wasn't the right thing to do. Even I can admit it, through my blind fury. But something that Charlie said still lingered in my mind. "It was all a part of the mission," she had said earlier. Turns out I'm a key component to a plan that I didn't get any say in. That changes now.

The car arrived in record time, with it being the dead of night, no traffic in sight. No words were exchanged in the Uber between the driver and I. I supposed it was my entire demeanor.

The arrival at my home was done efficiently. My things were gathered and I headed through my front door, greeted by the silence and stillness of an unoccupied home.

I carried my things up the winding staircase and made my way down the hall to my bedroom, the room that I had grown up in. I had considered moving into the master suite, where my father and mother had both resided during their lives, but I had left their room untouched.

I plopped my stuff on the floor beside my desk and landed belly first onto my king sized, pillow-top mattress. I laid like this for a moment. I knew I needed to gather myself. Pull it together. I didn't have the time to process all of this.

"Vee!"

I heard my name shouted from afar. I got up with a start and looked around to see where the voice could be coming from.

"Vee!"

They shouted again. I nearly fell out of my bed and hurled myself over to my window. And there he was. Our eyes met and my heart dropped to the floor. We locked eyes for what felt like an infinity, and then I snapped out of it and began sprinting out of my room, down the hallway, the stairs, and to my front door where he met me there. His arms wrapped around me and lifted me off the ground.

All of the sound and light disappeared from the room for a second that felt like eternity. Juniper surrounded me and the knots in my stomach unraveled as I inhaled his scent from the crook of his neck. He gathered us out of the doorway and softly closed the door behind us. His hands trailed down to the small of my back and I lifted up my head to meet his eyes once again. I closed my eyes and pressed my lips to his. The kiss was desperate and rushed, and I felt something from him I haven't felt before. I think it was fear. I only recognized it because I can feel it coming off of myself as well.

I pulled away from his kiss, "June, I was so scared."

He hushed me softly, bringing a finger to my lips. In the darkness, the only light coming from the streetlights outside, I studied his face. His eyes sunken in; he was tired, restless. His long, and delicate eyelashes blinked carefully as he returned my gaze. His finger moved from my lips and brushed away a single tear that escaped my eyes. I didn't even realize it had fallen.

"I didn't — I didn't know—" I stuttered but he stopped me from my stumbling words.

"Vee, please," he pleaded. He buried his head into my neck, "Don't. Not right now. Not yet." I could tell he was trying to remain calm, but his voice was hoarse and strained.

I realized how heavily we had both been breathing, gravity in the room was restored and it was like my feet had finally touched the ground. I felt afraid. I couldn't ignore the part of myself that didn't fully trust Juniper. But my body craved his touch. How could my body betray me? Why would my body want something that could hurt me? But I looked at him. And I saw how defeated he looked. He needs me.

"Come with me," I said to him softly. "You'll be safe here," I let myself out of his embrace and I locked the door and I fully armed my alarm. Nobody was going to be making it into this house tonight. Not without the entire neighborhood knowing.

I grabbed his hand and I led him upstairs, to my room, and into my private bathroom. He was quiet, but he knew what I was doing. The fluorescent lights revealed to me his hair, matted with sweat, and his arms covered in contusions. I began running the shower to let the water reach a warm temperature.

We began undressing. I finished before he did and I helped him peel his shirt over his head. I gasped when it revealed a deep purple bruise splattered along his rib cage. He looked ashamed.

That was from when the SWAT team took him down. Before he could finish his sentence. Before I was escorted away from him.

I shoved the memory down, and I guided us into the shower and let the water wash over him. He turned his back to me and he placed his head directly under the waterfall of water. I dispensed my body wash into a washcloth and began tending to him. Starting with his shoulders, making small circles until I reached the small of his back. He groaned softly as I went over his contusions, and I hushed him softly. He turned to me and I began to sooth the front of his torso. His hands went through his hair, fully immersing his hair in the water. I made the small circles of suds beginning at his shoulders, then collar bones, slowly making my way to his side so that I took extra care not to add more to his injury.

I lathered some shampoo in my hands and began massaging it through his scalp. I stopped suddenly, I felt something strange in my hand and saw the suds were turning a reddish brown. I looked at my hand and accessed what it was. Blood.

"June!" I said with fear.

He saw my hands and he quickly began rinsing his own hair. "I'm fine, that's dried blood," he tried to reassure me. He finished rinsing. And I took a quick rinse of my own, trying to avoid getting my hair wet. I moved him back into the water and I held him in my arms. He pressed his face back into the crook of my neck and my hands traced delicately around his back.

I don't know how my métier works. But if I really make other people stronger, this has to be the fastest way for people to regain their strength. Skin to skin. It was a hypothesis that I felt motivated to test. I think he did find strength in my arms. Because he returned my embrace, and his fingers and hands gingerly searched my body, and let the water cascade down his back until the water began to run cold.

I got out of the shower first and retrieved two towels for us. I wrapped mine around myself and wrapped him up in his. Using the corner of my own towel I carefully dabbed his face, absorbing the water droplets that trailed down his face.

After we dried off we headed into my bedroom. The sun was now fully risen above the horizon and it ambled through my windows. Juniper climbed right into my bed. Turning his back to me, and innocently curling into a ball underneath my white goose feather comforter. I began drawing my curtains so the sun wouldn't hinder our rest.

"Leave them open," Juniper said without turning to me. "Please."

I fulfilled his request and left the curtains open. I made my way over to the bed and laid my body next to his. My skin still bare, I wrapped my arms around his waist and pressed my skin against his.

Sleep finally found us. The last 24 hours were behind us.

It was well into the afternoon when I woke covered in an ice-cold sweat. I struggled to open my eyes, black spots obscuring my vision. My muscles felt stiff and worn out like I had been on a massive drinking bender. Why do I feel hungover?

I forced myself to carefully get out of bed, not to disturb Juniper, but as soon as I got up from my bed, I was attacked by a pounding headache, crashing and colliding in my temple and behind my eyes. I decided I must be dehydrated. I pulled my silk robe over my body and wrapped myself up in it.

I made the long trek to my kitchen to retrieve myself some water. Juniper slept soundly as I exited my doorway. My vision began to clear so I could get one last peek of him before I headed downstairs. He looked beautiful.

Making my way back up the stairs with two large glasses of water felt harder than it should. I did not feel like myself. I chalked it up to the last 24 hours I experienced. Juniper was taken from me and given back to me but it felt like I would never see him again. My trust in him wavered due to the lack of confidence from Collin and Charlie but the bigger part of me just wanted him near me.

I set one water on the nightstand next to him and took a sip of my own. I traveled to the other side of my bed and climbed right back in. My water was now on my nightstand, and I unwrapped myself from my robe. I pressed my body next to his again. He stirred slightly, awaking.

"Vee?"

"I'm right here," I said and held him a little tighter. He turned to face me in my bed and his thick brows were pulled together with his eyes closed. I felt his hands reach for me, cupping my face and reaching his lips to meet my forehead, leaving a soft and chaste kiss. Lightning struck through my body and I was no longer capable of forming words. Completely moved by a forehead kiss. Sounds like me.

My eyes closed, taking in the moment. Desperately just trying to exist in the present. A soft sigh escaped my lips, trying to settle in and exhale this brain fog. Juniper must have sensed something because he began stirring next to me.

"Baby, what's wrong?"

"Hmm?" I said dizzily with my eyes still closed.

"Something is off. Your skin is screaming."

My brain was slow to process such a unique sentence. "I just have a little headache, I'll be okay."

I felt him shift and turn, moving around the covers. "Fuck."

I finally opened my eyes, "June?"

"I knew... something wasn't..."

I looked at the man's naked form in front of me and remembered the deep purple bruise on his ribs, the contusions on his arms, now nearly completely faded. Like they just healed overnight.

"This isn't normal, Vee. I should feel like shit right now. Yesterday I could barely move. And you..." he turns to look at me. He uncovers me hesitantly only to reveal my own bruise from the plane landing, vibrantly purple. "Oh my God."

"Oh my God," I echoed. No, nope, no. This is too supernatural for me do not make me admit this.

He got up from the bed, panicked. I reached out for him worriedly, so desperately to hear what he's thinking. "June!"

"No," he scolded, "Don't touch me. I'm hurting you. I need to get away from you."

"Juniper, please."

"I should have known. I should have known that this would happen," He said beside himself.

I got up from the bed carefully and came closer to him while clutching the sheet over my body. "I didn't even know this was possible. This has never happened before. But now we know. Another extension of my métier. I mean... we knew I made other people with métier stronger, right? This kind of makes sense. I'm just making you stronger," he let me touch him. I pressed my body to his and burrowed my face into his chest.

"Nothing makes sense, Vee."

"That isn't true," I said, closing my eyes and taking in his scent. "We make sense, don't we? You found your way back to me," he burrowed his head into the crook of my neck. "This makes sense. You and me."

"Don't be kind to me right now."

"Why not?"

"Because I hurt you."

I lifted my head away from his chest and I grabbed his face with both of my hands, balancing the sheet that was covering me between us using only our bodies. I shook my head, "You did not," I emphasized. "Last night the thought had occurred to me that maybe I could make you strong again but it was just a theory. You cannot blame yourself for this."

His eyes beamed into mine.

"You have to believe me, June. You know I can't lie to you."

He smiled lightly, "You remind me of this all the time," his arms wrapped around me and embraced me.

"Do you remember yesterday morning?" I asked coyly.

"How could I possibly forget?"

"Can we please just go back to that? Just for a little while?"

He frowned and I could see him contemplating.

"We'll come up with a safe word. I know you're worried about hurting me. If anything hurts me-"

"Viridian, we don't need a safe word. I'll know if you're in pain. You're in pain right now."

"No, I'm not."

"You can barely stand."

"I don't need to be standing."

"You are impossible."

I smiled a crooked smile. "That's just part of my charm."

He shook his head slightly.

"Can you please just be kissing me now?"

He leaned his head down towards me and brought his lips to mine. Softly, carefully, like if he kissed me with any more urgency I would be blown to smithereens. My lips responded to his, slowly and passionately. This is all I've wanted from him. I like our version of normal. Something we could have kept if I had never left LA. I felt a tinge of regret.

I still don't know what happened to him in there. At the Domain. I don't know how he escaped.

But all I can do is be present, kissing his lips, being in his arms, our bodies connected again. How it's supposed to be.

I have never felt like this before.

The sheet fell to the ground and Juniper guided us to the bed. He laid me down across the bed and he laid next to me. I felt dizzy, intoxicated by his touch. His hand carefully trailed down my torso. He was listening to my body, I could tell. He was asking my skin how it wanted to be touched.

"Vee, I know what you want from me," Juniper whispered into my ear. I felt each word individually like each chord of a symphony. It tickled my brain and trailed down each nerve ending electrically. "But I want to hear you say it."

I was barely able to get out words. "Don't stop touching me," I pleaded.

"Where do you want me to touch you, baby?"

My eyes closed. He was really going to make me beg. "I-I can't-" I can't get these words out. And I felt him trail his fingers down to my opening. Teasing me to no end.

"So wet for me, already, baby? You are such a *good girl.*"

Fuck, I hate how much I love that.

I turned my body to his, his dominant hand still playing with me like he's only doing it for his own personal amusement. I kissed him hurriedly on his lips, parting my lips slightly and inserting my tongue into his mouth, tasting him. My hand wandered over his body and lightly caressed where his bruises once were, and then over his own hardness. Just as ready for me as I am for him.

"I want you now," I said pulling away from our kiss.

He smiled. "I'm not done with you yet, Vee. I'm having way too much fun," he pushed me back onto my back and quickly took my nipple into his mouth while his fingers inserted inside me. I let out a loud, involuntary moan. My eyes remained closed, as I allowed myself to feel every moment of pleasure. He began increasing the speed of his fingers inside me, and the pressure of his lips on my nipple began to hurt in a very pleasurable way.

Oh my God. He's going to make me cum.

"W-wait-" I tried to get out and then he took his fingers out of me and began aggressively stimulating my clit.

"I want to hear you baby. Does that feel good?"

All I could do was moan, feeling almost embarrassed by how quickly he can make me crumble.

I felt the pressure build and he could feel it too. He wasn't going to stop until I fell apart. I tried to muffle my moans but tears were forming in the corners of my eyes and I could no longer hold it in.

"That's it, Baby," he whispered.

The climax was like a tidal wave. I could no longer feel the embarrassment of how quickly he could do this to me so easily. I just felt hot and cold at the same time.

He removed his hands from my opening and he began tracing his fingers over my torso again. I turned to him. I was half laying on top of him. My face buried in his neck, letting our skin touch for just a moment. His arms wrapped around me and I returned his embrace. In this moment I was his. The climax still felt present, my skin was still singing. But it faded and the veil was lifted. My hands began searching for his pulsating stiffness.

I caressed it softly, teasing him. I slowly edged away from him and then over top of him. I smiled coyly.

"Your turn," I said playfully.

"Vee, are you sure?"

"Of course I am," I began sliding down to bring my face closer to his throbbing cock.

"You're really not in a condition to-"

"Hush. Your turn," I repeated. And I pressed a light kiss onto the tip of his cock.

I may not have Juniper's ability to just listen to someone's body. But it didn't take super powers to completely disarm a man in this way. I lubricated my mouth with my tongue, generating an adequate amount of saliva to maximize his pleasure. I inserted him into my mouth and began sucking lightly. I let my tongue stick out slightly to avoid any contact with my teeth, and I began playing with his shaft, swirling my tongue slightly.

He was responding to everything I did. His breath became unsteady and labored, and even let out some soft moans. I smiled around his cock as I listened to the noises that escaped his mouth. I bobbed my head up and down, creating a fast, maintainable rhythm. His hands ran through my hair, he grabbed a handful on each side, lightly, guiding me.

Suddenly he lifted my face off of him. "That's enough."

"What?" I said with saliva dripping from my mouth.

"Time to fuck you," was all he said. He lifted me off of him and pushed me onto my back onto the bed. My pussy was still pooling with desire. But he inserted one finger into me first and stimulated the roof of my opening, causing my body to twitch in anticipation. His finger set me free and he positioned himself over me and quickly inserted himself inside me, resulting in an audible euphoric gasp on my part. My eyes remained closed, practically overstimulated, just in the moment, wanting to feel every moment of him inside me.

Pressure. I felt pressure and pain. But so much pleasure came with it. He knew I liked it. But I also knew that this fuck was for him, it wasn't for me.

"Look at me, baby," he instructed. He brought his body closer to mine. Our chests were now touching and his face was centimeters from mine. I did as he told and I opened my eyes. He looked at me longingly. His eyes were so full of desire. I tried to stifle my moans, which incidentally just turned into whimpers.

"God, I love the noises you make," he said while bringing his lips to my neck. "They're so sexy," he said before placing a passionate kiss on my neck. "And they tell me how you want to be fucked," he began smothering me with kisses while each stride into me became more controlled, slower, but hard.

"I-I want..." I tried to tell him, "I want you to cum for me," I swallowed hard, trying to lubricate my drying throat.

He lifted his face from the nape of my neck and locked eyes with me once more. He quickened his pace and I tightened myself around his shaft. His breath became labored and a moan escaped his lips as he ripped himself out of me. I watched his cum cascade out of him and over my torso. I laid there for a moment. Eyes closed, catching my breath. And he collapsed on his back next to me. His head leaned on my shoulder, pressing his forehead to my skin. Then turned it upwards to place a small, tender kiss in the spot where he was resting.

"Well, my headache is gone," I said jokingly.

He laughed. He got up from the bed and headed to the bathroom to grab something for the inevitable cleanup.

After all the evidence had been wiped off of me he fell back to the bed, next to me. This felt so dreamy. When we're together it feels amazing but I have this fear deep down that we won't get to stay this way all the time. Juniper is practically on the run, and I'm basically harboring an alleged wanted criminal. But to feel like this, it's worth the felony.

"Baby, are you hungry? I can have the staff cook us something," the thought had just occurred to me. I have no idea when he had eaten last. I can't remember the last time I had eaten.

"If it isn't too much trouble I think that's a good idea, I think we should both eat," Juniper responded.

We gathered at the kitchen dining area. It was a modest-sized table next to a window overlooking the garden. Juniper had helped me get dressed and made sure I made it down the stairs okay. Even though I had already made that trip once this afternoon on my own just fine. He was just being overly cautious. Juniper ended up wrapping up in one of my thick bath robes, luckily I had one large enough for Juniper, but of course, it was a pastel purple.

We enjoyed a quick meal put together by my kind household staff. We sat in the remainder of the sun at the kitchen table and we somehow held on to our perfect little world as long as we could. It felt like LA. Like we could pretend we never left. Like I never found out about The Domain, or métier, like I could still trust him fully. I do trust him, but it's complicated when I have both Collin and Charlie on the fence about him. They just don't know him like I do.

I know. Famous last words.

"We need to talk, June. We've put it off long enough," I said, reaching my hand under the table to put my hand on his knee.

He sighed, "Fuck, Vee," he said softly. He looked so defeated. I feel bad for ending our bliss, but we need to come back to reality. "The airport… they honestly just knocked me out. The last thing I remember is being cuffed. But I was trying to tell you. They think I'm working with Walter."

I looked down. That's what Collin was trying to explain to me yesterday.

"To be clear, Vee, I'm not," he said with finality.

"I know that, June," I said while clearing my throat a little. I felt so nervous to hear what happened to him. I felt goosebumps erupt across my back like little needles stabbing me.

"When I came to, I was in some sort of basic jail cell. Nothing but a cot and a toilet in the corner. I was there pacing around and yelling to get someone's attention for at least an hour. It's hard to say how much time has passed. Could have been longer, could have been shorter. But then some guards came and sat me in an interrogation room. For the longest time I sat at a table alone. Even longer than I was awake in the cell. It was weird. It felt like psychological warfare. But my theory is that they knew they couldn't say anything to me. They knew about my ability. And they were waiting."

Something had just occurred to me. "Your métier, Juniper.

Have you ever heard of that term? That's what they call our abilities."

"Who? What?"

"The people that took you. The Domain."

He was taken aback and I saw all the color drain from his face.

"Oh my God, June, they didn't say who they were. You didn't know who-"

"Collin. Collin did this to me? Did this to *you*?" He was horrified. He was referring to how I was able to bring him back to almost full health, incidentally weakening myself in the process.

I opened my mouth to speak, ready to come up with some sort of defense for Collin, somehow, but Juniper was quick to stop me. He knew what I was about to do.

His body became rigid and slammed his fist down on the table. "Don't you fucking dare try to defend him," he angrily got up from his seat and stood with his hands in his hair, grabbing it into fists.

I gasped startled at his sudden, but seemingly reasonable anger.

"I thought he was my fucking friend."

"He still is," I tried to say, but I wavered with doubt peppering my voice. "He was trying to protect me."

He shook his head, "There is no one out there that you are more safe with than me, Viridian. I swear to fucking God."

I felt scared to speak. And I know he could sense it. He took a big deep breath in and exhaled sitting back down. His tone began to soften.

"I'm sorry, I'm not trying to scare you. Collin just put me in a very scary situation to get out of. I didn't know where I was.

And I just got lucky. That's all it boils down to. A guard told a lie, and that lie led me to a security pin that I used to sneak out of every locked door in that place. I waited for no one to be around, and I bolted as soon as I could. I got lucky again and was able to run all the way to the city transit station and get on the closest bus to your place. The lady in line in front of me took pity on me and paid my bus fare. Those bastards still have my phone and my wallet. I just got lucky, Vee."

I took in what he was saying but I still had more questions, "How did you not know you were at The Domain? Collin told me that's where you were. I was going to break you out but Collin resisted. He insisted..." I trailed off, deciding that including all of Collin's doubts about Juniper wouldn't be productive at this time.

"This wasn't the location that we toured in middle school, Vee. This was on the outskirts of town. And when I ran away, I wasn't exactly looking back to see where I was being held. But what I did see didn't have any signage. I escaped through a back entrance, very nondescript. And ran until I could find a familiar street. Luckily this town is on a grid system."

"But what happened in the interrogation room? What were they saying? What were they asking?"

His face went shockingly blank and I saw him reach to his head. The spot where I found the dried blood in his hair. He blinked slowly and responded, "It doesn't matter."

"It matters to me," I said carefully.

"A lot of their questions I had no answers to. I was hand-cuffed to my chair. One of the interrogators would ask a question, and when I couldn't answer or give them the answer they were looking for..." He couldn't finish the sentence but his hand went over his head. He didn't have to finish that sentence.

My throat felt like someone was squeezing it in their fist. I felt so physically ill.

I got up from the table and stumbled my way across the kitchen with a start. My entire body was shaking with fear and absolute betrayal.

Collin promised me that he was safe. Collin lied to me.

"Viridian?" Juniper called after me.

I began a trail up the stairs and June wasn't far behind me. I need to get that fucking cellphone.

Juniper was fast, but I was faster. I got to my room and found my cell phone in my backpack.

Juniper saw the cellphone and stared at me incredulously. "Who are you calling?"

I dialed Collin's phone number at lightning speed and held the phone up to my face fiercely. I waited for the line to answer.

"Vee? Are you okay?" Said Collin on the other end.

Coldly, I spoke, "You need to come over here. Right. Now."

9

Brain Damage

The phone conversation with Collin was fruitless. He was normally so composed, but in this case he sounded borderline frantic. But nevertheless he agreed to come to my estate and finally confront what he has done. He knows nothing of my newfound abilities and Juniper and I both agreed that we would be keeping that from him. I was still on edge. Knowing what I know now... I'm not sure who I can trust.

Juniper helped me into normal clothes. A fitted t-shirt with some comfortable jeans and even putting my socks on for me, bending over felt like a battle with my body. I didn't mean to, but taking on Juniper's ailments was hard on me. Harder than I wanted to admit. But I couldn't hide it from him. He knew exactly how much pain I was in.

In somewhat of a rush we both headed into my father's room

to find something suitable for Juniper to wear. I hadn't been here in a while. But this room remained untouched. Stepping foot in here I was instantly struck by his smell. It engulfed the room. The smell was a combination of freshly pressed laundry and some sort of overpriced cologne. It made me feel some sort of way that practically disarmed me, but I tried to shake it off. Juniper had been staying close to my side but he allowed me to make my way to his closet on my own.

I stepped inside and everything was organized by color. Mostly an assortment of suits. Black, charcoal, navy, and neutrals. I knew he kept his more casual stuff in his drawers. I pulled open a drawer and at the top of it laid a vintage band tee. It was the first thing I saw and it seemed to be the most perfect thing. I snatched it out of there and found a pair of black socks, some underwear, and some joggers. I wanted him to be comfortable in what I chose. This was something that more closely resembled what he would normally be wearing.

I stepped out of the closet and handed the clothes to Juniper. He looked at them for a second and considered.

"Is it wrong for me to be wearing your dead father's under-wear?"

"Oh," that was a good point, "Um... I just thought you'd want something clean to put on."

He smirked and nodded, "You're right, I'm just over think-ing," he dressed quickly and we exited his room and closed the door behind us and headed down the hall and to the stairs.

I had conquered these stairs already today but this time felt more daunting.

"I see you've met your final boss for the day, Vee," Juniper joked. "Let me just carry you."

I sipped in the air through my teeth. "No, I got it."

"Okay just let me get in front of you."

I obliged and allowed him to guide me down the stairs, while keeping my dignity intact.

We took a seat in the sitting room near the entryway while we waited for Collin to arrive.

"You know one thing for sure," Juniper started. "Whatever he says, he can't lie to me. I don't think I've ever been more in tune with my insight."

"That's true," I agreed. "No more confusion about anything. We're getting answers."

"And I know this came at a price, Vee. I don't take this lightly," He grabbed my hand and held it carefully between both of his. "I know you didn't know that I'd weaken you like this. But I just want you to know, I'm going to use this gift to do everything I can to protect you. No more emergency landings, no more holding cells, no more heartbreak. I promise you," he gazed into my eyes earnestly and I knew he was going to hold himself to it.

"And we're going to find Connor," he added. Hearing him say Connor's name hit me harder than the scent of my father's bedroom. So many mixed emotions. I have so much trust in this man before me, so many deep and complex feelings. But Connor... this man I had been inexplicably connected to my whole life. The love I felt for Connor... the love I still feel. It felt tainted by everything I have been learning. About myself, about the complex web of lies that my friends have been surrounding me with. I questioned it all.

"So I can kick his ass," I retorted.

He smiled, "Yes, baby. So you can tear him a new one."

Without warning, none other than Charlie Locke entered through my front door with a start.

It startled both Juniper and I, a result from both of our recent trauma, and Juniper instantly shielded me as if we were about to be in danger.

"Charlie?" I said confusedly. "Where's Collin?" Juniper was quick to stand down and act more casual as he could see we weren't in peril.

"Ah, yes. Collin sent me over to do some big-time explaining," she made herself at home in my sitting room. Sitting in a chair across from Juniper and I.

"And Collin couldn't be here because...?" I questioned, running out of patience. But trying not to take it out on one of my dearest friends.

"Oh! Hey," Charlie remembered something suddenly and began rummaging through her purse. She then grabbed out a cellphone and a wallet and got up to hand it to Juniper. "Here you go. Collin had me give these back to you. You're a free man. No one has it out for you, June."

"Did you... know that I was going to be here?" Juniper asked skeptically.

"Of course," she said matter-of-factly. "I had some super juice left over from hanging out with Viridian and as soon as she got home I got the insight that you two were together and safe. Collin is obviously worried sick but I reassured him," she shrugged. "He's tense as fuck, but he'll live."

I sighed. "I'm never going to get used to all of my friends having super powers." I'm also going to have to get used to people referring to the residual effects of my métier being called *super juice*.

She scoffed. "We've always been super heroes, Vee. Even you."

"And Collin," Juniper started, getting back to the topic on

hand. "What the fuck is his deal?"

Charlie shifted in her chair. While looking down she tried to explain. "He just still isn't completely convinced you aren't working with Walter on some grand evil scheme. But if Vee trusts you... That's all I need to know."

"Where's Collin now?" I asked.

"Oh. Well..." she was still avoiding eye contact with us. "He heard from Connor."

Every time I heard his name it pierced my stomach like a shard of ice. "What?" I said in shock.

"Connor needed Collin for something that couldn't wait. Then he called me to come over here because he knew you two were expecting him but he couldn't make it."

"Did he say what it was?" I asked.

"No, he said he couldn't tell me. I'm not going to lie, when it comes to Connor it's always been very secretive. Especially this past year. Something really changed in him after your dad died, Vee," her tone shifted. Her sugary voice, normally so unserious. But now... everything was gravely important.

I was brought back to my father's funeral. That was when he found out about my long affair with Walter. I had to agree, our friendship was completely different after that. He was so distant with me.

"You're right," I told Charlie. "He was never the same after that. But neither was I. We were both different."

There's no reason why Charlie and Juniper need to know. I just want to put that so far behind me. They don't need to know about Walter and I. I didn't even want Connor to know.

"But all of this is because of Walt, right? Everything that has happened? Everything goes back to him," Juniper chimed in.

Fuck, was I giving him some sort of signal? Ugh.

"That... Yes. Walter seems to be at the center of it all."

I was quiet. We all sat in that for a moment and Juniper was the first to speak up.

"I want to help. Tell me how," he said with conviction.

Charlie considered for a minute, "I don't—"

"I want to protect Viridian as much as you do," Juniper interrupted.

I scoffed, "You guys act like I'm made of porcelain and it's exhausting to me. Charlie, why don't you tell me how I should help myself. If I am soooo powerful," I said, rolling my eyes.

"You are, Vee, but—"

Poor Charlie, kept getting interrupted. "You know what?" I said. "I'm done working from the outside. I'm already in that fucking database. I know how to get into it whenever I want anyway. I'm going to the Domain and I'm demanding to be an... operative or whatever. Let me help. Let me in on these missions."

"Vee, you know that isn't up to me."

"And you also can't stop me."

Juniper softened next to me, "You are so not up for that kind of thing right now. And you know it. You could barely make it down the stairs."

"What? Vee," Charlie said concernedly. "What's going on? I just saw you yesterday and you were fine."

"I *am* fine," I said tensely. I gave a look to Juniper, annoyed with him, because we had just agreed we weren't going to mention our discovery of my additional ability. I got up feigning any sense of health, "Let me just get my shoes on," and then I immediately felt like the room was spinning and I couldn't get my footing. What the hell is happening to me? Why is my vision getting blurry?

I felt myself begin to tumble in place but Juniper reacted quickly and caught me by my waist.

"What the hell?" Charlie exclaimed concernedly.

Juniper sighed. "Her ability is more compelling than any of us could have thought. We all knew we were drawn to her as kids. I mean, that's why we all became friends. It was because of her," as he explained he set me back down on the couch. "But she seems to have a supplemental ability in addition to us being drawn to her, and feeling better when we're around her. But it runs deeper than that."

We wanted to keep this quiet, but if Juniper felt comfortable telling Charlie, then I knew I was safe. "Whatever happened to Juniper yesterday, any injury or affliction... Through prolonged physical touch, I was able to take it onto myself. Last night he was covered in bruises, and now they are almost completely healed and I think I might actually have a concussion because my vision is kind of spotty."

"Let me take you to the hospital, Vee, it's like you're just getting worse," Juniper pleaded.

"No," I said immediately.

"June's right," Charlie agreed. "But you can't take her to the hospital. They won't be able to help her anyway. The real world isn't equipped for this. Looks like you're going to get your wish, Kiddo."

"You're not serious," Juniper said opposingly.

"Yeah, the only people that can really help her are at The Domain. And June..."She paused. "I think you need to stay away from Viridian for a few days. I think you're making her worse."

"No," I said again. Seems to be my favorite word today. "Juniper isn't going anywhere."

"Think about it, we don't know the extent of this. You've never experienced this before and we don't know anything about it. Juniper still isn't back to his full strength and he could *literally* be draining you. Right now. Just sitting next to you."

"Fuck. She has a point. I hate it, but she could be right."

"Guess I'll just suffer then."

"Are you guys like, together?" Charlie questioned curiously. "Is this a thing? Oh my God. Oh my God. Guys. Are you..." She stopped herself because she saw how caught off guard I must have looked.

Juniper and I made brief eye contact and I didn't know exactly what to say because we haven't discussed it. I actually felt my face turn red. And now I probably look terrible because I didn't answer right away.

"What is this? Middle School? We haven't talked about it, Charlie. But as soon as we know, we'll tell you."

"*Oh,* 'We'll' tell you. Okay. Okay. I'm picking up what you're putting down," She said, winking her eye at the end. "Okay but on a more serious note. We gotta take care of our girl. Juniper, why don't you stay behind while I take Vee into the Domain and they can check her vitals and see if she improves just by being away from you for a while. Just a couple of hours, I promise. I'll get her right back to you."

"I don't like this," I said. "It doesn't feel right, Char."

"It's a good theory, Vee. Just to see how quickly you start to feel better. Regain your strength. I don't like being away from you either. Why do you think I chased you all the way to the airport in the first place? I wasn't going to let you go. Not without a fight," Juniper tried to reason with me. And while I was receptive to his reasoning, it didn't take away from this horrible feeling in the pit of my stomach.

If I was going to go to the Domain, it was going to be without him. I didn't want to accept that, but I had to.

I stepped out of Charlie's car and looked around at the facility. The first thing I did was light up. My first smoke of the day. Unfortunately I think Charlie was right in this case about getting some distance from Juniper. He really was draining me, and I already feel better.

It was an old building. Grey concrete bricks that towered up for stories. Little landscaping. A few bushes lined the building but the grass that surrounded it was turning gray.

It was uncharacteristically warm from a North East fall, but the wind still whirled around us providing a chill.

Charlie shook her head at me once she saw the cigarette. "If you do have a concussion, smoking is the last thing you should be doing."

I scoffed. "If I am as powerful as everyone seems to think, I think I'll be fine, Char."

She rolled her eyes at me and waited for me to take a few more puffs from my cigarette before I ditched it in the street.

Maybe I should quit smoking.

Eh, probs not.

The nicotine seemingly gave me some false confidence. Either that or I was being completely fueled by a furious desire to find Collin and Connor and kick both of their asses for putting me through all this shit when I could probably have been way more helpful to their cause.

I arrived through the entrance with authority. I glanced at the room before me and it was nothing like I had imagined. It was dingy and dated. There was wood paneling on the walls, and I'm not an interior design expert but that trend died in the 70s. Charlie sneaking passed me so she could head straight to the elevator.

"Come on, Vee," she chided as she lifted up a secret panel and entered in a code. The elevator doors flung open and she stepped inside and but I couldn't move. I watched her step into that elevator like she had used it hundreds of times, so confident.

Charlie scanned my rigid posture, and the fear and uncertainty in my eyes. And I watched as she realized. "Oh," she said softly, "Vee, there's no other way to get in. There isn't any stairs we can take. I'm sorry." She tried to explain.

"There's no other way?" I said to her, seeking confirmation.

She shook her head with empathy in her eyes. She knew I have struggled with elevators.

I softened my stance and I gathered myself, and I feigned confidence as I stepped over the threshold of the elevator and let the doors close behind me.

I kind of knew what I was getting myself into. I had the smallest idea, right? I was entering a secret facility in the business of espionage? They certainly blended right in. The elevator stopped descending and Charlie turned to me.

"You ready for this?" she said with a soft smile.

Before I could answer the door came open and I'm instantly blinded by flourescents, a room, a fucking stadium, sterile, and people in lab coats everywhere.

Charlie stepped out first and I followed closely behind her. She made her way down a flight of stairs and smiled and waved at some familiars. I maintained a powerful gait. Staying focused, holding onto my confidence to not embarrass myself. Besides, I was just a little dizzy before. My legs worked fine. I really was starting to feel better. No one knows that I just faced one of my biggest fears. Elevators.

We entered a wing of the Domain that gave me like Resident Evil vibes and left me with very little confidence to cling to. It immediately felt colder. The hallways were a stagnant white and Charlie led me to a vacant room, similar to a normal doctors office but without the anti-smoking propaganda littering the walls. It was blank. A small examination table, a counter with a sink, and chair were the only things that occupied this room.

"Babe, take a seat up there. I'm just going to grab Beckett," Charlie instructed.

I took a seat at the edge of the examination table, "Who's Beckett?" I tried to ask but Charlie already headed out the door.

This felt so weird. Why did I feel like I was just led into a trap? Then I reminded myself that I literally asked for this. This is what I wanted. And Charlie would never steer me into danger. Juniper would have warned me if he got a bad vibe from her. He would have never let me leave with her.

This anxiety is probably just a result of the absolute insanity that was my life the last few days. I haven't been able to get back to a routine at all. And being weakened. It felt like the worst hangover of my life.

I sat there for a few moments when a very tall man with a black mullet and a lab coat came through the door with a bunch of hospital equipment on a dolly. He wore black framed glasses and looked tense. I wondered if that was just how he always looked.

"You must be Viridian," he said gruffly. He instantly started rummaging with the blood pressure sleeve.

"Where's Charlie?" I asked worriedly.

"Oh, she got caught up with Collin."

"What?" Collin?

"You know them both right? Like you guys grew up together?" He ripped the Velcro apart and headed towards me. "Alright, give me your arm."

I reached out my arm and he wrapped the band around it and began pumping the sleeve full of air. "Yeah, we're childhood friends," I answered. "Why?"

"Just making small talk," He said nonchalantly. "I'm Beck, by the way. What brings you to the Domain?"

He said it so casually I wasn't even sure how to answer it. "I... I'm looking for my friend. And also... I'm kind of sick," I wasn't sure how specific I should be.

"Ooh yeah, you are a little sick. 145 over 95. Sounds like you've been under some stress," that's an understatement. "Are you feeling dizzy?" He asked.

"Yes, I've been experiencing some dizziness, some headaches..." He ripped off the sleeve and grabbed out a stethoscope.

"I'm going to listen to your heart beat really quick."

I was quiet as he listened to my heart for a moment. He pressed the end of the stethoscope to my back and I allowed my eyes to close and I exhaled slowly.

"Hmm," he said. "It's a little on the high side. Technically normal but it's 100 beats per minute. Are you a smoker?"

"Yeah."

"Yeah, you should quit smoking for a while. How's your caffeine intake?"

"I drink coffee every day."

"Yeah I mean, that's probably why you feel like shit," He grabbed out a thermometer and stuck it into my ear and grabbed nearly instantaneous results.

"Normal temp," he said. "Sounds like you need to lay off the nicotine and caffeine and just get some rest" he said shrugging. "But I still want to do some blood work."

"What? Blood work?"

"Grow up," he chided me.

"Excuse me?"

"Do you want to get better? Do you want to find out what's wrong with you?" He scolded me.

I couldn't believe this guy. So fucking rude. "I just want to understand why it's even necessary to draw my blood?"

He was quiet for a moment as he began to prepare a needle and syringe. "I am really good at what I do."

"What, is being an asshole your métier?" I snapped.

"No. I find solutions. I'm really, really good at finding solutions. When I was a kid, I diagnosed myself with cancer. First time a team of doctors had ever seen such a thing. I knew exactly how to treat my own disease. And you know what? I survived. So I'm going to be checking for brain injury biomarkers. With your blood I'll be able to determine your S100b protein level and your glial fibrillary acidic protein levels. If they're off, I'm going to suggest a CT scan next. If not, I'm just going to hand you straight off to Charlie and Collin so they can take you home and force you to rest and take away your cigarettes."

Wordlessly I held out my forearm and he prepped it with an alcohol wipe. I frowned. I did not like this man, but if finding solutions is his métier, maybe he can help me learn how to control mine. So I can be more useful to others. So I can help people without weakening myself.

"Now, you're going to feel a slight pinch," He said. And with no count down of any kind he expertly stabbed a vein in my arm and extracted my blood for further testing.

He pulled the needle out of my arm and quickly placed a bandage over my open wound and applied pressure with his thumb. "Okay, place your thumb over this and continue to apply pressure. I'll be right back, I'm just going to drop this off to the lab."

I did as I was told and continued to hold pressure over the extracting site. He left the room.

I better not have fucking brain damage.

There was a quick knock on my door and my face jerked to the clatter. Through the doorway Collin arrived and my expression immediately turned sour.

"I know you are mad at me," he said full of shame. "Will you believe that I am just trying to keep you safe? I'm desperately, desperately just trying to keep you as far away from this as possible and you're making things so hard."

"You can't keep me away from the danger when I'm at the center of it, Collin."

"You didn't have to be," he said in defeat. "but I digress. I'm here to take you in and get you registered. You'll be one of us, Vee. Well, hopefully more like Charlie."

"What do you mean?"

"Her métier is only randomly useful. Then there's people like Connor and myself... where our métier applies to all sorts of levels of advantages," he paused. "I never wanted you to be in the system."

"I've been in the system, stupid," me, remembering how I found myself in the Domain's database within 5 minutes.

"That shouldn't even be possible," he groaned, remembering that I told him that already.

"What exactly is your métier, Collin?" I asked changing the

subject. "What does it mean to be 'adept'?"

"Put plainly? I'm naturally good at everything. Not great, not an expert, but any new skill I need to acquire I am able to do proficiently on my first try. Why else do you think I can pick up any instrument and play it? That's just a party trick."

I rolled my eyes at him. "My best friends growing up," I stated with a twinge of annoyance as I began to list, "One naturally good at everything, and the other has a penchant for persuasion. Then Charlie? She just knows if people are dead? That is such a ridiculous ability."

"And you, who brought us all together. You're irresistible to us, you know," Collin said matter-of-factly.

I audibly groaned. Beckett, the massive, goth, scientist, burst through the door.

"Yeah, so, based on your lab results I see that you have a fun métier that none of us have seen yet. You're a nice little hero magnet. Collin will probably put you in recruiting immediately," he said absentmindedly while looking down at his research notes. I looked over to Collin who seemed less than pleased that Beck even mentioned how genuinely useful I would be. I had a little smug look in my eyes as I stared at him.

Beck continued, "And based on the blood tests you're clear for brain damage, so no need to worry there. Just keep an eye on your blood pressure, take it easy. But if you want to get back to normal faster, I'd say just spend a day with your sister."

10

It's All for the Best

"What?" I said confusedly. Sister? "I don't have a sister."

"Yeah, she was here the other day?" He said matter-of-factly. "Strawberry blonde, bitchy scowl on her face? Kind of like the one you're giving me now?"

My eyebrows furrowed together and opened my mouth to speak but Collin was quick to chime in. "He must be confused. We make mistakes sometimes," Collin said to me then turned to Beck. "She's an only child. She doesn't have any siblings," he said dismissing him.

I could tell that Beck wanted to argue but there was a power shift in the room. Based on his posture change, Beck seemed to make himself smaller around Collin.

"Well, anyway. Lay off the nicotine, lay off the caffeine, get some rest, I don't see anything concerning about your charts...

except for your strange, random DNA match."

"How did that happen?" I asked. "I don't understand."

Beck shifted uncomfortably and began to explain. "It's standard procedure. We always cross reference between other operatives to see if we can replicate previous diagnoses and treatments. The procedure recognized a relative in our system. But, like Collin said. We make mistakes sometimes," his last sentence came out unsure.

"Exactly," Collin chimed in. "Can I take her home?"

Beck exhaled. "Yeah, she's free to go," and he shrugged and exited the room.

"Why isn't Charlie taking me home? Where did she go?"

"I ran into her and put her on assignment. I told her I'd get you home. And also I'd get you started on the on boarding process. I get it, we've kept you in the dark long enough."

"I'm on your team, Collin. Just let me work with you," I tried to reassure him.

"You've been my best friend for my whole life, Vee. I just never wanted to see you in danger."

"Too late, huh, buddy?" I said with a smirk.

He shook his head and reached out his hand. I took it and he assisted me off the exam table.

"Connor is waiting for you in the parking lot," he said to me as we exited the exam room.

My heart skipped an entire beat. "He's here?" I said with my voice straining to stay calm.

"He's waiting for you in the town car. He has a lot of explaining to do."

I could hear my heart pounding in my ears, without another word I began sprinting out of the Domain with Collin running after me, calling my name, barely keeping up. The elevator ride was agonizing, my mind whirling. And finally, after days of thinking he was dead, the tears I had cried, the nights of nightmares, and for it to all be for nothing. Because he was alive all along. All reasonable thoughts had exited my brain. Nothing was going to keep me from seeing him. I grabbed Collin's hand in the elevator and forced him to hold mine. Two elevators in one day? I suppose I had to make it up somehow. But moments after grabbing his hand he realized what was happening. We didn't make eye-contact, but he held my hand back until the elevator crept up to our floor. We exited the elevator and I let go of his hand. We exited the Domain.

My eyes were scanning the parking lot wildly, looking for any sign of Connor. Collin pointed out the black town car with all tinted windows. Without a second thought I opened the door to the back seat and slid myself in. I locked eyes with him and I felt every tiny hair on my body stick out of my body.

"No," I uttered in a devastated whisper.

Collin closed the door behind me and gave the hood of the car two quick slaps and the driver sped out of the driveway.

"Hello, Honeybunny," His voice was smug, confident. "I've missed you." Connor wasn't in the car with me.

It was Walter.

I couldn't speak. I couldn't make a sound. I felt so terrified. So betrayed. It was Collin all along. Every fucking tangent he went on about keeping me safe... it was all bullshit.

Walter reached his long and bony fingers out to me, and I recoiled away from him. "You used to love it when I touched you. Baby, don't you remember? It wasn't that long ago."

As the car zoomed through traffic violently, I reached for the door handle and tugged at it as hard as I could, ready to jump out of the car, anything to get away from him. But the door wouldn't budge.

He grabbed me and pulled me closer to him and I shrieked.

"You're not going anywhere, Honeybunny. You've always been my little secret weapon. Even before I knew what you were."

I fought out of his grasp and inched myself as far away from him as I could.

He knew about my métier. He had the exact type of métier that Charlie had warned me about. She told me that not all of us were heroes.

"What do you want?" I finally spoke.

"I just want us back. You and me, Honeybunny. No one will be able to stop us."

"There was never an *us*, Walter," I spat at him. He stole years of my life, sure, but it was always in secret. Nothing about our relationship was real. And I was just young and naive enough to believe that was normal. That it was healthy.

"Of course there was," he said certainly. "Don't you want to hear my plans for us? How are we going to take over the universe?"

"God, not really," I can't believe Collin, right now. I felt nauseous. Like I was really about to vomit. How am I going to get out of this one? I need to come up with an escape plan fast.

"Your friend warned me that you weren't going to make this easy for me. But we can do things the hard way."

"He isn't my friend," I said acidly.

"Really? Because the way I see it he's just looking out for you. He watched you fawn over his brother for years, and for no reason at all, other than you were under his *thrall* for lack of better words. And he got you away from him, didn't he?"

I didn't answer. I was fuming. Seems that Walter Valentine

knew more about Connor, Collin, the Domain, everything… more than I did. And that just brought angry, traitor tears to my eyes.

"Don't weep, love," he said in a low tone, reaching up to my face to wipe my tears away and I recoiled from his touch yet again. "It's all for the best."

"I don't see how," my voice was straining. Desperately reaching for a calm but menacing tone, but only came off full of fear. I didn't want him to know how afraid I felt.

"This is just the beginning, Honeybunny."

The car pulled up to Walter's home driveway. Before I knew it the door I was leaning against was ripped open and two strong arms lifted me out of the car. No one I could recognize, a member of Walter's secret security team, ripping me away from my seat with one hand over my mouth, and another man grabbing my legs. I fought it so hard, kicking, screaming, crying, to no avail. I made eye contact with Walter who gave me nothing but a sad smile and a little wave.

"I'll see you at dinner! Boys, make sure she's comfortable."

They dragged me through the entrance of his home and up to the stairs. The men grunted as their hands grasped my wrists and ankles tighter.

I was in a daze, I couldn't believe where I was. I never should have left Juniper. The thought led me to this morning with Charlie. Juniper would have never let me leave with Charlie if he thought something was going on. Which means Charlie is in danger too. She has no idea about Collin.

The security guards back slammed into a door while opening it behind his back.

"You can't just lock me in here!" I heard a voice shriek. "Oh my God, Gwen!" The voice said once it realized it was me. I felt a certain level of shock, only one person called me that name.

Without grace, the two burly men set me on the ground and locked the door behind them. I looked around and realized where I was. This was Winona's childhood bedroom. Everything was white. White carpets, white walls, white bedding, white furniture, with the exception of her horse figurine collection that extensively lined her walls on shelves.

"Winona?" I was shaken to my core. The last person I had expected to see. She had helped me up from the ground.

"Are you okay? Oh my fucking God."

My surprise quickly turned into suspicion. I felt darkness grow behind my eyes, and ice surrounded my heart. "Of course, you're a part of this," I said coldly.

"Excuse me?" Her concerned face quickly changed to disgust.

"Of course you're working with your father, it all makes sense," I spat the words at her like bullets.

"Yes, Gwenore," She fired back with a sarcastic tone. "This is all part of his plan. I begged him to lock me in my childhood bedroom and throw you in with me. This is the *key phase* in his *master plan* to take over the world."

My eyebrows furrowed together, "Winona, there is no universe where we would be on the same side. You have always—" I stopped myself. I'm not sure why I did. But I looked at her, and I detected something different in her face. Behind all that anger I saw something, like she was hurt.

I started over, "Why are you here?"

She scoffed and took a seat on the edge of her pristine twin sized bed, "Where do I even begin?"

Something in her face, in her posture, something told me that she has had a hard week like I have. I kept my distance from her. I took a seat in her reading chair by the windows, which I had noticed had bars on them on the outside. The door itself had been equipped with a newly added lock that could only be accessed from the outside. There was no doubt in my mind that even if we charged through her bedroom door, ramming into it with maybe her dresser, or even one of her bigger horse statues, there would be a minimum of two guards waiting to tackle us down. No escape in sight.

"Looks like we have time to catch up on the last decade."

She scoffed again. "Like how you were fucking my dad?"

All the air was removed from the room. I knew that she knew, but she went right to where it would hurt me the most. I felt all of my blood rise to my face. I felt such sheer embarrassment.

"Is that relevant?" I tried to retort back confidently.

She sighed, "There was a time I never thought I'd... forgive you for that."

"I was a kid, Winona."

"I *know*," she said, "I know it wasn't your fault. I don't blame you for it, but at the same time..." She trailed off.

"You took Connor from me," I whispered, breaking the silence.

"Trust me, no, I didn't," she said with certainty, talking into her hands and then running them over her hair. "He's always been yours, Gwen."

It felt strange hearing these words come from her mouth. Something I probably always wanted to hear. But after everything I've gone through, thinking he was dead, then the certainty that he wasn't, but experiencing everything I did with Juniper... I didn't want Connor like I used to. I think part of me will always love him, but I no longer felt that deep connection to him that I always held onto so desperately.

This proves that maybe it was always his métier that held onto me. Every time that I felt so in love with him that it was like I couldn't even breathe, it wasn't real. But because of everything... my ability combined with his... wouldn't that also mean that there would be no one on the planet that could love him more than me? Even if it wasn't real? Even if it was against my will?

And attempting to sort this out now, in Walter Valentine's home, trapped in Winona's childhood bedroom, with my life long arch enemy, seemed to be the perfect irony.

Be careful what you wish for, kids. Because you might get it, but you'll get it at the worst possible time.

But I looked at her. Devastated to inform me of this. Completely beside herself.

"He's alive, by the way," she added, changing to a more matter-of-factly tone.

"I know."

"He came to find me after his funeral."

"What?"

"I don't know where he is now. Probably in some sort of holding cell at The Domain. Unless he got out of there. I don't know. Collin... he tricked us."

"He tricked all of us, Nona," I sighed.

She shook her head in shame. She inhaled deeply and exhaled loudly.

"Tell me everything."

And she did. She told me how Connor found her the night of the funeral, enlisted her to help him with his mission, how he told her about the Domain, métier, and her father's twisted plans.

"We found a quantum computer underneath my grandfather's old machine shed," she continued her story.

"That old barn that your grandpa would never let us go in?" I asked.

"Yeah, that's the one. We found the computer and then I immediately stepped onto a rusty nail and had to go to the ER of course, I'm still not walking normally yet. And then Connor had to finish investigating by himself. He was able to get everything up and running in there, in my father's secret lair. But he had to start decrypting everything and it ended up taking days to decrypt, even with the quantum computer. Cyber weapons were just the tip of the iceberg, Gwen. He turned himself into a cyber weapon."

"What do you mean?"

"That was his métier all along. He can manipulate technology, and he was using the quantum computer to come up with ways to make him more powerful. He has been studying métier for years. He knew about both of us, Gwen. He knew how you made him more powerful, and he knew being around me made his ability cease to work at all. He cracked the code. He was using the quantum computer to create a serum. And he was using himself as a test subject. He was successful. We found his journals. In them he explained that before he was just really good with computers, something that... science didn't need to explain. But being around you increased his power. He could start manipulating technology without being near it. He could will it to do whatever he needed to," She paused after this. I think she could see in my face that I needed a break.

"Collin and Charlie must have told me dozens of times that they wanted to keep me safe. That my ability needed to be kept a secret. That's why they kept me in the dark so long."

"Connor told me he never told anyone about my métier."

I thought back to my conversation with Charlie, outside on Collin's balcony. She had no idea about Winona. She just knew that she couldn't get a reading on her, it wasn't definitive of her having métier because Charlie thought that Connor's ability still worked on Winona.

"You were never charmed by him. Like everyone else," I realized.

"No," She scoffed. "I definitely wasn't."

"You actually genuinely like him."

"I mean, that's debatable."

I smiled and shook my head. "So your dad is as powerful as ever because of this... serum?"

Her face changed at the mention of her father. "There's something else I have to tell you."

"Okay," I said, slightly concerned.

"This doesn't have to change anything between us. I mean, the world's about to end and we're probably going to either be enslaved or killed."

"Nona."

"But while I was at Homeland... I found some old medical records. You wouldn't remember this but I wanted to give my kidney to my Grandpa and I had to do a blood test to see if I'd be a viable donor..."

"I feel like you're talking in circles. And for the record, I did know about this to an extent. Walter had told me that you both tried to donate a kidney to him."

"Walter Valentine isn't my dad."

I felt all my blood rush to my ears. "What?"

"Walt knew for years. That I wasn't his daughter. He kept it a secret."

"Winona," I whispered in horror, completely unsure of what

to say. Part of me wanted to comfort her. I wanted to be there for the girl I had considered to be my arch rival for over half of my life. "I don't know what to say."

She shook her head. "That's not even the craziest part, Gwen," she exhaled a little devastated laugh. Like she was grasping for her last shred of sanity. "We're sisters."

Spots clouded my vision, and I was brought back to what Beck said. *Just spend a day with your sister,* he had said. Winona Valentine, my perfect opposite. The girl that I had felt had gotten everything I wanted. Back when I was jealous of her for taking away Connor, or when I was foolish enough to envy her for having the privilege of having Walter at her own college graduation instead of mine, the argument that had led to our final separation.

I thought back to when we were kids, and we spent every waking moment together until her mom got sick and she just changed. And I started spending more time with the twins next door, and Charlie, and then Juniper, and I basically changed my name.

But Walter knew.

He knew that my dad...

"My dad... he...?"

"Yes," she answered quietly.

I sat in this silence. I can't sit here and pretend that none of this makes sense. But of course, everything is connected.

"Winona, I really don't know what to say. I don't know to apologize or... I'm..." I kept trailing off.

"None of this is your fault."

I sighed. "You're right. It's neither of our faults."

"Could you imagine how different things would be if every-one hadn't tried to keep us out of this world?"

"What do you mean?" I asked.

"Connor and Collin. They were in this web of highly-abled spies. They could have just clued us in and we wouldn't be here. There's a chance that you and I? We'd actually have a shot at being friends. If we had just known about métier. If we had just known about the Domain."

"God..." I sighed, "I need to understand why Collin teamed up with Walter. That's the part that still isn't coming together for me."

"Maybe he's just evil."

"An evil twin?"

"Too big of a cliche, huh?"

"Is there anything else?" I asked. "Anything more that you haven't told me?"

She thought for a moment. "There isn't much left to tell. After we decrypted Walt's plans from the quantum computer we headed straight back for the Domain. We met right up with Collin and he proceeded to separate us. Collin noticed my limp and suggested I get a follow up from Beck where he took my vitals and did some blood work. Collin came and found me and he sent me home. Said that Connor no longer needed any assistance from me and got me a car to drive me home," she sighed and wrung her fingers in her lap. "I didn't think anything of it until the car had two guards that immediately handcuffed me and ended up throwing me into my childhood bedroom with no escape. And trust me, I've tried."

"Do you know what's in the serum?" I asked.

"Based on Walter's notes? Your DNA, Gwen. There was a specific marker in your DNA that he was able to use the quantum computer to transmutate in the perfect elixir to help him reach his maximum potential."

I shuddered and groaned. "To think, I was the key ingredient to ending the fucking world."

"But not even the quantum computer was able to replicate it, Gwen. He needs you. He needs a constant stream of your DNA to keep making the serum."

I had seen a quantum computer in person once, but I never got to fully appreciate it. I never got to experience its power for myself. Walter was part of the reason why I had gotten into tech.

"This is the exact kind of danger my friends kept warning me about." I felt every hair on my body stand straight out of my body. "We need to get out of here."

It was quiet for a moment but I could see it in her face that she was scheming. "Gwen, I have an idea."

"Dude, please stop calling me Gwen."

"Stop calling me Nona," she retorted.

We both made this face like we knew that wasn't going to happen. I sighed. "What's the plan?"

You know how theatrical my father can be, she had told me. We were being walked to the intricately decorated Valentine Estate dining room. Winona had told me that he would do this. He would want to show off. We were being told that we would all be dining together and sharing a meal. We walked in a line, A guard in front, then Winona, then me, and ending with two more guards. Another thing Winona had warned me of. We weren't going to be able to make our escape before dinner. He was going to make us enjoy a meal together whether we liked it or not.

You're getting out of here, you're going to find Connor, and then you will come back for me. That's the plan, she said. *And by any means necessary.* I wanted to fight her on this but I didn't have time. She was right. I was in more danger being this close to Walter than she was. I didn't want to leave her behind.

We were seated across from each other. It was a grand table, able to seat over 30 guests, but there were only three place settings. One at the head of the table, which presumably Walter would be sitting. And the two at the end where Winona and I sat. The table however was fully decorated, hundreds of candles lit of all different heights and sizes, along a luxurious golden hued table runner. Overly lavish and theatrical, just as Winona had said.

She had known Walter as her father, but I had him as my lover. I let her think she knew him better than I did. Telling her that this was all predictable Walter behavior... this just didn't seem like the time.

She didn't know that this was the exact place settings he had arranged for our first dinner together. We had texted for a few weeks before he got me to suggest we share a meal together, under the pretense that he wanted me to know the right way a young woman should be treated.

I held my tongue. This was hurtful enough. He would love it if he got a rise out of me. And it would only hurt Winona, even though she would never say so. Even with our lost years, I knew her well enough to know she would never admit if something hurt her.

A member of the house staff filled one of our glasses with water in front of us. I embarrassingly chugged it as I felt more dehydrated than I had realized. But Beck was right about something. Spending time with Winona was all I needed to get back to my normal self. The dizziness was gone. But my cigarette craving felt unbearable.

Walter glided through the entrance of the dining room, beaming, smiling ear to ear.

"There's my girls!" He said. We both winced and said nothing. I saw Winona's face turn into a scowl. I had no idea what mine looked like, I tried to remain apathetic but nothing but fear was boiling underneath the surface.

"Honestly, Viridian, I thought you'd be more happy. Isn't this what you begged me for? For years?" He said gleefully with malice.

I didn't respond. I couldn't. I felt so ashamed. There really was a time that I dreamed of this. That we shared a home, and openly had meals together. Granted, Winona wasn't in any of my fantasies. I knew even then that she would never approve, and back then I was so misled, so misguided, so lost, that I didn't even care. He was right. There was a version of me that begged for this. But she isn't here anymore.

"Leave her alone," Winona hissed. "And we aren't your girls, Walter," she spat out his name. She was so quick to protect me, loyalty that I have not earned from her. But it will be repaid ten-fold if we live long enough for me to show it to her.

He chuckled and beckoned for his staff to bring us our salads, marking that our dinner had officially begun.

"I... I'm just so excited. I have my two secret weapons finally here, to finish what I started years ago. It actually started with Victor," he said in between bites of his Caesar salad. "Victor was the one that introduced the concept of developing our very own quantum computer. Something I know you're both familiar with, yes?" He paused but he knew we would not be responding.

Winona nor I had even begun eating the food in front of us.

We questioned if it was even safe for consumption.

"Anyway, boring Victor, he just wanted to use it to increase our edge in the security world, like we weren't already the leading company. But I knew it was capable of so much more. So we started the project together on the fifth floor, Research and Development. And it was getting closer and closer to being complete, having me on the team definitely sped up the process, if you haven't figured it out already I have a certain *métier* for technology," he emphasized the word, toying with us. Teasing us. Letting us know that he's been in on their secret world for long before we had any idea.

"Ah, Victor. He was like you, Viridian. He had that penchant for making the rest of us a little bit smarter, sharper, wittier, stronger... you name it. But it seems when he passed on his genetics, you were the perfect storm."

I shuddered internally. I couldn't let him know. Collin's betrayal. He must have been working with Walter for years. I just wish I could understand why.

"But my own daughter... the opposite. A living, breathing void. I couldn't do anything when she was around. I never questioned it until my father's health began declining and we both tried to donate our kidneys. It actually almost slipped by me. But our blood test results. My blood type being B negative and yours being AB negative I knew something was wrong. It was practically fresh in my mind that your mother, Winona, my beautiful bride...She was also B negative. Years of being in and out of hospitals and doctors visits, things like that stick with you. This might not mean anything to you, but two parents with a B negative blood type cannot parent a child with an AB negative blood type. I retested your blood many times, thinking there had to be a mistake. But then I got suspicious... and I tested your DNA with Victor's... and that's how I found out. I guess it makes sense. That Victor would create a better version of his own métier, and then of course, its perfect opposite. All within weeks with each other. Isn't that just *wonderful*?" He put so much sarcastic emphasis on that last word. I could tell each word was laced in pain.

My father certainly wasn't a perfect man. But to have an affair with his best friend's wife... under everyone's noses. It was unforgivable. I can't help but agree.

"So I decided to hit him back, close to home, and I decided to make his own daughter fall in love with me. I couldn't go after his own wife, after all. She left him years ago. The perfect revenge, isn't it? It was all going according to plan. The quantum computer was almost finished. I had you, Viridian, in my back pocket. I was ready to propose to you. I just had a few more things I needed to complete."

"Was it ever real for you?" I whispered. "Any of it?" I felt tears brimming in my eyes. It wasn't because of Walter. Well, it was. But it was sheer loss, it was the devastation I felt. Will anything I feel for anyone ever be real?

He set down his fork, his plate now clean. He lifted out his hand and cupped my cheek. "Of course, it was real. Maybe not in the beginning. But I felt so drawn to you I don't think I could ever let you go."

Oh, so it's just my super powers.

"I want us back, Viridian. Don't you? Don't you remember how good things were?" He pleaded.

The staff took away our salads and began setting out the main course.

"I... this doesn't feel right, Walter," I said quietly in devasta-tion.

I looked up from my plate to take a quick look over at Winona who wasn't making eye contact with either of us. I couldn't get a read on her at all. I couldn't tell what she was thinking. But her words repeated in my head, *by any means necessary*, she had said. This is how I'm going to get out of here. I'm going to have to seduce Walter. And she knew it.

He looked at me. And there was something in his eyes that gave me this underlying certainty that I was going to succeed. I was getting out of here. Tonight.

"What can I do?" He begged. Stop being a creep is a start.

"Let me stay with you tonight. Show me, remind me, how good things can be."

"I'll make the arrangements," he said with a final tone.

I might actually have to sleep with him. *Fuck.* What would Austin Powers do?

But do I have the audacity to go through with it? I've had sex with him before. He was my first. A girl never forgets her first. If you can disregard the fact that he's a deranged super villain, I've lived a normal life. The first to have sex with to first heartbreak pipeline.

Juniper might not forgive me for this. And it's something I had to decide whether I could live with it. Juniper might not forgive me, but Connor would. And that felt so dark to even think. I felt guilt for comparing the two of them.

Winona finally looked up at both of us. She turned her attention to Walter. "Where do I fit into all this?"

"Winona, you're always going to be my little girl."

Her posture changed, she became more rigid, and began retching. "No. You said I was part of this master plan. How do I fit into this?"

"Of course," he began. "So the serum I was able to develop

using Viridian's DNA has become so successful, I had the idea to sequence your DNA next. As more of an offensive weapon. I have ideas of harnessing your métier and making all of my enemies, anyone that had the ability to stop me, completely incapable of using their métier. Better yet, remove their métier permanently. Not everyone is worthy of that kind of ability. I think we can be the judge of that."

"You have got to be kidding me," she said in disgust. "If you think for one second I would willingly provide to you my DNA—"

"I'd be careful what you say next, Winona," Walter warned sternly.

He could make her disappear. I knew how she was my whole life. She never had a close group of friends. She repelled more than just heroes. I never questioned it. But I know now, I have to protect her.

I tried to kick her underneath the table but my foot wouldn't reach without me making it obvious. She was too far away.

"You're fucking disgusting," she spat at Walter. And she turned to me, piercing me with her pale blue eyes, "You both are. I can see what you're considering. You're going to really... Really? Truly? You're going to choose him?"

She's playing the part. But I'm not sure what exactly she's playing at. But I know she wants me to play along with her.

"He's been the only father you have known for the past 24 years. You're not going to choose him?" I questioned.

"Are you fucking serious? He ADMITTED to manipulating you as revenge!" She shot up from her seat and kicked her chair behind her. "And *what?*" Two guards quickly collected both of her arms and began restraining her, and dragging her back to her prison cell of a bedroom. "You're just going to give him *the benefit of the doubt?*" God, she's really selling this.

To remain natural, I said nothing. I feel like the old version of me, the version that Walt liked the most, would just be quiet and unsure what to say. I looked down as she screamed in frustration and got dragged away. All part of the plan. I was getting us out. I just had to follow the plan. This is the plan. This is the plan. This is the plan.

Walter reached his hand out and set it on my thigh and caressed lightly with his thumb. "She'll come around. And I know you need convincing too. But I promise, you'll never have to feel lost again, Viridian."

I feigned a small smile, and set my hand on top of his. I tried to dredge up the old, warm feelings I felt for this man. Before it was replaced by disgust and shame.

I needed to hold on to them if I was going to sell this.

"I want to believe you, Walter. This past year has been..." I couldn't look at him.

"I know. But we can put everything behind us. It's all part of the plan. I'm getting ready for a massive merger between The Domain and V Corp. Collin and I have been preparing for this transition all year. Nothing will be able to stop us."

The mention of Collin made my heart feel like it was being gripped inside my chest. "How did you and Collin start working together?"

"He reached out to me, actually. It wasn't long after Connor began his employment on the fifth floor. You know, I'm glad I fired him. Everything that occurs on the fifth floor is supposed to be highly classified, but what's the first thing he does? Tell his twin brother. Infuriating. Total grounds for termination," I had a feeling that the last word was a double entendre. I knew that Connor had faked his own death to get out of Walt's radar.

"I didn't know Connor was working at V Corp at all. How did... Why did you keep that from me?"

"That one wasn't intentional. You know how you've been since Victor. You let me take the reins, and so I did."

He was right. I was on autopilot. It's even possible that... actually it's entirely likely that Walter protected me. The board could have stripped me from my position months ago. It was probably more like 1% him protecting me 99% him knowing that he'd have an easier time controlling the company if he kept me around. The girl on autopilot, that wasn't fully aware of what she was signing off on. But really, I attended a few board meetings a week, but that was about it.

I never touched anything on my plate, even after Walter's reassurance that it was perfectly fine. But I felt so unwell, a level of nausea that I wasn't used to. To think this morning I could barely put my own socks on my feet, Juniper had done that for me. And then after spending a few hours with Winona, I was back to my old self. Walking normally. No spots in my vision. No vertigo. But it was all replaced with this sick feeling in my stomach.

Walter assured me he'd be right behind me, but he had a guard lead me to his room without him. The guards didn't even touch me. I followed closely behind him. I thought it was strange, that it was just the one guard when every other time it had been more than one. But we were silent as we bee lined down the corridor and up the stairs. Something had caught my eye. Something so foolish on his part. But on the back belt loop, there hung none-other than a carabiner. And on that carabiner was an assortment of keys.

This was the moment that my entire life had been leading up to. I haven't had the itch like I did when I was younger. My friends knew I did it. But I've never been truly caught. I was able to get close enough to that mother fucker while we climbed that stairs that I was able to effortless unlatch the keys from his belt loop without even the slightest inkling that he noticed. The keys were already jangling from climbing the stairs so the noise didn't seem out of place. And I shoved them into the back pocket of my jeans as we made it to the top step. Now I can save Nona too. We didn't have a plan for that besides coming back with back up but if I have these keys I can get her out myself. All I'd have to do is get the guards to step away from her door for one minute.

I followed the guard the rest of the way to Walter's room. A room we had been in together many times. It wasn't that difficult to have sleepovers. We had it down to a science back then.

Everything in his room was washed gray. Grey hardwood floors, gray furniture, gray walls, gray bedding delicately assembled on his king-sized bed. I knew that's where he'd want me to be. I made myself comfortable, and sat on the edge of his bed, and waited for him.

I didn't have to wait long. He made it to the bedroom and his coarse, rough hands held my face. Bringing our lips together, in what he may assume to be a passionate kiss. But I did not kiss him back. I was stone. It didn't stop him. But I guess the twisted ones don't really pay that much mind.

I just need to stay in control. The faster I get him to fall asleep, the faster I can grab Nona and get out of here. And I knew exactly how I would make him fall asleep. I was going to have to finish him. How's that for a double entendre?

He pulled away from the kiss and he looked at me deep in my eyes. His hot breath creeping up my nose, speaking softly seemed to make it worse, "How about a little trust exercise?"

"What do you mean?" I questioned.

He headed to his night stand and pulled out a long thick piece of ribbon. A blind fold. I weighed the options in my mind. I considered it. If I agreed to this, at least I was guaranteed to not have to see him. In a way it reminded me of when June and I had sex for the first time. I couldn't see anything. If anything else, at least I could try to pretend I was with June. I could pretend I was with someone that made me feel safe.

He held it out to me and all I did was nod. I turned my back to him and I felt the blind fold go over my eyes and he tied it securely behind my head.

I didn't have time to consider the consequences of what I had just done. All I could do was be grateful that it worked. I laid there, bare, with Walter loudly snoring next to me with his arm still around me. I didn't have time to feel disgusted. I didn't have time to feel ashamed.

I had to be quick about this. Quick and careful. I was able to slither away from underneath his arm without him stirring once. Honestly, he just made this too easy for me and it kind of freaked me out. I carefully gathered my clothes and quietly put them over my body. Again, getting flashbacks to this morning, remembering Juniper helping me get dressed in the first place. I hope he's okay. I pray to God he's just waiting for me to get home and not out there searching for me or something. I need him to be okay or none of this is even worth it.

I put my ear to the door first, checking for any sign of Walter's security detail, but I heard nothing over his obnoxious snoring. I put my hand on the door knob and softly turned it, hearing some soft clicks of the mechanism and pulled the door open.

I got lucky again. No guards. I felt my back pocket, the keys were still there. I stood in the hallway, my mind racing, knowing I needed to come up with a distraction so I could get whatever guards by Winona's room away so we could make our exit.

I had no doubt that in this maze of a mansion, the front door would be armed. The home of a security mogul? Are you kidding me? It's going to be so tightly armed. If I just opened the front door like an idiot, all of his security would be alerted. I would need to be quick. Which gave me the perfect idea.

I bolted discreetly to his front entrance while scanning my eyes everywhere, making sure I was not being detected. I made it to the front door and quickly opened and shut it. I saw the sensor on the top corner silently turn from green to red and knew that I had about five seconds. I crouched down and ran to the kitchen where the second staircase to the upstairs was. It was the longer way to Winona's bedroom but it was the best chance I had to make it to her.

And I was right. I heard a stampede of mountain men come running for the front door. I even turned behind me and saw them all run outside, a full on commotion. The chances of this also waking up Walter were high. I turned the corner and made it to the stairs and sprinted to Winona's room. I made it and I reached for the keys in my back pocket. I scrambled with them in between my fingers. I made it to the third key in the lock and finally found a match. "Nona, it's me!" I whispered through the door while I got it to unlock.

Winona was at her door ready to jump out. "Fuck, Gwen, took you long enough," she huffed. She made it out of the door. "Follow me."

"Where are we going?"

She didn't answer but we made our way down the servant quarters stairs and to the kitchen, making a turn to a door I hadn't realized was there. We went down a hallway through that door, and found a staircase heading down to a basement that I didn't know existed.

"We're finishing this, once and for all," She said through gritted teeth. Down the staircase we found the Valentine Estate's panic room, complete with a control center, monitors, buttons, LED lights flashing. The monitors showed the security detail all rushing back inside, they realized that we hadn't escaped yet.

"What are we doing in here? We need to get out of here," I said, with a slight panic in my voice.

"Hold on, okay?" And she ran over to what seemed to be a large safe with a numbered keypad on it for entry. She began entering in multiple sequences of numbers and it wailed a horrible sound at us as it continued to fail.

"Nona, please, let's just go. We can come back," I pleaded. If we didn't make it out of here, everything I had done would be for nothing. I couldn't let that go. I destroyed myself.

She tried one more time and she got it to open. *"Fuck yes."* she celebrated.

She whipped the door open and there it was. It was a metallic silver substance. A dozen vials of it. All sitting there, defenseless against two little girls like us. She grabbed one vial and popped it open.

She stared at me with a sparkle in her eyes. She lifted it up in front of her, "One for me..." she said before she shot it down her throat like a shot of whiskey.

"Winona!" I screamed. "We don't know if that's safe! We

don't know what that's going to do to you!"

She then grabbed the whole tray and slammed it to the ground, "...And one for the homies," she finished her phrase, terrifyingly coy. "Come on, kiddo. I'm hero repellent, and you're a super villain magnet. I just gave us our best chance," she grabbed both of our cellphones out of there and she handed mine to me. "Let's go."

"Oh my fucking, God, Nona," I said at my wits end.

She grabbed my hand and she led me out of there. We exited the estate through the back entrance in the kitchen.

The cold October air hit my bare arms so quickly, making it hard to ignore despite the adrenaline pumping through my body, the absolute daze I was in, allowing Winona to lead us up to a fence and me clumsily climbing over it. But by some miracle we made it over and into somes yard, continuing our sprint, and my lungs absolutely burning.

We made it to the street, it felt like we were almost in the clear when multiple cars turned the corner. All black, SUVs, roaring loudly as we could hear the acceleration. Fuck fuck fuck fuck fuck, the word repeated in my head.

Winona was losing speed and I could see her begin to limp in front of me and I grabbed her before she could fall to the ground and had us both crouched beside some bushes.

"Nona, we have to keep going," I said in between heavy breaths.

"My foot..." she said with anguish. Her eyes were pressed shut and her eyebrows were pushed together.

"Fuck, your foot," I realized. I just remembered she was still recovering from stepping on that nail earlier that week.

"Nona, we have to keep going," I pleaded. "Where can we go?" This was her neighborhood after all. This is where she grew up.

She opened her eyes and she started to orient herself. She looked around at her surroundings. "Okay... there's a party store a couple blocks that way. Tons of cameras, tons of bystanders. We'll be safe there for a second and I'll try to call Connor. He'll get us somewhere safe."

I didn't even want to think of what to do if he didn't answer. If he was out there, being detained against his will too. But who else could we call? I'm at a loss. It felt like we were running out of people we could trust.

"Okay," I straightened our position and lifted her arm over my shoulders to help her walk and she shook herself away from my help.

"I got this, it's just a little bit farther," she said determinedly.

"Nona," I said with concern.

"No, it'll slow us down."

Nothing about this was slow. She led the way as we crossed through more backyards and she clumsily hopped fences. I wasn't far behind her, but stopping for a moment seemed to help her. Or maybe somehow, me being near her gave her some strength. It was unlikely. Everything I knew about her made it seem like she was completely unaffected by all métiers. But maybe because we shared blood...it'd be different. But she also took a hit of that super juice, for lack of a better word, so she was even more unlikely than ever to be able to gather strength from me.

I watched Winona run out into the street without checking any of her surroundings, into five lanes of Rock Island traffic. She wove through the road rage drivers and I tried to keep up behind her when she almost got hit twice. My ears were ringing and my heart beat could be felt through my finger tips. I kept trying to look out for her when I saw her, inches away from her doom, stumbling, falling down and I lunged at her with all of my might pushing her to the sidewalk, getting her out of the traffic.

I heard the sound before my vision began to fade out. The sound of machinery and glass crunching, such an unnatural sound. It was the sound of me being massacred by an environmentally-conscious mid-sized sedan. The last thing I saw was Winona safe. And the last thing I felt was my cheek hitting the asphalt.

<h1 style="text-align:center">11</h1>

<h1 style="text-align:center">Role Model</h1>

Connor

You try to plan ahead, anticipate every move. But with Viridian things are different. They always have been. Since we were kids I have found that she had two very unique abilities. She was a magnet to other people with métier. Which explains our friend group. Me, Collin, Charlie, and Juniper. Even Walter Valentine. We honestly couldn't possibly help ourselves. We have this inexplicable attraction to her that none of us could comprehend. Which brings us to her second, complementary ability, how she makes us stronger just by being in proximity. This is her métier. We all have métier.

But I needed her away from me. I was getting too close to something, something that could hurt her. Which is why I faked my suicide. I needed her to believe I was gone. It seemed like the only solution at the time.

My existence truly brought her so much pain. She experienced *my métier the absolute worst because when I was with her, it made it so strong, so enhanced. My charisma was just off the charts. My ability to persuade people is honestly unmatched. Being with Vee she probably had no choice but to fall in love with me. But I could never be sure if she truly felt that way or if it was just my métier. Knowing this, and trust me I've known this for a long time, I couldn't let her know how I felt about her. So I had to set her free from me.*

Never in my life did I think it would end like this. Seeing her this way. So broken and frail. It was entirely my fault. Collin warned me it would be bad. But I thought if I was able to stay away from her she would be able to move on, be herself, without any of my influence.

I sit in a chair near her bed in the recovery room. She's resting with tear-stained cheeks. I sit in anguish knowing that I put her here. Unknowingly, yes, but this was entirely avoidable.

I wanted to hold her hand, but I worried that it would be more for my benefit than hers. I do not deserve any such comfort.

Suddenly, she began to stir uncomfortably and I heard the faintest whimper escape her lips. I stood up from my chair and came near. Her eyes still not opening but she tried so hard to make a coherent movement, to steady herself.

"Connor?" she got out weakly.

"I'm here," I said quickly. She responded with another whimper.

"Stay," she strained to say.

"Don't try to speak," I said with concern, "I'm not going anywhere."

Finally she opened her eyes and she saw me. Something was different in her eyes. Something that wasn't there before. She almost looked like she was trying to recognize me. I must have looked different.

I slowly reached out my hand and placed it onto hers. She felt strangely cold to the touch so I let my hand engulf hers. Within seconds she stopped stirring and her eyes closed once again, she was able to catch her breath and nodded back to rest.

Just because she woke up does not mean she's okay. She has a long road ahead of her.

"I," She started and I was jolted with surprise, "understand why you did it," she said in a whisper.

I was dumbfounded. She could be talking about so many different things. I felt her fingers interlock with mine weakly.

"Never again," She continued. She was talking about my rude departure. Faking a death is definitely unforgivable. Yet look at her, unconditionally, she's still my girl.

I knelt down to her, down on my knees, holding onto her hand carefully. In agreement I say softly, "Never again. I promise."

She stirred slightly and I felt her gather her strength so she could bring my hand to her lips, giving it the softest and most delicate kiss. Her eyebrows were furrowed together.

"Vee," I begged. "Please save your strength," I felt her hand hold mine a little tighter than before. "Please, Vee," I responded.

"Hold me," she said unfurrowing her brows. Her eyes looked into mine, pleading.

I questioned this act, wondering if that would be best for her in her current state. One of her arms casted like a mummy, and her cheek bandaged up from the impact of the collision. But who was I to deny her? If this is the only thing she asked of me, how could I take this from her when I owe her so much. So carefully to not disturb any of her injuries I let go of her hand and tucked her into the covers and made myself a spot big enough to lay next to her on top of the covers. I cradled her in my arms. I saw her lips curl up into a satisfied and comforted grin. Her eyes closed and I pressed *my nose into her hair and inhaled. She smelled like she always did. Expensive shampoo with a lingering hint of Marlboro reds.*

She wasn't supposed to ever see me again. And now that she was, I regret that this is how we've found ourselves together again. I only wanted to protect her from me. Enough time has passed. She shouldn't still be impacted by my charisma. Which means that whatever feelings she has towards me, they should at least have a fraction of merit. But I didn't want to get my hopes up.

So I held her until I heard soft little snores between each breath. I had so much to explain to her. I wondered what she already knew. She said she understood. But to what extent? All I knew is that this is where I was supposed to be all along.

I day dreamed how I wanted it to go. Vee would wake up and she would ask for me and she would just forgive me, and I would hold her, and we would both be okay. The perfect resolution to the most unforgiving week since my funeral. But even in my fantasy, I knew deep down, with Viridian things never go how I plan.

I never planned that my brother would betray me. I didn't think he could. I didn't think anyone could. But even my métier couldn't stop the darkness that grew inside of him. How quickly he could sell all of us out. My own blood. We shared a womb.

But I was not in her room, by her side, so I would be the first one she saw when she woke up. No. I abandoned that right when I let her think I was dead.

It's been days since Viridian was admitted into the hospital. How Winona tells the story, Vee saved her life. She was crushed by a vehicle that was about to hit Nona who was unable to move fast enough. All while running from the clutches of Walter

Valentine. Winona called for an ambulance and they arrived at the hospital together where Winona was finally able to call me. I had just escaped from my own prison, one that Collin knew would never hold me for long anyway, when I could persuade any of those personnel to set me free. He just kept me in isolation for a few hours, which incidentally made me stronger so I could detox from spending so much time with Winona, and as soon as a guard came to check on me I was basically free. I just grabbed my cellphone and dipped. I was already on my way to Winona's apartment, thinking that was where she was.

But I arrived and I called Charlie, who was completely frantic upon arrival and immediately asked where Juniper was. And I felt my body get heavy, and my heart get clouded with jealousy. I had no claim over Viridian. I never did, and especially not now. But he is the one that gets to sit in that chair, hold her hand, and be there when she wakes up.

I can't help but feel like it should be me.

But I'm not allowed to feel this way. Not when I have a beautiful girl that sits next to me in the waiting room, anxiously stirring, waiting for Viridian to wake up. This girl, who has put up with so much from me, all of my bullshit, all of these mixed feelings, and still stands by my side. She loves me for me, and it's crazy. But I love her too. I haven't told her, but maybe I should.

But I also feel like... How can I tell Winona Valentine I love her if I still harbor all these feelings for another girl? Not just any girl, but her sister. Someone she shares blood with? Someone I have loved for years. Someone who I know has loved me back for just as long.

I will tell her I love her the day I can be sure that she will no longer feel second best to someone. That's what she deserves.

Charlie has been in and out of the hospital since Vee's admission. I needed someone I trust to handle everything at the Domain.

That's where Collin was now. But Walter, of course, is completely missing.

Collin was in solitary confinement. Until I know where to put him next. There's no handbook on how to deal with a situation like this. What to do when you're betrayed by the person you trusted most. I'm just living moment to moment. Hoping that as soon as Vee wakes up, I'll know exactly what to do.

Just in that moment, Juniper emerged around the corner and got our attention. "She's awake!"

Nona was quick to her feet and sprinted to her room. I didn't know if I was supposed to follow her, I just stayed where I was. I felt afraid to see her. Maybe she wouldn't want to see me. Maybe she blamed me for everything. She should blame me. But I had just been stuck in my thoughts thinking that the second Vee woke up I would know what to do, but I'm still at a loss.

I wanted to see her. But all I do is hurt her. All I have done is hurt her.

Nona wasn't gone for long. Maybe 5 minutes.

"She isn't talking yet," Nona said. "She's still regaining her strength. But I had to let her know she was safe and taken care of. The nurse is with her now. I'm sure she'll be taking visitors soon."

I sighed. I didn't know what to say. She took a seat in the chair next to me and brought her hand over mine.

"She's okay, Connor," she reassured.

I sat there, staring straight ahead at the wall ahead of me, then just looked down.

"It's weird seeing Vee with an age appropriate boyfriend," She joked, trying to lighten the mood. "I know Juniper is supposed to be your arch nemesis but he seems pretty normal."

I allowed my tongue to wet my lips, and I shook my head, "Yeah, I guess," she wasn't wrong. We spent the past couple days with each other. With Winona around, none of us had the ability to use our special advantages, so we were all just regular people. It had its advantages and disadvantages.

She didn't need me here. I think I was still holding onto this fantasy, this story that I had written for myself, that she'd wake up and I would be the first person she wanted to see. But that wasn't real.

I wonder if she had a similar realization while I was gone. That we both made up this story in our heads, like we were supposed to be together. But it probably really was métier versus métier, working against each other. Me being drawn to her, and her being overwhelmed by my ability.

But she didn't need me here.

"C–" Winona had started saying my name, and remembered that I had assumed Collin's identity while out in public. We stripped the brown hair dye out of my hair so I could go back to how I used to look, more of a sandy blonde color. "Collin," She corrected herself.

I had no idea what she was about to say to me but I began collecting my things and stood up from the chair. "I need to go."

"What?"

"I'm sure she'll be out of here by tomorrow. I'll make it a point to see her then. This just isn't the place. After everything..."

"After *everything* don't you think you owe it to her to stay?" Winona snapped.

"I owe it to her to let her have some peace," I said in return, solemnly.

Winona's eyes burned into mine, like I was betraying her somehow. I ripped my eyes away from hers, and exited the hospital without looking back.

Viridian

"Vee?" His voice was like honey.

My eyes felt heavy, and I felt like something gigantic was sitting on top of me, like I couldn't move. But I felt so cold. Everything except for my hand, I wanted to feel more of that warmth.

"Viridian?" He spoke again, calling out to me, bringing me out of the dark haze I had spent hours drifting in.

I made a low sound, a sort of whimper. I couldn't get the words out. I felt a hand caress my arm.

My eyes blinked open and I saw him, he had a sort of angelic quality. His eyebrows thick with concern and his luxurious eyelashes framing those deep brown eyes full of worry. Juniper. He made it. He was here. He was okay.

"Everything is okay, Vee. You're doing great, babe," he said while his hand began to caress my hair, brushing it out of my face.

"I'll be right back, I just want to let your nurse know you're awake," he said softly and began stepping away but I felt my heart beat faster, with the monitor itself rising with it.

"No," I croaked out. That's all I could do. It's all I could muster. And I felt a tear slide down my face.

And he came right back to me and got on his knees, kneeling next to me and being at eye level. His hands returned to mine and held it between his before leaving a soft and chaste kiss. "You're safe, baby. You're safe. I promise."

His words. It took me back. What was it? Yesterday morning? I couldn't have been out that long. There's no way. But he promised me, *No more emergency landings, no more holding cells, no more heartbreak.*

After another soft kiss to the top of my hand I let Juniper step away from me. *No more heartbreak*, he had swore to me. And I believed him.

"I *need* a second with her! I have to tell her something. Get out of my fucking way, don't touch me!"

It was Winona. I could hear her voice carry from outside the door. It actually made me smile. It's strange how quickly everything in your life can change. Just two days ago there was a version of me that would dread seeing her. But now I'm just so happy to see her face peering through the doorway, making eye contact with me, seeing the relief in her eyes.

"She can't talk yet, but I know she can understand us. She's in there," Juniper came from behind and she immediately turned around.

"I don't need you crowding us, buddy. Just give me like 5 minutes to talk to *my sister*." and she shoved him out of the room and closed the door.

She rushed to my side and crouched down as Juniper had, she squatted down to eye level and gave me this soft, relieved smile. "You did it, Gwen. You really did it. You were amazing," she said softly.

"I'm not going to have much time before a nurse comes charging in here to take your vitals or whatever, but I just want you to know...*no one knows*, Gwen," I instantly knew what she was talking about. "I just told them we were able to distract Walt long enough to escape and we used those sticky fingers of yours to our advantage. That is *your* secret and *your secret* only. You don't have to ever mention it again. As far as I'm concerned, it didn't happen, okay?"

She didn't even know. I didn't tell her what I had done. But she just knew.

Even with my inability to speak, I was speechless.

"But if at any point...just come find me," she reassured me. Right now I'm just in this place where I'd like to pretend... but she wanted me to know I could talk to her.

The nurse came in shortly after she told me this and the nurse had her exit the recovery room while she checked my vitals. The nurse shut the door behind her when Winona was no longer in sight.

I couldn't talk to Winona about that. I couldn't tell anyone what it was like. I'd rather let it eat away at me. But she protected me, she seemed to keep doing that. That left me with one thing I didn't have to worry about. At least one.

The nurse spoke to me softly. "Don't try to speak, yet, honey. I'm just checking your vitals," she did the usual tests, and ran a light across my eyes and had me follow it.

"Can you lift your hand for me?" She asked.

And with some effort I was able to get my hand up from its position and hold it out in front of me.

"Very good. Now I want you to answer some questions for me. What is your name?"

I swallowed roughly and tried to lubricate my dry throat before answering. "Gwenore Viridian."

"That was very good," she assured me. "Can you tell me how old you are?"

"Twenty-four," I responded through my cracked throat.

"Okay, you can rest your voice for a minute. You're doing great. I'm going to come back with some water and some food from the cafeteria and I'll send your boyfriend back in here. I'm not going to allow extra visitors until you're more comfortable talking, okay? You don't need to push yourself. Your body needs all the time it takes to heal."

"What..." I tried to get out. "What happened to me?"

"You experienced blunt force trauma from a pedestrian-vehicle accident. Sounds like you were a hero, kiddo. You pushed your sister out of the way. She had her own injuries when she arrived and we got her all wrapped up. We kept you in a coma to reduce any more swelling to your brain. When the car hit you it dislocated your shoulder and fractured your ulna, and then when you hit the pavement you sustained some trauma to your brain. Your arm will be casted for a couple months, with a few more months of physical therapy, but you'll be back to normal in no time."

"Thank you," I whispered. This was so much. I was just trying to get away, I can't believe I got hit by a fucking car.

"There's one more thing, Miss Viridian," the nurse began slowly. "When they brought you in we saw you had a lot of bruising, trauma that didn't correlate with your collision, contusions that would resemble... sexual assault."

I could audibly hear my heart skip a beat. But she continued. "We performed a rape kit. We found seminal fluid. You've been in this coma for three days, but it isn't too late if you would like emergency contraception."

"Yes," I choked out.

"We have counselors here at the hospital, plenty of resources at your disposal, and people here that would help you file a report if you wanted to press charges," she stated calmly.

My mind was whirling in circles. No, No I would not be pressing charges. It wasn't rape. Was it? Was it rape? I knew what I was doing. I just wanted this to go away.

"Did you tell anyone about the rape kit?" I whispered.

"Only your sister knows."

It's crazy how last week I could barely stand the sight of Winona. And now she's my sister. She filled the role so quickly. I went from having no one... But now, we're the only family we have.

"Thank you," I whispered again. The nurse left and sent Juniper back in her place.

I gathered all of my strength and shoved myself to one side of the hospital bed.

"What are you doing?" He asked concernedly.

My eyes met his and I whispered, "Hold me."

He gladly obliged and finished the job by getting me more to one side of the small hospital bed. I turned from him and felt him snake his arm underneath the crook in my neck and placed his other arm over me, over my right arm, the one that was wrapped up tight in a cast. Of course. My dominant hand. Luckily, I still seemed to have use of my fingers.

He cradled me. "I never left your side, Vee. I got here as soon as Charlie called me. Winona has been here too. And Connor."

"Connor?" I whispered in shock.

He buckled uncomfortably next to me. "We've been calling him Collin, though. He's sort of...assumed his identity. Perks of being an identical twin, I suppose."

"Convenient," I whispered in agreement. Made me wonder where Collin was during all of this. Or where Walter went. Things I'm sure to find out soon. For now, I just needed to focus on my recovery.

I allowed myself to be soothed by Juniper. Someone who has been nothing but loyal to me. Has never betrayed me. And always wanted to take care of me. It's worth noting the irony of being tired after waking up from a coma. But my eyes felt heavy, my limbs felt heavy, I felt so completely out of control.

I gathered enough strength to take my "good" arm to bring it over to June's hand so I could lace my fingers in between his. And just for a moment I could pretend that everything was right in the world. No matter how badly I low key just wanted a cigarette.

Recovery was a grueling process of no one leaving me alone. It was welcomed at first. Winona essentially moved in with me to take care of me along with Juniper. There were just things that I needed that I wanted to remain mysterious from Juniper. Showering in a cast was kind of a feat. My right arm, while my fingers were functioning, there were some positions that my cast did not allow me to position myself in such a way. There was a point when she shaved my left armpit for me that made me forever in her debt.

I remember the conversation I had with Winona. She told me I could talk to her about anything. She was with Juniper and I when we got settled back in at my estate. And I asked her if she would be willing to move in for a while. She didn't make me say it. But we both knew I needed her there for more than one reason, but the biggest being I wasn't ready to be honest with Juniper yet. And I knew as soon as Nona's métier wore off, Juniper would know everything. I would not be able to keep that from him. With Winona there I could lie, or at the very least, omit the truth. With Winona here, that's just one thing I don't have to worry about.

I owe Winona so much.

I'm grateful that Juniper hadn't tried to be intimate with me. We will kiss, he will hold my hand, and we fall asleep in each other's arms, but he can hear my body, and he knows something is going on with me. Thankfully, he also hasn't pressed me about my nightmares. And I know as soon as he touches me like that... he'll just know. He'll know everything.

But after a follow-up appointment with my doctor, they cleared me to drive. They said I can be independent. The help was amazing, but I just want to get back to normal. Whatever that is.

I wish I was still in LA.

I left June at the house and I made my first errand on my own. My last bit of business. There were two people I needed to see. And luckily, they were at the same place.

The Domain. An alleged real estate development company, but a real life underground secret organization. Where I could find both Connor and Collin.

Connor, who has avoided me since I awoke, since I was discharged from the hospital. And Collin, who put me there in the first place. Charlie said that Collin wasn't talking to anyone. No one understood his motives. No one knows why he did what he had done. But that changes today.

Charlie had already explained to me how to get there. There were a few days where Charlie had been left in charge and she got me fully in the system. She replaced all the keypads with fingerprint scanners to increase security. Especially with how easy it was for Juniper, and then eventually Connor, to escape. It was actually kind of laughable. I had full clearance now, officially an operative. Charlie was eager to step down when Connor came back. She lived more of a nomadic lifestyle, going wherever her spirit tells her to. She's laying low for now because she's been helping taking care of me, but I'm sure the second this cast comes off she'll be headed to Ecuador or Palau or something.

I walked through the Domain and brought myself to that first elevator, I took a few deep breaths in preparation to face this fear again. I don't think I will ever stop being afraid of elevators. I scanned my finger and took myself to the bottom level where they kept the holding cells.

My heart was racing, but I remained composed. I had rehearsed what I would say to him so many times. But suddenly my mind just went completely blank. I had no idea what he would say to me. If he would speak to me at all. He had remained silent this whole time. Charlie told me it was chilling. He didn't try to defend himself. He didn't try to do anything. He was completely mute.

I knew exactly where to find him and I followed the numbered signs leading me to his cell. I knew it was a cell within a cell. And as soon as I opened the doors, he would see me.

And my hand shook as I reached out and pressed my pointer finger on the pad. It recognized my fingerprint and the red LED light indicated itself green, I turned the door knob, and I let myself in.

Not ready to make any sort of eye contact, I entered with my back facing the door. Allowing it to close with my eyes closed, waiting to hear the click of the lock mechanism.

I turned around and there were those eyes. Big. Full of tears. Provoking a visceral reaction within me, awaking an anger that I knew lived deep inside me. He was not himself. His hair was in disarray, and his facial hair patchy and unkempt. My former friend that stood in front of me was practically unrecognizable.

I watched him scan over me. Seeing my form. My face no longer bandaged, but with purple and blue bruises framing the contusions from when my face hit the street. My arm wrapped up tightly in a sling. But standing. I was broken, but I was still standing. And I wasn't the one in the cage. He was.

I walked closer to the enclosure. A standard square surrounded by metal bars with nothing but a bed and toilet combo, smacked in the middle of the room. I saw a small stool next to the wall of the room itself and dragged it closer to him. I was still far enough away that he couldn't reach me. I took a seat. And we just stared at each other for another moment.

"Is there anything you'd like to say to me?" I tried to speak evenly, but even I noticed the fluctuations in my tone.

He broke his gaze and looked down.

"Collin? Collin Parrish. After everything we've been through?"

He continued to look down. This fueled my anger more.

"How many times did you lie to my face? And tell me you just wanted to keep me safe? God, you must have said that like a hundred times."

I paused again, seeing if I could get any sort of reaction from him.

"You know what's really fucked? Walter told me that you were trying to help me by getting me away from Connor. That I was sooo under his spell that you saved me from him. Walter really tried to spin it. I'm not sure how long Connor has been back, but I'll tell you what, he has stayed sooo far away from me," I vented.

"What?" He said, finally breaking his silence. "You haven't seen him?"

At first I was taken aback by his voice. It was so hoarse and morose. I took a moment to answer him.

"No," I sighed. "I haven't."

"That doesn't make any sense. Everything he did was for you, Vee. He didn't know about anything. He wasn't going to. I did everything I could... and now he... I just don't get it," he said gravely. He finally looked up at me and made eye contact. I watched a tear fall from his eyes. "I'm glad you're okay, Vee. You were never supposed to be hurt."

"Well, fuck, Collin," I didn't even know what to say to him.

"Would you believe me if I told you I tried to do right by you?"

"No," I said plainly.

"Walt... he was in his final stages with his serum. I knew he was going to try to reach out to you to get more of your DNA to make more... I did everything I could to keep you away from him. That's when I sent you off with Juniper. I figured you'd be safer with him, an old friend, get out of Rock Island, get a chance to breathe."

"But the plane, Collin. What the fuck was that?"

"Walter. He... perfected the serum and started going a little power crazy. Taking your plane down was a two-birds, one-stone kind of deal," he admitted.

"What? Me and Juniper?"

"No," he said regretfully. "You and Connor."

My face twisted in confusion. "What? Connor was dead."

"Walt... he knew that Connor had faked his death. And he

wanted him to come out of hiding. And he knew that Connor would have no choice but to stop his investigation and come find you to make sure you were safe. Walt was never going to kill you, Vee. You were at the center of all his plans... and I did everything I could to delay him. I really did. Until I couldn't," He wept.

I stood from my stool and walked straight up to his prison, grasping the bars, "How could you work with him?! Don't you know what that man has done to me?" I screamed at him in agony. "How? Explain how something like *this* happens!"

"You would never understand, Viridian!" He sobbed.

"Well, make me understand, because I'm not going any-where," I said through gritted teeth, my own traitor tears falling freely.

"You don't know what it's like... to grow up... and be good at everything. Be good at literally everything...and *still not be anyone's favorite,*" He spoke so darkly. So full of hate. Something he's been holding onto for decades.

I let go of the prison bars and backed away from him. I couldn't stop shaking my head.

"You did all of this? You teamed up with Walter Valentine... because you're jealous of your brother? Are you *fucking kidding me?*"

He scoffed through his tears. "I told you. You wouldn't understand."

"You're right. I don't."

"Perfect grades, lead the football team through countless victories, off the charts GPA, Valedictorian... and I didn't even get to give a speech at graduation. I wasn't even voted class president. But you know you know who got to give the speech at graduation? You know who was class president, Viridian?"

"This is fucking pathetic, Collin. Holding grudges over shit that happened in high school? Are you fucking kidding me?"

"It didn't stop after high school, Vee. It just got worse. Connor heard that I wanted to get out of our parents business, away from the Domain. I didn't tell him I applied at V Corp but I did. I wanted to lead the R&D department, the fifth floor, and I didn't get the job, Viridian. Summa Cum Laude at MIT and I didn't get it. But you know who did?"

Connor did. But I didn't know about that until recently.

"He walked right into HR, told them he wanted the job, and they just gave it to him. He didn't know I had applied for it, but he also didn't know that he had just applied for the job that was rightfully mine. He had no credentials. He doesn't know shit about tech. I'm surprised he was able to decrypt that quantum computer as fast as he did. That's when I went straight to Walt myself. He saw something in me. Took me underneath his wing... but at the same time it wasn't like that. We were equals. We were going to change the world."

My throat felt like it was being crushed. "I don't know who you are. Apparently I never did," I said devastated.

"Vee... don't be like this. Please, just try to understand. I just had to get away from him. Or get him away from me. I needed a chance."

"You had your chance, Collin. You made a choice. A bad one," it was all I had left in me to say. I couldn't hear any more from him.

I turned my back and started heading to the door.

"I know what you had to do, Vee!" He shouted from behind me, but my back stayed turned. "I know how you got away. Very classy, Viridian. You're such a great role model. Just *fucking* your way out of situations."

His words burned in my ears and I felt my heart shrink into nothing. With my back still turned I spoke, "If I were you, I'd go back to not talking," and I unlocked the door, and left him behind to rot.

With the door closed behind me I felt the sobs erupt out of me. How did I get myself here? Why did I let this happen to me? I felt my back slam into the door and I slid down to the floor and allowed myself a moment to myself. How did he know?

Collin knew. And he used it against me. I cheated on Juniper, but I did it to save the people I care about. Walter was only going to get more powerful if we hadn't gotten away. He was going to make a weapon that stripped people of their métier. Who knows if he would have done the same to me once he could finally figure out a way to make the serum without me still being kept alive. It was only a matter of time.

It doesn't matter if we never took the time to clearly define what we were. Juniper has done nothing but be kind to me, and take care of me, make me feel safe... and now I feel like I'll never feel safe again.

Is this all I'm good for?

Not now. I can't do this right now. I can't.

Get up, Viridian. Get the fuck up.

I scrapped myself up off the floor carefully, doing things one handed is harder than it sounds. And I made my way to the elevator. I didn't have time to falter, to crumble under the crippling fear I had of them. I would finish cleaning up my face in the reflection of the chrome in the elevator. I'm going to be fine.

I went the short distance to the elevator and pressed the button and waited for it to arrive and I felt myself begin to fall apart again. I don't have fucking time for this. The doors opened and quickly there were arms wrapped around me. I felt this wave of warmth surround me. An old feeling that had been missing from me that finally returned to me.

The arms gathered me into the elevator and it began ascending.

"I came down here as fast as I could," he said looking into my eyes, and holding me by my shoulders. Finally. It was Connor.

The tears flowed faster than before and my face crashed into his torso, grabbing onto him so hard, so desperately, and he matched my embrace and held me back.

"I know I should have come to you sooner, I'm sorry, I was being a coward," He said into my hair.

And I just wept. Words were not flowing, but hearing his words, hearing his voice for the first time in a long time. It felt overwhelming to me, and it felt like I would never be able to stop crying. God, I just missed him so much.

"Vee, what can I say? What can I do?"

I lifted my face from him and I felt my lip quiver. "Do you have a cigarette?"

We ended up lighting up right in his office.

"This feels so wrong," he said. "Should you be smoking?"

"Shouldn't you be dead?" I quipped back, and did a nice slow inhale. This was my first cigarette in over a week. The way they treat me at home, like I was made of porcelain, they would not give in to the broken girl and let her smoke.

He clicked his tongue. "Fair," he responded while inhaling his own cigarette.

"Should we be smoking in here?" I questioned.

"Eh, I own the place," he flicked some ash into an old coffee mug and set it in between us.

"You know what's absolutely crazy?" I started.

"Hmm?"

"It feels like no time has passed, like nothing happened. And now we're just back on our bullshit."

He scoffed, "Like I didn't pretend to be dead and hide a secret organization from you or keep you in the dark about your super powers?"

"Yeah, no, none of that happened. We're just a couple burnouts smoking cigarettes in your dad's office. Kid stuff," I said with a cheeky grin. He laughed. The sobs were behind me. Crazy what a cigarette and a few minutes with your best friend can do for a girl.

We finished our cigarettes and stabbed them out in the coffee mug.

"What took you so long?" I asked, breaking the silence.

"Well, first I saw you on the security cams in the cell with Collin and then I saw you leave and I ran down there as fast as I–"

"No. You know that's not what I'm talking about."

I saw him, contemplative. I noticed something new on his face. He had painted on a little beauty mark in the corner of his mouth to match Collin, to be more realistic to the identity that he was assuming.

"I saw you laying there in that hospital bed, comatose, and I got scared. Because I knew that I put you there. And I couldn't handle it. I ran away, Vee. I'm sorry," He said genuinely, his voice sprinkled with fear.

"But, Viridian. I can't keep this from you. But I heard every word that was said in that cell. Everything Collin said. And never... did he mention to me how he felt. We never discussed...

If he had just told me he was feeling that way... I could have backed off. I really could have. I don't have to be... this person that my métier makes me. It's why... Why it's so great with Winona. She hates my fucking guts, Vee. It's amazing," he finished rambling, "But God, just..."

Oh my God, please for the love of God do not mention what I think...

"Collin is so fucked up, for accusing you of fucking Walter to get away. You would never do that," he said, shaking his head in total disbelief.

My entire posture changed and I felt the blood drain from my face. I honestly felt like I was going to be sick. I felt something crawl up my insides. I was going to be sick.

I felt my hands go over my mouth as I scanned the room for the nearest trash can and by some miracle I was able to locate one just in time for the bile to painfully exit my body.

"Vee? Oh my God," he said concernedly, rushing to my side, holding back my hair. My slinged arm hung close to my body and my free hand gripped the trash bin while I was retching on my knees.

I felt another wave of nausea. And I felt the grime pass through my throat, poisoning my tongue, and making my eyes water from the pain.

I stayed there for a moment longer before getting up slowly. I used my free hand to wipe my face of any leftover debris. "Yeah I mean, I smoked that cigarette kind of fast... it was my first one in over a week," I tried to play it off. But Connor couldn't be tricked.

"I didn't know, Vee. I'm sorry that I... If I had known—"

"Stop. There's nothing to talk about."

"Was there really no other way?"

"What?" I said in shock.

"Like that was the only way for you and Winona to escape?"

I was quiet. Just...completely dumbfounded that he even asked me that question. To be frank, it seemed ungrateful. Sure, Walter is still out there, but the super juice supply is gone and now he's on the lam with no resources. I stopped him from getting more powerful.

"You know what, Connor? I've asked myself that question every day since I did what I had to do."

"I trust you. I trust your judgment," he tried to back track.

"No, I think you were about to fucking slut-shame me." I spat at him angrily.

"No. It was just a question. I swear."

"Yeah, say that in front of June," I rolled my eyes at him. Both of us know that we can't lie in front of him. With the mention of Juniper he shifted gears.

"Does he know?"

"No."

"Are you going to tell him?"

"No."

"Don't you think... he's going to just find out?"

At least now I was too angry to throw up again. "Connor, what the fuck?"

"I'm sorry. I see how much this hurts you. I'm sorry I'm making this worse. Does anyone know? Have you told anyone?"

"Winona knows. I didn't tell her. But she knows. And apparently Collin knows. So that's super fun. And now you. And it's funny. Before I bargained with myself, before I lowered myself to this sub-human level to allow myself to fuck my way to freedom, you know what I thought?"

He shook his head and sighed. "No."

"I thought that Juniper might not ever forgive me for this, but you would. You were the one that I thought... even if every person on the planet wouldn't understand, you would be the one to forgive me."

"Forgiveness? Forgiveness for what? You didn't do anything wrong, Vee," he inched closer to me.

"If I didn't do anything wrong... why do I feel this way?" My lip quivered. "Why do I feel like... the absolute lowest form of being on the planet? A fucking bottom-feeder. A fucking parasite. Scum of the fucking earth."

"I can tell you right fucking now. You are none of those things. You are the wittiest, and the funniest... the coolest chick on the planet, Vee. Someone everyone wants to be around."

"Wrong. I'm the one who all the weirdos want to be around."

"Ah, see, there's that sense of humor."

And I pulled away from him. And looked at him in the eyes. And saw something that wasn't there before.

He broke eye contact, then the embrace, and then the silence, "It was never going to be us, was it?"

And I thought for a moment. Slightly off put by the sudden change of topics. But it never occurred to me that this was something he thought about. I had always assumed I was alone in that day dream. But after being apart from him and finally reuniting I knew for sure.

"No, Connor," I said with a hopeless smile. "It wasn't ever going to be us."

"I always thought it was gonna be us, Vee."

I felt nearly ill, hearing him say those words. A sentence I never thought I would hear escape his lips. Something I've always wanted to hear. This was the person I fell in love with as a child. And I knew that if we were going to ever have our moment, it was now. But I didn't want it anymore. All of the magic... it was completely gone. The reality set in. And I had come to this realization that he was never mine.

"I thought that for a long time, Connor. I'm still your girl. But not like that," I struggled to get out those words, but I knew it was true.

He sighed. "Well, that settles that doesn't it?"

"You gonna go home and tell Winona you love her?" I asked.

"You gonna tell Juniper?" He returned with a question.

"Don't. I need more time. I love him, I deeply care about him, but I want to be right in myself before I do that. You and Nona have history. Don't make her wait any longer. Life is short, you know? It's not everyday you find someone who can see through all your bullshit," I reasoned with him. Honestly referring to both me and Juniper as much as his relationship with Winona.

"It's not every day you find out you have a half-sister."

"It's not every day you find out you have an evil twin."

About the Author

Jessica James is a Saginaw Valley State University graduate with a degree in Communication. She likes to stay involved in her community any way she can. When she isn't writing novels she is writing music, sewing dresses, mixing cocktails, and rewatching Buffy The Vampire Slayer. She lives in Saginaw, Michigan with her plants. Photo Courtesy of Josie Fife.